Mystery of the Missing Quilts

a novel by

Jan Cerney

American Quilter's Society

www.AmericanQuilter.com

Located in Paducah, Kentucky, the American Quilter's Society (AQS) is dedicated to promoting the accomplishments of today's quilters. Through its publications and events, AQS strives to honor today's quiltmakers and their work and to inspire future creativity and innovation in quiltmaking.

DIRECTOR OF PUBLICATIONS: KIMBERLY HOLLAND TETREV
JUNIOR EDITOR: ADRIANA FITCH
COPY EDITOR: CAITLIN TETREV
GRAPHIC DESIGN: SARAH BOZONE
COVER DESIGN: MICHAEL BUCKINGHAM
PHOTOGRAPHY: CHARLES R. LYNCH

This book is a work of fiction. The people, places, and events described in it are either imaginary or fictitiously presented. Any resemblance they bear to reality is entirely coincidental.

Cover photo credit: Boston Dry Goods Store. N.d. Photograph. Los Angeles Public Library, Los Angeles.

American Quilter's Society
www.AmericanQuilter.com

Additional copies of this book may be ordered from the American Quilter's Society, PO Box 3290, Paducah, KY 42002-3290, or online at www.AmericanQuilter.com.

Text © 2015, by Author, Jan Cerney
Artwork © 2015 American Quilter's Society

Library of Congress Cataloging-in-Publication Data

Cerney, Janice Brozik.
   Mystery of the missing quilts : a novel / by Jan Cerney.
      pages ; cm
   ISBN 978-1-60460-210-4 (softcover : acid-free paper)
   1. Quilting--Fiction. 2. Women missionaries--Fiction. I. Title.
   PS3603.E74M97 2015
   813'.6--dc23
                                        2015018197

Jacob's Ladder

CHAPTER 1

1901

I hope I've made the right decision, Sara fretted as she looked out of the train's window at the snowy white landscape flashing past her. She was already missing her loved ones at the mission, and she hadn't even been a day on the train. This monstrous beast that her Lakota people called the iron horse was taking her away to Boston, far from everything dear to her.

Sara brushed the escaping tendrils of her raven black hair back from her bronze face. She glanced out of the corner of her eye at the sleeping Maud who puffed out bursts of air from her vibrating lips.

Sara slouched low in her seat as Maud's loud whistling drifted throughout the railroad coach, initiating stares and whispers from other passengers. She turned slowly and peered around at the strangers. Seeing a few curious eyes looking her way, she inched as far away as she could from Evangeline's mother.

Shame on me, I shouldn't be feeling this way. She reminded herself, Maud and her husband Frederick were kind enough to take her home with them to Boston to live, until she matriculated into the nursing school for the spring semester.

Maud had money to spare, wore the latest fashions, and she considered herself the pinnacle of society, but Sara thought she seemed so unfeminine and less stylish at the moment. She rolled her eyes. Sometimes, she just didn't understand these white people, but she would never admit it to Evangeline who had been pushing her to learn the white ways since she was a young Lakota child at the mission.

Should I wake her? But what would I say? Then I would be embarrassed!

Sara's eyes searched for Maud's husband Frederick, wishing him to return to his seat. She had always considered him a practical sort of fellow, but he wasn't around to help at the moment. Frederick had left them both to visit the smoking car.

I'll let him take care of the situation when he gets back. Sara retreated into her space, coiling herself like a hibernating animal when she finally decided to open to the third chapter of Elijah's book that Evangeline had shoved in her hand before she had left the Mission.

"Read this in case you miss home," Evangeline had told her with tears filling her eyes. Sara hadn't been gone one day, but she already felt like her lifeline had been severed to all she had known.

Even before her cousin Elijah had married Evangeline, he had written the book she held in her lap. She turned the volume over in her hand several times, remembering the story behind the book. Evangeline had encouraged him to write of Swift Bear's life before she had gone back to Boston. Elijah took her advice and had spent hours visiting with the old man and recording Swift Bear's stories of the Sioux when they lived a free life before being relegated to the reservations. Sara had always enjoyed books, but she never got around to reading this one.

Her grandmother Red Bird also had told her stories about the old days. She fondly remembered sitting on a pallet near the crackling fire in their tepee listening to Red Bird's soothing voice lull her into the past, recalling days of a nomadic plain's life. The stories seemed like a fairy tale to her then. From reading the first two chapters of Elijah's book, she realized Swift Bear's stories were of the same era of her grandmother, but told from the male perspective.

Red Bird could do anything, she thought. She knew about medicinal plants and expertly tanned hides and beaded. When the missionaries introduced her people to quilting, Red Bird had enthusiastically adopted the new art form. She had attended the sewing sessions with the mission women and helped to make quilts, including the last one, the Jacob's Ladder quilt. For some reason the Jacob's Ladder quilt with Red Bird's handiwork disappeared and no one knew what happened to it. Sara would have loved to have that quilt with her now as a reminder of her grandmother. To wrap up in it would be like having Red Bird's arms around her.

Just as she settled in, Frederick returned, smiled at Sara knowingly and jiggled Maud's shoulder. She awoke with a start, blinked her eyes several times, and nervously adjusted her bodice and straightened her skirt, perhaps realizing that she might have been making a spectacle of herself.

Maud wrinkled her brow and then pursed her lips as she looked at Sara. "We'll have my dressmaker design you the most fashionable dresses when we get to Boston," she said as if they were in the middle of a conversation.

Sara knew the look. She had seen Maud use it with Evangeline many times. "You don't approve of what I'm wearing?" Sara asked, smoothing her conservative navy and white dress Cassandra had sewn for her.

"Oh no...what you're wearing is fine, but you'll be competing with the more affluent girls at school. It costs money to attend nursing school in the East, and you'll want to look the part."

"I see." Sara knew Maud meant well, and she wanted to be appreciative of all the family had done for her. After all she could have applied for a grant to attend school, but they insisted they would pay for her tuition.

"We don't want you to be a needy student. You have position. Don't forget it," Maud had insisted.

Sara liked the clothes Cassandra had sewn for her before she had left for Boston, but she forced a positive response. "Thank you, Maud, I'll look forward to the dressmaking sessions."

"We have so much shopping to do. I just can't wait to buy you everything you need. I miss not having Evangeline near." Maud clapped her hands together in memory. "Oh, we used to go on the most fantastic shopping sprees. Now there's Willow, of course, but Evangeline's denying me the pleasure of shopping for her, too." She frowned.

Oh, great, Sara thought, remembering Evangeline's advice. "Be firm with Mama. Tell her exactly what you want." Sara knew it would be easier said than done. It never worked for Evangeline, except when she decided to become a missionary. Then both Maud and Frederick eventually accepted her decision, but it hadn't been easy. She would worry about Maud later. She let the conversation lapse and returned to her book while Maud picked up a ladies' magazine.

As Sara began reading Elijah's book, a panorama of unspoiled views opened up before her, a way of life predating her own that would never be again. She felt swept away in the tide of change and felt she too would have resisted the drastic changes like some of her people had. While living at the mission, Evangeline and Elijah's encouragement had carried her to a place she was unsure of, yet desired, to her own consternation. Her own people would probably not approve of what she was embarking. They would look down on her, and she would be ridiculed if she still lived among them. To become like the white people was not acceptable to most of them.

She settled back in her seat and began to read Swift Bear's words, words that took her to another place and time.

When the days were good, buffalo, deer, elk, and antelope grazed in the tall grass, waving under a blue sky. White, puffy clouds floated above an unspoiled land. It was a happy time. The women sang as they set up the tepees on the fresh earth. The men hunted and the women butchered, cutting strips to dry on their racks while chunks of beef boiled over the fire. Swift Bear had said, "Ah, the smell of fresh meat made my stomach growl in hunger." The parfleches would not be empty for the winter. Tepees gleamed white along the river where the grass was green and good for the ponies. At night the moonlight shone against the rugged land playing tricks on Swift Bear's eyes. As a boy, he thought the queer shapes were ghosts dancing, but he could not show he was afraid.

Sara couldn't show her fear either. She closed the book, thinking of her Grandmother Red Bird, who had taught her of the herbs and roots she should gather to use for sustenance and healing. For some reason, she thought of her a lot today. Losing her had been difficult, but then Evangeline convinced Elijah, her cousin, to let her live with her and the teacher, Mary, at the mission. Sara remembered wanting to learn about everything. Some of her friends struggled with school or simply didn't care, but she found it fascinating.

Sara desperately wanted to hold on to the memories, but they were fading. She tried her hardest to remember her father and mother, but she couldn't. She recalled only her grandmother who always seemed old to her. Then there was Evangeline who was kind to her when she was just a young girl. Evangeline talked to her the first day of school even though she would not answer because of fright.

Sara had never seen a woman with such light skin and blonde hair. She laughed at her actions now. It was impolite to stare, but occasionally when Evangeline wasn't looking, she would sneak a peek at this different looking woman. What would she say to such a person? She hardly spoke a word to her for the longest time. Little did she realize then, Evangeline would become her best friend. She grieved for her when she left the mission to return to Boston to marry James. Now she had left Evangeline and Elijah.

Oh, I hope I made the right decision, she worried again.

– – – – – –

"Now make yourself comfortable in Evangeline's old room," Maud told Sara once they arrived back at the DuMont home in Boston. Maud bustled about the bedroom like an overprotective hen. "I had the room redecorated when I knew Evangeline wasn't coming home to stay. I couldn't come in here without thinking about her," she said sadly. Maud adjusted the white lace curtains that now hung at the window.

"You took down the red velvet drapes," Sara said, glancing at the windows.

"Evangeline liked to sleep in a darkened room, but personally I like lots of light, so I gave them away. After James died, Evangeline spent too many lonely moments in this once darkened room." Maud shuddered and opened the wardrobe that stood empty. "As soon as the dressmaker comes and begins making your new clothes you'll have this filled up in no time." She spread the clothes hangers apart while counting them. "Now then, I'll let you settle in. Supper is served at 6:00."

"Thank you," Sara said as Maud left the room, her skirts rustling. Paying attention to time was a habit Sara learned to acquire. Her peoples' lives weren't regulated by a clock.

She looked around Evangeline's old room, grateful that she would be sleeping here for a while before she left for nursing school. She remembered this room from the two times she had come to Boston to visit, once with Elijah and the other time with Cassandra. The cabbage rose wallpaper she had always admired had been covered over with a green fern-like print that evoked a cool retreat along with painted white furniture, which replaced the upholstered pieces she had remembered from before.

Sara opened her trunk and took out her favorite quilt named for her Indian name, Morning Star, and spread it out on the celery green bed spread and flopped herself into its familiar comfort. Totally exhausted, she felt like a nap but a glance at the bedside clock told her she had less than an hour until supper. She lay there and closed her eyes thinking of Evangeline's advice to her. "God has plans for you. Pray about it."

Was this His plan? She thought. God's plan always confused her. How did anyone know what God's plan was? If this was it, His plan had taken her so far from home and the people she loved. She knew several of her people who had returned from school at Carlisle. Once they got home they never wanted to leave again. She hoped the nursing school was nothing like the stories she had heard about Carlisle.

Sara dozed off to be awakened by Maud, gently jiggling her arm. "Sara, we're waiting on you."

Sara rubbed her eyes then jumped off the bed. "I'm sorry. I fell asleep," she said. Feeling self conscious that she hadn't changed her clothes for dining, she followed Maud downstairs.

"There's our girl," Frederick said enthusiastically as Sara entered the dining room.

"She fell asleep," Maud explained.

"I don't blame you. I could have taken a nap myself." He winked.

Sara placed the cloth napkin on her lap and waited for Frederick to say the prayer.

Afterward, Maud rang the bell for the maid to bring in the first course. She entered and brought the serving dishes around to each. Sara helped herself to the beautifully prepared food, although she didn't feel hungry.

"I've been thinking," Maud said while heaping mashed potatoes and gravy on her plate. "I should have the dressmaker over this week to begin sewing. I have the newest pattern books. You definitely need a new coat for winter. We'll take a look at them tonight after we've finished with supper, Sara."

"Oh, there's plenty of time for that, Maud. Let the child settle in," Frederick suggested.

"She won't mind. I'm anxious to see what we can come up with. After all we only have a few weeks in which to create a fashionable wardrobe."

Sara sat quietly not knowing what to say. She liked the time she had spent sewing with Cassandra at the mission. She and Cassandra had come to know each other just by working together. Each had carried emotional scars of the past, although they never discussed them, they seemed to have a silent understanding between them.

After dessert, Frederick left for his study and Maud and Sara retreated to the parlor. You sit here by the side table, and I'll bring in the books. Sara did as instructed and waited until Maud lugged in two large pattern books with stylish ladies on the cover. "I haven't had much time to look through these. Oh, won't this be fun?" Maud puffed.

Sara nodded as she flipped through the pages of thin white women modeling fashions she thought much too extravagant for school.

"Now, if you see something you like, mark it with these pieces of paper," Maud instructed.

While Maud looked through one book, Sara searched through another marking the simplest dresses she saw. Maud looked over to Sara's book and perused her choices. "Oh Sara, these are much too plain. You won't draw any attention dressed like that."

Sara didn't want to draw attention to herself. She recalled Evangeline telling her to stand her ground with her mother. "But I'd rather be simple," she blurted out much to her own astonishment.

"Oh nonsense, we'll see what the dressmaker says. I like these. Have a look."

Sara took the book and opened to the pages Maud had marked. It didn't surprise her, Maud's choices were much out of character for her. No way would she wear these ostentatious creations clearly meant for someone else. Somehow she would get her preference across to the dressmaker. "I appreciate what you are suggesting, but I like something much like what Cassandra has sewn me."

Maud heaved a deep sigh. "We'll see. Now go on up to bed, I'm sure you're tired."

"That I am," Sara said, relieved. She had already met her match with Maud, and she hadn't been here even a day.

— — — — — —

Since Sara had been to Boston on several occasions already the tall brick buildings of the city didn't overwhelm her as they did on her first visit. They still seemed cold and unfriendly, not all in symmetry with Mother Earth. She recalled how her people detested living in the square buildings, preferring buildings built in the symbolic circle. She smiled when she remembered Swift Bear spending time both in the square log hut and in the tepee, which he preferred.

Sometimes she had almost forgotten she was Lakota on the inside. Living at the mission when she was very young taught her the white way, but she was still Lakota every time she looked in the mirror. Her features, dark skin and black hair, reflected her heritage.

She approached the school's administration building, reminding herself to keep her head held high like Evangeline insisted she do. She had learned from her people that to look at anyone in the face was considered disrespectful, but in the white world it was acceptable.

"Hanging your head, like you do, makes you seem inferior," Evangeline had told her.

Sara smoothed the skirt Cassandra had made for her several months ago before she had left for Boston. She felt comfortable in it and chose it for this first day of school. It suited her. Since she wouldn't be living with Maud and Frederick during the school session, she brought along the fashionable dresses Maud had chosen, and the dressmaker had sewn for her, storing them in her overly large trunk. Someday soon she would wear the dresses that had turned out to be a compromise between Maud and her tastes of style but not now.

Today, Sara was grateful Evangeline had been careful to pre-register her and fill out the paperwork to meet all the requirements, so there would be no surprises when she arrived. She feared the unknown. It took all the courage she could muster to continue with her registration.

"Sara Fletcher?" asked a woman with a tight bun that accented her pinched face.

Sara nodded, forcing to keep her gaze directed toward her.

"I am Miss Andrews. I oversee all paper work and assist with enrollment." She shuffled through the papers. "It appears everything is in order. I see you received your schooling at a mission and Santee Training School?" She peered over the rim of her wire rimmed glasses.

Sara nodded.

"I hope they taught you well." She sniffed. "Our school is

known for its high academic standards." She ran her finger over Sara's academic records. "I see you earned superior marks. Nursing is a demanding field of study."

Sara nodded but said nothing to this woman whom Evangeline would advise she respect, but she disliked her condescending tone. She fought hard not to drop her gaze.

"Do you have any questions?"

Sara shook her head.

"You're not very talkative, are you?"

Sara remained silent.

"Hmmm...well then, I'll have someone show you to your room...oh, you will have a roommate. I do hope you were made aware. This may be temporary, however." Miss Andrews left her desk and opened a door to an adjoining room. "Miss Beal, would you please show Sara Fletcher to her room."

A young girl about Sara's age appeared wearing a smile that immediately put Sara at ease.

"This is Sara," Miss Andrews said to the young brunette.

"Hi, Sara. Call me Amy. Welcome to Cliff Point Nursing School."

"Thank you," Sara managed to mumble.

Amy led her to a room off a hospital wing. "I hope you didn't let Miss Andrews intimidate you," Amy said concerned. "Don't feel bad if she did. She does that to practically everyone."

"I'm used to it. Evangeline reminds me that I'm anybodies equal. I try not to forget."

"Good for you."

Sara ran her hand over the smooth oak woodwork on the staircase as they ascended to the second floor of the hospital. Finely polished wood floors glowed under her feet. Their footsteps echoed down the long hallway to her room. Music streamed out of the open door into the hall.

Sara cast Amy an inquisitive glance.

"Oh, that's your roommate Lois. She loves classical music."

Sara identified the piece as Wagner's "Ride of the Valkyries." She learned about it when she had attended Santee. One of her instructors had been an aficionado of classical composers.

"Yes, I know it. The rise and fall of the notes reminds me of warriors riding over the plains on a buffalo hunt."

Amy stopped short. "I hope you don't mind my asking, but are you Sioux?"

"No, I don't mind, and yes I am."

"We get very few of your background enrolled here." She hastened to add. "But we are so glad you have enrolled in our school. It's one of the best."

"My...mother selected it for me," she said surprised that she had just described Evangeline as her mother. *But why wouldn't I?* She thought. *She has been like a mother for a long time now.*

Amy introduced the two roommates then turned to leave them alone to become acquainted. "I'll find someone to bring up your things."

"Thank you," Sara said to Amy as she left the room.

An awkward moment ensued. Neither girl knew what to say to each other. Sara sensed that Lois attempted her best not to stare. However, she felt Lois looked at her when she thought Sara wouldn't notice.

Should I just come out and say I'm a Lakota girl from a South Dakota Reservation, she wondered. Sara hadn't been too self conscious of being Lakota until she had spent some time in Boston when she began to notice the stares.

A young man deposited her large trunk in their room, setting it down with a thump. Lois's eyes grew wide when she saw it. Maud had insisted Sara use this large trunk trimmed in brass.

"My, that's a beautiful trunk. I don't think I have ever seen anything like it," Lois commented.

"Thank you." Sara didn't imagine that anyone would be

impressed, but her roommate sure was.

As Sara unpacked her newly acquired wardrobe, Lois couldn't help watch as she hung up each delectable creation. Obviously forgetting her manners, Lois unabashedly asked, "Who designed your beautiful clothes?"

"Oh, Maud DuMont's dressmaker from Boston."

"Is Maud rich?"

"Yes, I would say she is."

"Aren't you lucky! I may have a few nice clothes, but nothing like you have," she gushed as her eyes devoured each garment.

"I expect we'll be in uniform some of the time."

"I suppose we will, but you will certainly stand out in the frocks you have just hung up."

"It wasn't my idea to stand out," Sara said quietly.

Lois ignored her remark. "I think we're about the same size. Could I wear some of your frocks sometime?"

No one had ever asked to wear her clothes before. "That's fine with me."

"Oh, I think we'll get along splendidly," Lois predicted. "I heard the music."

"I hope you don't mind if I play classical music from time to time. I wanted to study music but my parents insisted I become a nurse, so I would be able to support myself," she said disappointed. "They think music is frivolous nonsense as a career. Why did you decide to come here?"

"I studied to be a teacher, but I helped our doctor out on rounds and discovered that I like helping sick people. I mentioned it to my...mother, and she thought it a great idea."

"Where are you from?"

"South Dakota."

"Hardly anyone comes here from South Dakota."

"It's a long ways from here." She simply said, deciding not to tell her all the details.

"I'll look it up in the atlas the next time I go to the library."

"Where do you live?"

"A small town in Connecticut, it's not far from here."

"Then you'll be able to go home often."

"I suppose."

"Any brothers or sisters?" Sara asked.

"One sister. She's younger than I am."

"What about you?"

"A...sister named Willow. She's just a baby."

"A sister that young! How can that be?"

"I just call her my sister."

"Oh. I guess I don't understand."

Sara decided to tell Lois about her past. She knew Lois was too inquisitive to let the matter drop. "My real mother and father died when I was very young. In fact, I don't even remember them. My Grandmother took me in and raised me."

"That's terrible. What did they die from?" Lois asked as she sat on the edge of her bed in expectation.

"Some sort of illness. Anyway, I lived with my Grandmother Red Bird until she died...of old age. Then Evangeline who was a missionary at the Cheyenne Mission asked my cousin Elijah who was studying to be a pastor if I could come and live at the mission and stay with Evangeline and another teacher, Mary. He finally agreed. Then I moved to the mission."

"Oh, this is interesting. Tell me more."

Sara sighed. "Within a year, Evangeline left the mission to marry a man from the East. Mary left shortly after that, too. Then I was left with Elijah and his mother Cassandra. She had a hard life and was almost unapproachable, but we eventually became friends, and the best part is when Evangeline came back to the mission and married Elijah."

Lois interrupted. "Wait a minute. I thought you said she married someone who lived in the East."

"Oh yes. I got ahead of myself. You see, this man was named James and he died at sea. She was so distraught that

Cassandra and I went to Boston to see her. Cassandra asked her to come back to the mission. She did and that's when she married Elijah. They have a little girl named Willow."

"And you refer to Evangeline as your mother?"

"I decided it was much easier than explaining this long story. Besides, she is like a mother to me."

"What a fascinating life you have led. My family is just ordinary—a mother, a father, and a sister."

"You should be thankful you have always had a home and people to love you."

"You're right. Sometimes I take my family for granted. Did you...live in a tepee?"

"I did."

"Wow. Wait till the other girls hear about this."

"I'd rather you wouldn't repeat what I told you, not just yet anyway. I don't want to explain my life's story to everyone. I think it's best I settle in first."

"Oh, alright. I'll keep quiet. But you will tell me more, won't you."

"After a time. Right now I would like to finish my unpacking."

"I'll leave you alone for a while, if you don't mind. I have a friend who lives down the hall."

"I'll be fine," Sara said, watching her new roommate dash from the room. She hoped Lois wouldn't break her promise to her.

— — — — —

Sara watched Mrs. Dobbs, the nursing instructor, as she entered the classroom absorbed in the papers she carried. She carefully placed them on her desk and reshuffled them before she spoke to the class. "I have an announcement to make about your residences. I know some of you are quite cramped in rooms you have to share. In my hand I have a list of places where you will be able to work for your room and board and also be able to perform nursing duties as part of your training. I took the liberty of assigning some of you a position. While I meet with each one of you, I'll pass out a study assignment you can work on in the meantime.

Sara's heart fluttered. She knew she would be one of the students reassigned. She glanced at the study questions on anatomy the instructor handed her. She enjoyed these formal classes and wished there were more of them even though it had taken a while for her to become used to the stares from the other girls. She wasn't sure if it had been because of the clothes she wore or the dark color of her skin. Her heart had sunk when she realized she was the only Indian in the nursing classes, but Evangeline had told her she might be.

Evangeline's words echoed in her ears every time she began to feel afraid or inferior. "Hold your head high," Evangeline had drilled into her mind.

Sara's teachers had taught her well. She had no trouble keeping up with the curriculum. In fact she topped her class in academics, which made her the envy of her classmates, but she ignored their stares and whispers. She began her tenth study question when the instructor called her to a table.

"Now Sara, I have chosen you to care for an elderly lady who lives in the city. She lives within walking distance to the hospital. She's an invalid and has worked with our program for several years. She has a few other medical issues that I have listed here." The instructor handed the file folder to Sara. "You will live with her for the remainder of your training."

Sara looked over the notes her instructor had made. The duties listed were so much like the jobs she performed at the hospital. Her heart sank once again. It was more housekeeping and menial duties instead of what she actually wanted, more academic studies.

"Any questions?"

Sara shook her head, picked up the folder, muttered a thank you, and walked to her desk.

After class dismissed, Lois bounced over to her side. "What assignment did you get?"

"Taking care of an elderly lady, a Mrs. Mattie Wilkes."

Lois grimaced. "Oh, I've heard of her. Nobody has a good thing to say about the woman."

"I've had experience with older women." Sara defended her ability to manage the assignment. "My Grandmother Red Bird was old and Cassandra isn't exactly old, but she can be cantankerous."

"You're so brave," Lois commented, her eyes wide with admiration. "I wish you luck just the same. When will you have to leave?"

"Within the week. I might as well begin to pack and make more room in the closet for your clothes. In fact, why don't you choose a few of my frocks to keep?"

"Oh, I couldn't do that!"

"Well, why not. When will I ever find time to wear them? You know we put in ten to twelve hours shifts at the hospital, sometimes seven days a week, and now I will be caring for Mrs. Wilkes. How am I ever going to keep up? And I certainly won't have the time to wear fancy dresses."

Once back at their shared room, Lois could barely contain her excitement as Sara opened the wardrobe closet door and began to study which clothes she should keep. "Obviously I will keep the plain dresses the apron we wear will cover." Sara held up a few nicely tailored garments. "Cassandra put so much care into these. I can't part with them. Maud bought me a couple I'll never wear." Sara thrust the lavender one up near Lois's face. "You'll look good in this one. Take it."

Lois gasped. "Are you sure?"

"Yes, yes, I'll never miss it. Hmmm, I suppose I had better keep one Maud bought me, just in case she comes to visit."

Sara saw Lois eagerly eyeing her olive green traveling suit with a hat to match. "Here, take this one too."

"Really? Oh, you are just too kind. You know I will miss

you. I think we could have become good friends."

"We'll still see each other. I'll be scrubbing floors, and you'll be washing dishes." Sara laughed.

"I get the feeling you were you expecting more from nurses' training."

"I shouldn't have, but yes I was. I wanted to learn more about medicine. Not just how to bandage a wound and fluff a pillow. After all we're just women and shouldn't expect much, but living with Evangeline made me forget the world isn't always fair. She always made me believe I could accomplish anything."

"I know what you mean. I'd rather compose music than empty bed pans any day, but my father thinks that nursing is part of the Christian duty."

"I would think music would be too."

"Perhaps for the wealthy, but I have to confess that my family isn't wealthy," Lois said. "My father works two jobs to send me to training, so I owe it to him to do the best I can while I'm here. I hate to tell him I'm exhausted and overworked."

"That's exactly what we are."

"I thought I might be the one reassigned, since my family doesn't have money."

"But they don't know that as long as you can pay the tuition."

"I guess you're right."

Sara frowned. "As for me, I think they've made an assumption I might be needy."

"Why do you think you're so interested in medicine?" Lois asked.

"My Grandmother Red Bird used to take me with her when she harvested the herbs and plants for healing. She knew how to help the sick."

"I know nothing about it. Would you be able to do that now? I mean, find the right plants."

"I'm afraid I've forgotten too much and we wouldn't find

many of them in Boston."

"Have you ever considered studying to be a doctor? You're so smart, the best in the class."

"Oh, Lois, that's very nice of you to say, but how many women doctors do you know of? And an Indian doctor at that."

"Well, maybe none, but you could be one of the first. You're brilliant, unlike me. I'm just getting by."

"Nice thought. It takes years of study, and I can't expect Maud and Frederick to fund my education."

"I suppose not. It was just an idea."

Sara thought Lois's idea was right on the mark. But it was a dream she couldn't possibly hope to obtain. Or could she?

CHAPTER 2

The trees and shrubs had overgrown the expansive Victorian shrouded in snow. Sara could barely see the ornate jutting lines and scroll work on the towers and turret underneath the dense vegetation. She counted two tower rooms, one turret, and at least three porches. She thought it was an awfully big house for just one woman.

"Mrs. Wilkes lives here alone?" She asked her instructor Mrs. Dobbs who accompanied her to her assignment.

"She does except for her cook who doubles as a maid."

"Does Mrs. Wilkes have a family?"

"She had a daughter, Isabel, who died a while ago in a riding accident. Mrs. Wilkes was injured in that same incident. A granddaughter comes to visit her quite often, sometimes staying for a lengthy spell."

The driver pulled the carriage up to the main entrance, jumped down from his perch and opened the door for the two women. An efficient middle-aged woman, wearing her brown hair in a severe upsweep, answered the door and ushered them into a dark hallway.

"So this is the new one?" She commented.

"Yes, Mrs. Burns, this is Sara Fletcher. Sara, please meet Mrs. Burns."

Sara bowed slightly and briefly smiled.

"I'm sorry to rush off, but I have other students to place. I'll see you at the hospital, Sara." With the hurried introduction over, Mrs. Dobbs left Sara in awkward silence.

Mrs. Burns cleared her throat. "Did Mrs. Dobbs tell you how this arrangement works?"

"She did. The way I understand it, I take care of Mrs. Wilkes when I finish my duties at the hospital and also care for her on Sundays."

"That's correct."

"Do you room here?"

"I do. I have a room off the kitchen, but don't disturb me in the evening after supper. Sunday, I usually go out and don't return until late evening."

"I understand."

"Now then, I'll take you to your room, so you can get settled. You'll meet Mrs. Wilkes at lunch. Your room will be one flight above Mrs. Wilkes's room," Mrs. Burns told Sara as they climbed the first flight of well polished walnut stairs. "We have a system where you can communicate with Mrs. Wilkes in the room below you. I'll let you unpack."

"Where is Mrs. Wilkes now?"

"She's in her room below you. I wouldn't disturb her just now."

"Oh, I won't."

After Mrs. Burns left her alone, Sara surveyed the room where she would be sleeping for the remainder of her training. A small upholstered gold chair sat next to the tower window with a lamp table nearby. Oh how she would have liked to sit down and rest for a while. She had spent the entire morning disinfecting the surgery rooms. Instead of resting, she went to the matching dressing table, pulled out the ornately carved bench, sat and removed her hat. She gazed into the walnut framed mirror, examining the look of strain upon her face.

I can do this, she thought. *Nothing has every defeated me before, why would I let it now.*

She rose and peered out the tower window only to be met by thick overgrown trees frosted with snow. The looming trees high above her tower window blocked out cheery sunlight. She sighed and then opened her suitcase and hung up her nurse's uniforms and two dresses in a dark walnut wardrobe. According to Mrs. Dobbs, she would have little time for herself other than when Mrs. Wilkes's granddaughter visited. Mrs. Burns could attend to Mrs. Wilkes in a pinch, but she had too much to do with cooking, cleaning, and laundry.

Sara laid one plain beige dress on the bed draped in a heavy dark brown spread. She smoothed the wrinkles from her dress with her hand. She changed into it and placed a white uniform apron over it and then pinned up her raven black hair. She shivered and decided to wrap her beige shawl around her shoulders before she set off to explore the house.

Stepping out into the hall, she wished she had someone to show her around, but she knew she must become familiar with the layout in order to perform her duties, so she set out alone, beginning with the second floor on which she would be residing. For some reason she discovered she was tiptoeing down the hall to the next room. She laughed at herself.

Whom would I be disturbing? Ghosts from the past?

Relieved, she found most of the doors open. She peeked in the bedroom next to hers and found it to be austere and silent. It seemed almost a replica of hers in arrangement although it appeared to be more masculine with brown striped wallpaper, a leather chair and a larger bed. She wondered which male relative used this bedroom.

She moved on to another bedroom down the hall. A

few books lay on the lamp table. Lace dollies and violet patterned wallpaper added a softness to counteract the dark furniture. Sara would have preferred this room as no trees blocked the view and sheer curtains hung at the windows, allowing more light to filter in. A thought crossed her mind that this was probably the bedroom in which Mrs. Wilkes's granddaughter stayed when she came to visit.

The sunny window invited her to gaze out onto what could be an immaculate flower and herb garden in the summer. A middle-aged man whom she never noticed when they drove up earlier was shoveling the walk. She watched him a while and then noticed Mrs. Burns came out and visited with him. He must be the handyman or the grounds keeper.

No doubt she's giving him instructions, she thought.

Sara continued exploring the second floor only to discover she had seen the last of the bedrooms. There were a few rooms with the doors closed, but she left them alone and progressed up the stairs to a third level.

At the top of the winding staircase, she heard an ethereal tinkling sound. She discovered she was tiptoeing again when she located the source of the music from this third floor. Outside near a window, a burgundy glass globe with suspended matching beads clinked against metal tubes producing the delightful sound. Again she could look down on the gardens from this vantage point and could even sit in a variety of cane and soft cushioned chairs near the window.

Odd, she thought, *who would have time to sit here in what appears to have once been a large ball room? Mrs. Wilkes would not be able to come up here, unless it was her granddaughter that enjoyed this spot where one could look out on the gardens as well as the city.*

There were no rooms per se, just an open area with a few book shelves, chairs, the wind chime, and a telescope. Sara had seen telescopes in books. She couldn't resist looking through it. The city certainly appeared larger when she peeked through the lenses.

What would the stars and the moon look like? She asked herself. Some night she would have to come up and see.

Thinking she should check to see if lunch was ready, she took one last look around, her gaze resting on a mural of a fountain and flowers painted on the far wall. She thought it pretty and would have studied it closer, but felt she had tarried long enough. She descended to the first level and peeked in the dining room. She saw no one sitting at the large walnut Chippendale table. Mrs. Burns noticed her and invited her into the kitchen.

"I'll go and get Mrs. Wilkes and while I am gone, please fill these water glasses and set them on the table. Sara did as she was told, noticing that Mrs. Burns kept an impeccable kitchen. Mrs. Burns wheeled Mrs. Wilkes into the dining room just as Sara set the last glass on the table.

Sara stood motionless as she scrutinized this woman whom she would be caring for. Mrs. Wilkes appeared to be in her late sixties, well groomed, but as fragile as an orchid. She wore her hair in a graying bun, puffed up at the crown. For a brief moment Sara saw a resemblance of someone, but she just couldn't place who it was. After Mrs. Burns pushed the wheelchair to the table, she introduced Mrs. Wilkes to Sara.

"Pleased to meet you, Sara. I hope that you have found your accommodations satisfactory?" She said mechanically as she placed a linen napkin on her lap.

Sara sat rigid in her chair. "I have," she mumbled unintentionally.

"You have looked the house over?"

"I did. I went up to the third floor. Was...was the top floor used as a ball room at one time?" she squeaked.

Mrs. Wilkes stiffened, and then waved her hand. "I don't know. I've never used the third floor. Nowadays, I don't explore beyond the first floor."

"I see." Sara wanted to ask how long she had been an invalid but thought it would be impolite to do so.

Mrs. Burns dished up a plate a food for Mrs. Wilkes before she passed the bowls and platters to Sara. The food appeared to be well prepared, but Sara didn't feel like eating. She placed a small sampling of each item on the monogrammed china plate."

"Heaven sakes, girl, you need to eat more than that to keep up with me," Mrs. Wilkes bellowed. "Mrs. Burns pass the food around again."

Sara shrunk inward, but placed enough food on her plate to cover the monogrammed W.

"That's more like it. I don't starve my help. I might scare them off, but they don't go away hungry."

The two women ate the remainder of the meal in silence. Sara had no idea what to visit about, so instead she sat wondering what Mrs. Wilkes did to scare off her help. A scenario of ghastly incidents played through her mind.

"Sara and I will have tea and dessert by the fire," Mrs. Wilkes told Mrs. Burns when she finished the last bite of roasted chicken and pushed her plate away from her.

"Yes ma'am. Make yourself comfortable and I'll bring it in," Mrs. Burns answered. "Sara, wheel Mrs. Wilkes into the parlor, please."

Sara assumed her first duty assisting Mrs. Wilkes into the parlor. Thankfully, she was familiar with this particular model of wheelchair and glided Mrs. Wilkes's emaciated form into the adjoining room effortlessly.

"Close to the fire, please. I'm always chilled to the bone, beside the lamp table," Mrs. Wilkes instructed.

Sara did as she was told and then stood by her employer's side waiting for further orders.

"Put another log on the fire and seat yourself."

Sara selected a small log from the brass wood box situated near the white rock fireplace and placed it on the ebbing fire, and then she chose a settee nearby and sat on the edge of the gold and green chintz upholstery with her hands folded and placed in her lap.

Mrs. Burns entered and set the tray containing the steaming tea pot and delicate, rose edged china cups on a low table in front of Sara. Mrs. Burns poured the tea and handed Mrs. Wilkes the cup and saucer. Mrs. Wilkes grasped the saucer with both hands and clenched her face in concentration as she brought the tea cup to rest upon her knee.

"Thank you," Sara murmured as she took the cup and saucer Mrs. Burns offered her. Sara waited for Mrs. Wilkes to take the first sip, and then she too drank the tea that was a bit too weak for her taste.

"I sliced the orange marble cake for you and placed it on plates," Mrs. Burns explained. "If you would like more just ring for me."

"The cake looks good," Mrs. Wilkes remarked. "Thank you Mrs. Burns," she said to her housekeeper and cook.

Mrs. Wilkes sipped her tea slowly while seemingly scrutinizing Sara. "Tell me about yourself, Sara."

"There's really not much more to tell. I've led a simple life in South Dakota."

"But you are now attending nurse's training in Boston. Surely, no one of your...background has done that before?"

Sara set her cup and saucer down. "No, I guess not. Evangeline made sure I had every advantage."

"And who is Evangeline?"

"A missionary who taught me and took care of me when my grandmother died. She's been very good to me."

"What about your parents?"

Sara cleared her throat. "They died when I was very young."

"I see. You haven't had an easy life." Mrs. Wilkes paused. "I might as well tell you I don't have the best reputation for sociability. In fact, I suspect many of the young nurses have shed their share of tears while working for me." She stared at Sara intently. "But I suspect you're different. You haven't been pampered."

Sara sat quietly not knowing how to comment.

"The school told me you're an exemplary student and come highly recommended. I always ask for the finest. If they can survive me, then they'll be ready for anything."

Sara nodded, not sure how to respond to this woman who reminded her of someone.

"Now then, we'll go over the ground rules. I'm an early riser. I wake at 5:00 a.m. I like to bathe in the morning, get dressed and be ready for breakfast at 6:00. After breakfast, I sit in the solarium and read until 8:00. Thank goodness, I still have my eyesight. If the weather permits, I visit the gardens. If I have appointments, they are usually scheduled for 10:00." She stopped to take a breath and then rattled on. "Sometimes my granddaughter or banker comes by. Lunch is at 12:00 and by 1:00 I'm ready for a nap. At 3:00 another bath and a leg massage. I have arranged with the school that you shall attend your training from 8:00 to 3:00. The remainder of the time you will be with me. Oh, yes and you should know that I don't often sleep well at night. I may call for you. Any questions?"

Sara mentally replayed the schedule and shook her head.

"Very well, off with you. I'm going to sit here awhile. Mrs. Burns can put me to bed tonight. If I need anything during the night I will call you through the tube."

Sara nodded, set her half finished tea and her untouched cake on the table and left the room while mulling over the schedule. It didn't seem to be too rigorous for her. She already knew she wouldn't have a day off, but perhaps while Mrs. Wilkes was resting she could do some personal errands.

Before Sara climbed into bed she noticed the tube above her bed that Mrs. Wilkes referred to. *An odd contraption,* she thought. *I wonder if I'll hear her.* She sank into bed thinking this was her last night of freedom for some time. Oh, well, she reminded herself it won't be forever. It didn't seem like she had been asleep long before she heard Mrs. Wilkes's voice blurting from the tube above her bed.

"Sara I can't sleep. I need you to fluff up my pillows and rearrange me."

"I'm coming," Sara managed to say into the tube, and then she groggily climbed out of bed confused if she should get dressed in her nurse's uniform or just put on her robe. "Oh dear," she worried out loud, deciding her robe would do.

She turned on the gas light when she entered Mrs. Wilkes's bedroom. In the soft glow of the light, Mrs. Wilkes appeared especially thin and fragile. A ruffled collar on her bed jacket framed her transparent paper thin face. Two tired, agonizing eyes peered back at Sara, who flinched, detecting a hint of familiarity in the older woman's face. *Odd*, she thought. "How can I help?"

"Elevate my head. I feel like I'm drowning in this feather bed."

"Are you in pain?"

"I'm always in pain."

"Do you take pain medication?"

"Sometimes, yes, but not tonight. I'd like a cup of strong tea instead."

"I'll see what I can do," Sara muttered after she had fluffed the pillows and moved Mrs. Wilkes into a sitting position.

Neither the pillow fluffing, leg rearrangement, nor the hot tea satisfied Mrs. Wilkes entirely. She produced a book from which she requested Sara to read. Sara turned the book over in her hand, glanced at the title, *The Oregon Trail* and determined this book was one which she hadn't read before. She opened it and read without enthusiasm, mangling the words as she fought to stay alert.

"Sara is that the best you can read?" Mrs. Wilkes complained.

"It must be the lighting in here," Sara muttered.

"Finish the chapter. Perhaps I'll be sleepy by then."

Sara picked up the pace and attempted to read with interest and inflection. Finally by the time she finished the chapter, Mrs. Wilkes's eyes were closed. Sara pulled up her covers, turned off the light, and tip-toed from the room. As she climbed the stairs to her room above, she detected a whiff of lavender near the steps.

From an atomizer? She thought. *But whose?*

– – – – – –

"How is your first month going with Mrs. Wilkes?" Lois asked Sara one morning while both girls were on their hand and knees scrubbing the surgery room's floor. "You haven't said much about her, and I've been afraid to ask."

"Oh, all right, other than I don't get much sleep. It's a good thing I don't have to use my brain today, or I might be in trouble."

"Today we are just cheap labor," Lois remarked. "Wouldn't it be grand if we could really do something important?"

"Quit your dreaming," Sara said wearily as she thrust the brush into the bucket.

"Did Mrs. Wilkes keep you up all night?"

"She couldn't sleep, so I had to read to her again. I was so tired I could hardly see the print."

"Is she mean like the other nurses have said?"

"I don't really know yet. I've only been there one month."

"So she's treated you fairly so far?"

"Yes, I would say so," Sara said. "She's often gruff but that doesn't bother me."

"I hope she isn't mean for your sake. I do miss having you around. If it gets too bad, just come back and live with me."

"Thanks. I'll keep that in mind, but I think I can manage."

Lois's face became serious. "Have you heard any strange

noises in the house?"

"Noises? What do you mean?"

"Well I don't want to worry you, but some of the girls who stayed there before said the house was haunted."

Sara ceased her scrubbing. "You mean ghosts?"

"Oh, I don't think they ever saw one." Lois laughed nervously. "Listen to me. I sound like I believe in ghosts."

"You don't?"

"Of course not. Do you?"

"Well...I'm not supposed to...but my people believe in evil spirits."

"Like the devil?"

"Spirits mostly. My people are deathly afraid of evil spirits."

"Oh dear, I guess I shouldn't have said anything."

"No it's okay. It's something I have had to work through."

"When you said I'm not supposed to, were you referring to when you lived at the mission?" Lois asked.

"Yes. Like I told you before Evangeline and my cousin Elijah are missionaries and are doing their best to convert the Lakota to the white man's religion."

"Well, just forget I said anything about ghosts."

"Not so fast," Sara said. "I want to know more. Who are these ghosts?" By now both girls were sitting on the floor, scrub brushes in the buckets.

"I really don't know much, but one girl said she heard noises from the floor above her."

"Did she ever go and see what it was?"

"No way," Lois said. "She was scared to death. She slept with her door locked and a chair or two against it."

"Was she the only one that heard noises?"

"Another girl said she heard voices. One sounded like an old lady crying out."

"It could have been Mrs. Wilkes," Sara rationalized.

"From the top floor?"

Sara shrugged. "Have you ever been in the house?"

Lois's eyes widened. "No."

"Would you like to come and visit me sometime?"

"And look for ghosts?" Lois asked, incredulously.

"Sure why not."

"I thought you and your people were afraid of spirits?"

"I didn't say that I was afraid of spirits."

"Oh, because the missionaries convinced you there is no such thing as ghosts?"

"That might be it. Come by after we get done here. Mrs. Burns will be gone this evening. I'm to prepare supper for Mrs. Wilkes. I'm sure she won't mind if you come by."

"Oh, I don't know."

"Even better. Stay the night."

Lois's eyes widened. "Are you kidding me?"

"No, I'm serious. There's nothing to be afraid of."

"Could...I stay in the same room with you?"

"Sure, I see no problem in rooming together. Besides, you aren't going to hear or see anything out of the ordinary anyway."

Lois hunched up her shoulders. "Suppose you think I'm a ninny?"

"Maybe." Sara smiled teasingly.

"Alright, just to prove I'm not afraid, I'll spend the night, but I'll have to tell Mrs. Dobbs where I'll be," Lois told her.

"Good, I'll meet you by the rear door when we've finished for the day."

Lois nodded and returned to the cleaning task. They met one another at about three o'clock and stopped by Lois's room, so she could pack a few things for the stay over.

"Do you miss rooming with me?" Lois asked while stuffing a few essentials into a small brown bag.

"Sure. But I'm getting used to living at Mrs. Wilkes's. She's not so bad, other than being a little demanding."

"I would be dead tired trying to keep up with your schedule." Lois closed her bag and slung it over her arm. "Okay I'm ready."

Once they entered the Victorian, Sara reached for Lois's hand and led her into the parlor.

Mrs. Wilkes looked up from her reading; her face wore a sour expression. "Well, who do we have here?"

"This is my friend Lois. She's also training to be a nurse. I hope you don't mind me inviting her to supper and to spend the night."

"Oh, Sara, will you ever learn to ask permission first." Mrs. Wilkes' face softened unexpectedly. "As long as it doesn't interfere with your duties, I suppose it will be all right just this once. It will make more work for Mrs. Burns, washing sheets and all."

"I knew I shouldn't have come," Lois whispered.

"Don't pay attention to her," Sara whispered back. "She's quite brusque, but I don't mind that anymore."

Lois rolled her eyes. "If you say so."

"She's staying with me in my room. So there won't be extra sheets."

Mrs. Wilkes heaved a sigh. "Oh, all right."

"I can go back to my room at the hospital, Sara. I don't have to stay," Lois protested.

"It's fine, Lois. You're staying," Sara said under her breath.

"I'm especially hungry tonight," Mrs. Wilkes said. "I hope you make something extra delicious."

"I'll get to it right now," Sara said thankful that Mrs. Burns had left specific instructions for their meal.

After a satisfying supper Mrs. Wilkes, Sara, and Lois returned to the parlor, where Sara served them applesauce cake and tea. When the plates and cups were cleared away, Mrs. Wilkes shared her day of aches and pains.

Lois merely nodded. She had hardly said anything all night except for thank you and becoming restless, she offered to wash up the dishes while Sara sat and kept Mrs.

Wilkes company.

Mrs. Wilkes grew weary and asked Sara to take her to her room. After Sara tucked her in to her satisfaction, she returned to the kitchen for Lois. "Let's go up to my room. Maybe we can explore a little before bedtime," Sara whispered.

"This is your room?" Lois seemed surprised when Sara led her to the second floor bedroom. "It's much larger than the one we shared. What's this?" She pointed to the strange looking tube above her bed.

"This is how Mrs. Wilkes calls me."

"A little too often I suspect?"

"I usually hear from her about two o'clock. I have to fluff her pillows, fetch her a cup of tea, and oftentimes I read to her before she falls back to sleep. Don't worry, you can just stay here and rest while I tend to her needs."

"Good. I hate to get up in the middle of the night," Lois shivered, pulling her sweater around her. "Where are we going to explore?"

"I thought I'd take you up to the third floor. There's a great view from up there."

"Is it safe?"

"I'm still here, aren't I?"

"Let's get it over with." Lois shuddered. "I have to prove I don't believe in ghosts," she said more to herself than to Sara.

Sara laughed. "Follow me." Sara took hold of Lois's hand and led her down the gloomy hall to the stairway."

Lois chattered, both from cold and anticipation. "Does anyone stay in these rooms?"

"No. The granddaughter might stay in one, but I haven't met her yet."

"The doors are closed. Have you been in these rooms?"

"All but one. No ghosts there."

"What's in the other room, then?"

"It's locked."

"Locked. Which one?" Lois's glance darted back and forth

among the rooms. "Now that's spooky."

Sara pointed to the locked room. "There might be valuables in there. One day I'll ask Mrs. Wilkes. I think she's beginning to like me."

"I would say so. She's not as mean as I thought."

"See, I told you."

The young women ascended to the third floor where Sara lit a gas light. "Gosh, it's hard to see in the dark. I should have brought you up in the daylight, but we won't have time in the morning.

"Ooh, I don't like this room." Lois stood immobile. "So big and creepy."

"Just concentrate on the view through the big window." Sara found herself whispering.

Lois tip-toed up to the viewpoint and conceded it was a magnificent view of the city. "There's even a telescope."

"Have a look through it."

Lois warily took hold of the telescope to peer at the city. Immediately Sara thought that the telescope was in a different position than when she had last seen it. Who moved it? She wondered. She didn't dare make any comment to Lois. She was too nervous already. "Want to explore this room?" she asked Lois, attempting to keep her tone steady.

Lois jumped at the sudden sound of her voice. "I don't think so. The floors creak and there are dark shadows in the corners. What was this room used for?" Lois asked, backing away toward the stairs.

"I believe a ballroom. I asked Mrs. Wilkes about it, but she had little to say." Sara turned to leave. "It's bedtime anyway. Let's turn in."

The young ladies returned to Sara's room and after some conversation, they called it a night. As usual Sara was awakened at two o'clock by Mrs. Wilkes's demanding voice. She tended to her as she always had, leaving Lois to her sleeping. At about three o'clock she returned to her room to find Lois awake. "Why aren't you sleeping?"

"I'm glad you're back. I thought I heard something," Lois said breathlessly.

"Like what? Where are you, anyway?" Sara pulled at the covers.

Lois emerged from underneath a mound of blankets, barely able to get the words out of her mouth. "Someone was shrieking."

"Shrieking? I've never heard such a sound. I think your imagination is running away with you. It was probably the wind," Sara said, although she didn't think it was particularly windy this night.

Lois sat up in bed, her hair disheveled and her eyes as large as the moon outside. "I swear I heard it coming from the third floor. I don't know how you can sleep on this second floor all by yourself. It's so big and creepy. Do you mind if we lock the door and put something up against it?"

"I always lock the door."

"You do? So you're scared, too?"

"I wouldn't say scared. More like cautious."

Lois grimaced. "Let's slide something against the door."

"Okay," Sara agreed too willingly. She jumped out of bed and pushed a chest against it. "There, now let's try to get some sleep."

Sara lay awake, listening to the still night. *Did Lois hear something?* She wondered. *No it couldn't be,* she decided, realizing Lois's uneasiness was getting to her, too.

CHAPTER 3

Sara was reading in the parlor when Maud came by the Victorian to visit one bright and cheerful Sunday. "I was hoping I could take you away from here for the day," Maud suggested when Sara answered the door. "Let's go shopping or do something fun."

Sara was pleased to see Maud even though she was a bit eccentric at times and totally absorbed in fashion. Unfortunately, fashion was not one of Sara's interests, but she knew Maud meant well.

A change of scenery would be the best medicine for my tired and overworked soul, Sara thought. "I have to stay. Mrs. Burns is out for the afternoon and someone has to be here for Mrs. Wilkes."

"Do you ever get any time off? We miss you and would like you to come for a visit."

"I don't have any time for myself except for a couple hours while Mrs. Wilkes is resting." Sara wrung her hands. "I would like to come and spend some time with you, but I just can't." She had felt uneasy ever since Lois spent the night with her. It would have been pleasant to sleep somewhere else for at least a night. She had been straining her ears every evening after Louis's stay, listening to the house, but she never heard the shrieking Lois claimed to have heard.

"Well, I think it's dreadful," Maud sniffed. "I came to tell you Evangeline is coming to Boston to testify and put that vile man who tampered with her estate away. This time Elijah is coming with her and Willow. You just have to get some time off to see them."

"They're coming here?" Sara's face beamed with happiness. "I'd love to see them, but how can I? My training sessions and caring for Mrs. Wilkes take all my time."

Maud straightened her shoulders and firmed her jaw. "I'll just have a word with Mrs. Wilkes and convince her you're needed at home for a few days."

"I don't know if that is such a good idea. Mrs. Wilkes can be cantankerous."

"I can too if I have to. They're working you to death, and I am going to do something about it. I suppose you are even committed to all the weekends?"

"I work at the hospital on most Saturdays and care for her on Sunday."

"My, my. That's just criminal."

Sara attempted to soothe Maud's ruffled feathers. "While Mrs. Wilkes is sleeping we can visit. I'll brew us some tea, and you can tell me about Frederick and Gertrude. Is she still with you?"

"She is, poor soul."

"I find it almost unbelievable that Gertrude was James's mother and Evangeline's mother-in-law, and Evangeline didn't even know it," Sara said.

"It is an odd case. Frederick and I felt a responsibility toward her when we found out she had no place to live where she wouldn't be in danger from Ethan Halloway."

"You and Frederick are so kind. I don't know how to thank you for all you have done for me, too."

Maud smiled. "Just bring me a cup of strong hot tea."

Sara left to brew the tea. While the water was heating, she tiptoed to Mrs. Wilkes bedroom to determine if she was still sleeping. She stood still for a moment listening at the door. The doors were extra heavy and muffled the sounds from the hallway, but Sara could faintly detect voices.

That can't be, she thought. *No one has entered the house since Mrs. Wilkes retired for her nap.*

Soon the whistle on the teakettle began to sound, and she rushed to the kitchen to remove it from the burner. She shook as she poured the water into the teapot. While she let the tea steep, she went to Mrs. Wilkes room again, but this time, she didn't hear anything.

She must have been talking in her sleep, Sara decided and joined Maud in the parlor.

"Here's our tea. Good and strong." Sara poured herself a Maud each a cup. "Now back to Gertrude. Does she still live with you?"

"She does. When Ethan Halloway is put behind bars, we'll find a suitable place for her," Maud said. "Evangeline would never forgive us if something happened to her."

"Evangeline told me that she didn't remember anything about her past. Is her memory improving?"

"I don't believe the doctor has made much headway. She tends to stay to herself, but she has been quilting with the nurse we hired to take care of her. Some days I hardly know she's in the house."

"A sad story," Sara conceded.

Maud set down her tea cup. "Are you happy here?"

"It's all right. I do miss being with you and Frederick." Sara didn't dare say anymore or Maud would move heaven and earth to make her happy.

"I could talk to the training facility. Perhaps I can exert

some influence."

"No, no, it's just fine the way it is."

Maud tilted her head to one side and narrowed one eye. "Are you sure?"

"I am." Sara averted her gaze. A call from Mrs. Wilkes room set her on her feet. "I think Mrs. Wilkes is up."

"Remember I want to have a word with her. I'll stay right here until she's ready to receive me."

Sara left Maud and opened the door of Mrs. Wilkes' room and glanced around. No one was there besides Mrs. Wilkes other than the faintest scent of lavender and nothing looked disturbed.

"Good afternoon. Did you rest well?" Sara fluffed the pillows.

"Yes, I think I did." Mrs. Wilkes yawned.

"Maud DuMont is here to see you."

"I don't know anyone with that name."

"She's the lady that escorted me to Boston from the mission. She's Evangeline's mother."

"Evangeline?" Mrs. Wilkes massaged her forehead. "The woman you consider like a mother?"

"Yes, she's the one."

Mrs. Wilkes scowled. "What does she want? I'm still rather tired."

"Oh, I think she just wants to meet you." Sara was hesitant to say anymore.

"Perhaps another time." Mrs. Wilkes waved her hand in dismissal.

"You don't even have to get out of bed if you don't want. She can come in here."

"What? The way I look...like I'm helpless." Mrs. Wilkes fluffed her hair.

"It's just a suggestion. It'll take just a moment to lift you into the wheelchair." Sara began to feel the pangs of disappointment. She did want to spend time with Evangeline,

Elijah and Willow. She had missed them so much. "I'll tidy your hair, put on a little powder and you'll be ready to go."

Mrs. Wilkes groaned. "If you're that insistent. Let's get this over with."

In a few moments, Sara wheeled Mrs. Wilkes out to the parlor where she introduced the two ladies, and then poured Mrs. Wilkes a cup of tea.

"I understand that you have taken a personal interest in Sara?" Mrs. Wilkes said, beginning the conversation.

Maud set her jaw firm and dispensed with the pleasantries. "Yes, my husband Frederick and I are quite fond of her. That's why I'm here."

Mrs. Wilkes lifted her brow. "You have some complaints."

"No, no, not at all. Evangeline, Elijah and their young daughter Willow are coming for a…visit. We would like Sara to join us for a weekend, but she says she needs to work to fulfill her obligations. I'm here to see if you can release her from her commitments for this one weekend."

Mrs. Wilkes directed her gaze toward Sara. An inquisitive glint appeared in her eyes. "I see. Sara has said nothing to me about it."

"Sara didn't know. I'm speaking on her behalf."

"I depend on Sara so much. I don't know what I'd do without her."

Sara held her breath. At this moment, she wanted nothing more than to be with her family. She felt sorry for Mrs. Wilkes, but she had to admit she was homesick.

Mrs. Wilkes glanced at Sara apparently noticing her bated breath. "I'll see what I can work out. Perhaps my granddaughter can spend the weekend here with me and take over Sara's responsibilities."

"Thank you," Sara and Maud said in unison.

"Write down the date, Sara, so I don't forget," Mrs. Wilkes said.

The roar of Frederick's motorcar outside on the street announced Maud's departure.

"I'll walk you to the door, Maud," Sara said. She hugged Maud and waved to Frederick before she returned to the parlor. "Thank you for letting me have some time off."

"I've been selfish. I apologize. I should have asked you before now if you wanted a little respite."

Sara shrugged. "It was my job to stay here and care for you."

"Family is important. I forgot."

"But they're not really my family by blood, other than Elijah. But they have treated me like I am."

"Nevertheless, you need to be with them. You are so lucky to have people who love you." Mrs. Wilkes held out her empty cup. "Now, let's have another cup of tea."

———————

It was in March when Frederick came by Mrs. Wilkes's home to pick up Sara for a weekend at the DuMonts. Evangeline and her family had already been there a while to take care of legal matters.

Sara had packed a few things and was waiting anxiously in the parlor when Frederick drove up in his motorcar. As soon as she heard a noise outside, she peeked out the door. She was hoping for a carriage.

"I see you're ready," Frederick said, holding the car door open for her.

"You brought your motorcar?" She edged closer to the auto.

He laughed slightly. "You've never ridden in one of these have you?"

"No, I have not." She moved closer, inspecting the strange contraption. "I've seen them dart around the street, but I didn't know I would have to ride in one of them. Are they safe?"

"Just as safe as a carriage, but you do have to pay attention when you drive one of these. There are some really wild drivers out on the streets."

Sara drew closer, studying the interior. "It does look comfortable."

"Slide in and get used to it. I'll get in, too, and explain how it works." Frederick waved his hand with a swooshing motion as if to help her in the car. "Now then," he said, when he climbed in beside her, "there's a motor that powers the car under the hood—"

She covered her ears. "My, it makes a lot of noise."

Frederick nodded. "Yes, I guess it does, but you'll get used to it. We'll start out slow."

Sara grabbed on to her seat as he edged the car away from the Victorian. "Does this car go fast?"

"It can. Want me to show you?"

"Oh, no, this is fast enough."

After a few minutes, Frederick glanced quickly at her in concern. "You okay?"

"I'm getting used to it I think." Her grip on the seat hadn't lessened.

Frederick waved and honked to passers-by. Sara startled at the horn.

"Some of those motorcars are going mighty fast," she observed.

"It won't be long and the motorcars will be replacing the carriages."

"I suppose. Times are changing," Sara said.

"Everyone's so anxious to see you."

"And I'm anxious to see them." Sara relaxed a little and looked out the window. She had forgotten what the rest of Boston looked like other than Mrs. Wilkes's Victorian and the hospital. "What style is your house?"

"My, where did that come from? Are you studying architecture, too?"

She laughed. "No, just curious. Mrs. Wilkes lives in a Victorian, I know. I was just wondering about your house.

"We have a modified Victorian, not as ostentatious as Mrs. Wilkes's, but a Victorian, nevertheless."

"Does yours have secret rooms, secret passageways and such?"

Frederick glanced at her in puzzlement. "No, not that I know of. Why do you ask?"

"Just wondered."

"Have you found one in Mrs. Wilkes's house?"

"Oh, no. I just heard about them. Why do some houses have them?"

"Some builders were eccentric and included them in their designs. Others used them to hide slaves."

"I find that very interesting."

"Ah, here we are," Frederick said, pulling up beside the house. "Be careful, you might be mobbed with people. They're dying to see you."

Sara stepped out of the car and gazed at the house. "I've missed this place. More than I can say."

"You should wait inside the car and let me open the door for you. That's what gentlemen do." He bowed slightly.

She covered her mouth in embarrassment. "I didn't know."

Frederick scurried around to her side of the car and folded his arm around her shoulder and escorted her to the door. Before they had a chance to turn the knob, Evangeline flew outside and threw her arms around Sara.

"I've been so worried about you. My, you look thinner. Are you well," she said, holding her at arm's length.

"I'm fine." Sara shrunk back from the attention. "No need to fret over me."

Evangeline frowned. "Nursing's hard work isn't it?"

"It is, but it will be worth it."

Inside the house, Sara coaxed Willow into her arms.

"She remembers me." Sara nuzzled the child with coos of endearment. Elijah placed a comforting hand on Sara's shoulder, and Maud smiled at the reunion.

"Mabel has made all your favorites for lunch," Maud announced. "Let's make ourselves comfortable and catch up on all the details."

Sara held Willow in her arms and settled in her favorite chair. She didn't realize how tired she had been until the soft chair cushioned her weary body.

"Tell us everything, Sara," Evangeline encouraged. "Is the school everything you hoped it would be?"

Sara didn't want to complain that nursing training wasn't what she had expected, but Evangeline would eventually pry everything out of her. "Most of the training takes place at the hospital. We learn by doing, mostly the messy clean up jobs."

Maud wrinkled her nose. "That doesn't sound too interesting to me."

"I do enjoy the academic lessons, but they don't happen as often as I like."

"And Mrs. Wilkes how does that work out?" Elijah interjected.

"She has quite a reputation with the students, past and present, but we seem to get along well. I don't know much about her other than she lost a daughter to a riding accident. The same one in which Mrs. Wilkes was crippled. I fear the incident has drastically changed Mrs. Wilkes forever."

Evangeline appeared sympathetic. "How did the accident happen?"

"The horses spooked and threw the riders."

"Oh, how dreadful," Maud said compassionately.

"Enough about me," Sara insisted. "Evangeline, how did you come out with your case against Ethan Halloway?"

"Halloway and his partners in England were found guilty of fraudulence and tampering with James's and Gertrude's estate. He's behind bars I'm happy to say." Evangeline shifted her gaze to the window. "Henry should be coming by soon. If it wasn't for him, we might not have cracked the case."

"I remember you talking about him. He's the detective who's fond of Mabel's cooking?" Sara asked.

Maud laughed. "He certainly was and still is for that matter. We invite him by every once in a while. He's become a friend of the family." She lowered her voice. "In fact, he has taken Mabel out on drives in his motorcar."

Evangeline grinned with conspiracy. "Is it because of her cooking or Mabel herself?"

"I don't know, but they seem to enjoy each other's company." Maud smiled.

"And where's Gertrude?" Sara asked

"She's upstairs with the nurse," Maud said.

Sara placed Willow on the floor to play and straightened her skirt. "Has her memory improved?"

Maud sighed heavily. "The doctors have been working with her for several months and they have made some progress, but she refuses to remember the accident with the boat that killed her husband, and almost herself."

"She knew who I was," Evangeline said. "She seems in better spirits, and she has been sewing quilts again. Thankfully not the Storm At Sea, but patterns with cherry motifs. She still doesn't remember her son James at all and becomes annoyed when I mention him."

"Now that she's in no danger from Ethan, Evangeline and I will look for a care facility for her," Maud explained.

"I'm happy she's making progress," Sara said.

"We all are." Maud's face saddened. "I hope she will be happy in a care facility."

Evangeline leaned into Maud and patted her hand. "She will be, Mama. You have done so much for her already."

"Your father insisted we care for her," Maud said absently. "He was so fond of James."

Evangeline cast a furtive glance at Elijah. "Yes, I remember."

An awkward silence lapsed, and Sara seized the opportunity to change the subject. "I miss the mission. Tell me about everyone."

"Of course they all miss you, Cassandra especially. They are keeping busy with the students. Our enrollment remains steady, and of course I have filled in for you," Evangeline said. "I enjoy going back to work. Sometimes Willow goes to class with me when I can't find anyone to watch her."

"Or she comes to the church with me," Elijah added. "Although, it's hard to work on a sermon when she's around."

Sara yawned. "I bet. She's an active one. Are the ladies still quilting? You know, I especially remember the Jacob's Ladder quilt they made when I was quite young. I remember my Grandmother Red Bird working on the quilt."

"Oh, I do, too." Evangeline laughed. "I was just learning to sew and Red Bird was so patient with me."

Just visiting with her family caused her weariness to slip from Sara like a silk jacket from her arms. She sighed in contentment. "She embroidered a red bird on the quilts she made."

"Yes, she did," Evangeline recalled.

"I wonder what happened to the quilt. It was the last one Red Bird worked on. I feel terrible that no one knows where it went," Sara said.

Evangeline picked up Willow and bounced her on her knee. "It disappeared while I was gone, too. I asked about it but nobody knew where it disappeared to."

Sara frowned. "I guess it's gone forever."

"Cassandra thinks it disappeared when the mission had such a turnover with staff," Evangeline said. "I certainly don't want to accuse anyone, but it's a possibility. I wasn't there, of course. I had returned to Boston. What do you think Elijah?"

"I don't really feel like I should judge either, but we had mission workers coming and going," Elijah said, uncrossing his feet. There was a couple who came to the mission for a while. And then there was this younger woman who wanted to return east and continue her education. Most of the time we were understaffed."

"I really don't remember the young lady," Sara commented. "Why is that?"

Elijah stroked his chin. "I believe you weren't at the mission very much then. We let you visit at Santee for awhile to see if you liked it there."

"We'll never know what happened to the quilt," Evangeline said, shaking her head.

Sara scowled. "I guess not. I just have to accept I will never see Red Bird's last work again."

Evangeline jumped up from her chair, startling Sara. "Henry's here. Can you hear his motorcar?"

"It would be impossible not to." Maud grumbled.

Evangeline flew to the door, hugging Henry as he stepped over the threshold.

"My, my. I didn't expect such a reception." Henry laughed as he regained his balance.

"I apologize for my exuberance. I was just speaking of you and discussing how you solved the case involving Ethan Halloway."

Henry joined the group where Evangeline introduced Sara and Elijah to him.

"We are grateful to you. Solving the case brought my Evangeline and Willow back to me all the sooner," Elijah gushed in appreciation.

"It was a doozey, but glad to help. Heard your case against him went well." Henry fixed his attention on the door to the kitchen.

Maud noticed and commented. "Lunch should be ready."

Henry settled in a chair to wait.

Sara was surprised that a past employee had become such a good friend of the family. She studied his casual manner and his genuine concern for them all. Perhaps, she thought. He can help me. "Excuse me Mr. Knox, but I was wondering if you could direct me on how to find out a history of an old house here in Boston."

"Call me Henry. Everyone here does."

Evangeline interrupted. "I didn't know you were interested in history, Sara."

"I think she's referring to the old Victorian of Mrs. Wilkes where she now resides," Frederick added.

"Oh, I see," Evangeline said.

"Something special about that house?" Henry raised his bushy brows.

"Not really. I just would like to know who the previous owners were and such."

"Did you ask Mrs. Wilkes?"

"She doesn't like to talk about such things, and if she does she becomes upset and irritable."

"I see. I could look into it if you like."

Sara had no money to pay for his services and regretted that she had brought up the subject.

Frederick spoke up and gave his permission. "Why don't you have a look? Besides, that will give you an excuse to pop in from time to time," he said with a wink.

Maud joined in the conversation with an afterthought. "I was only in the house once, but I found it odd that there were hardly any accessories like paintings, knick-knacks, and such. In fact, I thought the furniture rather shabby and the house poorly decorated or should I say lacked decoration."

"Mother," Evangeline scolded. "That's not a nice thing to say. I'm sure Mrs. Wilkes does the best she can, being an invalid and with no one around to help her but a paid staff."

"I didn't mean to be judgmental. I just thought it was peculiar."

———————

Within a week, Sara stopped by Henry's office at his invitation. She was surprised at the number of old books that haphazardly filled rows upon rows of book shelves. Stacks of books were also heaped on his desk in jigsaw fashion, as well as notes scribbled on irregular pieces of paper scattered among an array of folders. A worn brown couch occupied the corner with a rumpled dingy blanket draped across the arm rest. Sara imagined he slept there on occasion.

Henry fanned the air with one of the crinkled manila folders. "I have some information on the Victorian."

She sat in a chair across from his distracting desk. "Good, what is it?"

"Nothing out of the ordinary. It was built by Sam Cummings in the 1840s. His wife's name was Henrietta. He built onto the house in the 1850s, by adding a turret. Rumor has it that he harbored escaped slaves for a short time. When the authorities began to suspect him, he desisted. Now, why he added a turret puzzles me." He pushed himself away from his desk and paced the floor, tapping the folder on his hand. "A turret wouldn't hide slaves as there is no entrance to the ground level. Unless...unless it was a cover-up. Yes, that's got to be it." He spun on his heels to face her.

"I don't follow you."

"I bet he was actually doing something else to the house, but he constructed the turret as a diversion to the public. You know, outward appearances."

"You mean he could have been adding secret rooms or such?"

His eyes brightened with discovery. "There would have to be tunnels, too."

Sara nodded in agreement.

"It's quite possible that no one would pay attention to the extra lumber he brought in for the turret. I sure would have liked to have been there to see how he managed the ruse." Henry rubbed his hands together in thought.

"What else did you find?"

Henry glanced back at the folder. "Sam died in 1870, and I found no record for Henrietta's death. In fact, I could find nothing about where she lives, or if in fact she's still living." He peeked in the folder one more time. "The house was transferred to R.D. Wilkes and his wife Mattie in 1880."

"That would be Mrs. Wilkes, the woman I care for."

"Do you want me to find information on her?"

"Oh, no. That wouldn't be right. Spying on my employer?"

"I see your point, but if you change your mind, I can do that."

"Are there any house plans?" Sara asked. "Plans of the rooms and such?"

"No, nothing of that nature. Like I said, the information is quite sparse."

"Thank you. I appreciate your research. If you come across anything more, please let me know. "

"I certainly will."

"Do you think a stop at the library would give me information on how people helped slaves to escape? Maybe I could pick up a few clues."

"It's worth a trip. Would you mind if I come with you? I have an idea."

"Come along if you like. It's just a short walk."

"How about a ride in my motorcar?"

"No thanks. I'll meet you there."

Henry laughed. "Very well."

The visit with Henry had piqued Sara's interest in secret rooms, slaves, and tunnels. She approached the librarian's desk and asked her for the information she needed. In no time at all, the librarian produced books and articles on the Underground Railroad, the system of safe houses to hide and move slaves to freedom. Not knowing anything but what she briefly had studied in school, she found the subject fascinating. To think she was living in such a house, a house that gave refuge to slaves during the day, a place where they could eat a meal and rest before they continued their trek to the north under the cover of night.

People who ran the safe houses had to be brave to risk being arrested and maybe their own lives for the sake of the slaves, she thought.

Henry joined her at a library table where she was immersed in slave history.

"Our talk got me to thinking about the Cumming's family," he said. "I'm sure the library has something on such a prominent man."

"A good idea." She was beginning to appreciate Henry's skill as a detective.

"Did you find anything interesting?" He asked.

She flipped through the pages of a history book. "Indeed. The slave issue never crossed my mind much until now."

Henry spoke briefly to the librarian, and then sat at the table with her. Shortly the librarian brought out a book on noted personalities associated with Boston's history. She had marked the page for him with a brief biography of Sam Cummings. Henry read it and then pushed the book over to Sara.

Sara read with interest about Sam Cummings. She learned he was involved in civic and communities affairs. He had been a staunch abolitionist and had used his money to further the cause. His wife's name was Henrietta, which she already knew, but she reread the part that discussed their daughter. Her name was Mattie? Mrs. Wilkes first name was Mattie.

"Henry, Mrs. Wilkes first name is Mattie. Could this be a coincidence?"

"Not if Mattie and R.D. had the title transferred to them. It's not so unusual for children to inherit or even buy their childhood home."

"So Henrietta Cummings would be Mattie's Mother?"

Henry nodded. "Looks that way."

"And you said that you could find no death record for Henrietta?"

"That's correct."

"Mrs. Wilkes' mother could be alive?" She asked in amazement.

"She could."

"But Mrs. Wilkes has never talked about her."

"We could visit the cemetery and see if Sam Cumming's wife is buried beside him. The article tells us where he was interred."

"Good idea. When?"

"Right now. It won't take long."

Her eyes widened. "In your motorcar?"

He grinned. "I'll drive slow, promise."

Sara agreed much to her own consternation. But Henry did drive slowly as he promised, and they arrived at the cemetery without incident.

Henry hopped out of the car and opened the door for Sara. This time she waited as Frederick had told her to. "Now to find the family plot," he said with gusto.

Sara could tell by his actions that Henry loved his work. Evangeline had told her that he was good detective, and so far she agreed. He was a funny sort of man, but she liked him.

One glance at the huge cemetery told her finding the plot would be no easy matter. Headstones of every shape and size covered the cemetery. Years of family ancestors had been buried here, so unlike their little cemetery at the mission where her Grandmother Red Bird was buried.

The wind moaned through the evergreens and played with her scarf. She tied it tighter and bent her head into its force. She shivered at the thought of spirits and reminded herself what Evangeline had told her. Henry decided they should split up in their search. They each took a different section of the cemetery and hunted for the grave of Sam Cummings.

She marveled at the engraved headstones, taking to heart the sadness of each one, especially the infant graves often marked by a little lamb. She knew it was hard to lose loved ones, no matter the circumstances.

Nearly an hour passed before Henry waved his arm. "Over here, Sara." She quickly strode over to where Henry stood beside a large granite monument with the name Cummings engraved in large letters. His birth date and date of death were also engraved at the bottom. The name Henrietta and her birth date was etched beside his, but no date of death had been recorded.

"She's still living," Sara said breathlessly.

"It appears so, but don't take it as a definite yes. In my line of work, I encounter surprises all the time," he warned.

"What does this information tell me?" Sara questioned Henry.

He stroked his chin. "Maybe Mrs. Wilkes' mother is alive somewhere."

CHAPTER 4

Mrs. Burns had left the house to run a few errands, and Mrs. Wilkes was taking her Sunday afternoon nap when the beckoning sunshine pulled Sara outdoors for a stroll. She hadn't explored the five acre grounds since she had arrived in January.

Sara slipped into her wool winter coat and black boots and left the confinement of the house. Breathing deeply of the fresh cool air, she set off to inspect the property. A short walk led her to a dilapidated riding stable and carriage house partially hidden behind a large copse of evergreen trees. She quickened her pace when she heard the neigh of a horse in the paddock. As she rounded the corner of the stable, a sway back, black horse looked up at her with soft lipid eyes.

"It is a horse," she said out loud, clasping her hands to her mouth.

She slowly approached him and stroked his head. She surmised he was the carriage horse that no one used very often, but she didn't care if he had seen better days. A horse was a horse and she had missed one since she had moved to Boston. She had nothing to offer him, not even a carrot.

Next time I'll bring him something, she reminded herself.

After another stroke of his nose, she left him to inspect the out buildings. Pushing open the door of the stable, she entered the building, distinctly smelling like horses; however, the aroma of earthy scents had never offended her. In fact, it reminded her of days when she rode freely over the prairie with the other children in camp. Her horse was her best friend then.

One of the stalls appeared to be in use, but the others looked untouched for years. Poking around the building, she located a small amount of tack that hadn't hardened and dried out. Someone had been oiling it and keeping it supple. A well kept saddle drew her attention. She ran her hand over the smooth leather, her fingers tracing the monogram *IW* near the pommel.

Isabel Wilkes, Sara quickly surmised. *They kept her saddle? But why wouldn't they?* She returned to the other saddles, looking for other monograms, but there were no more. Obviously the saddle with Isabel's monogram had been a special gift.

Her heart leaped when the door burst open and a man stepped inside. "What you doing in here?" his harsh voice demanded.

She stumbled back a few steps. "I...I was just looking around."

"Who are you?"

"I live here." She folded her fingers into fists and willed her voice to stop shaking. "I'm the nurse, Sara Fletcher, who takes care of Mrs. Wilkes."

"Does she know you're here?" The gruffness hadn't left his tone.

"No. I left her napping. I didn't think she'd mind." Sara was beginning to make out who the man was. She had seen him from the distance but never up close. "You the gardener?"

"I am, among other things."

"I wanted to get out of the house a while. I found the horse. Would you mind if I visit him from time to time." Her courage mounted.

"You'll have to ask Mrs. Wilkes. She's the boss here."

"Does he have a name?"

"Simon."

"Are you the one that cares for him?"

"I do." His tone was curt. "Mrs. Wilkes insists that we keep up the carriage and the horse for...for when her granddaughter comes to visit." He cleared his throat. "You ask a lot of questions."

"I'm sorry. I like horses."

"I got to go and tend to my duties. I suggest you ask Mrs. Wilkes permission before you go nosing around." He turned his broad back to her and stalked off.

Sara had yet to visit the carriage house. Should she defy his orders? She asked herself, craning her neck to see where he went. She saw that he had disappeared around to the front of the house.

Mrs. Wilkes might be waking up, too, she thought. *Oh, just one peek*, she decided.

She sneaked to the side door, opened it and peered inside at something shrouded in a canvas cover. She guessed it was a carriage. A buggy had been jammed into a corner, and a variation of family relics had been tucked into shelves and hung on walls. She didn't dare investigate any more at this moment. Mrs. Wilkes might be awake and calling for her.

On her way to the house, she spied the gardener who was doubling as a handyman repairing a shutter. He paid her no mind when she slipped past him and into the house. There was something about his appearance, his shifty eyes and that hawk like nose made her uneasy. He hadn't even told her his name. Hurriedly, she skipped up the steps to her room and listened at the tube. She heard nothing from Mrs. Wilkes, so she removed her coat and boots, sat in the chair by the window and read, waiting.

Within half an hour, Mrs. Wilkes called Sara to her room. Dutifully, Sara descended the stairs and came in to find Mrs. Wilkes trying to sit up straight against the pillows.

"Could you fetch me a cup of tea?" she asked.

Sara assisted her and then brewed a pot of tea in the kitchen, which she shortly brought to her room. As she poured the tea and handed it to her, Sara asked about the stable and the horse in the paddock.

"I probably shouldn't have gone out there without asking you, but I needed to get outside for a while."

Mrs. Wilkes scowled. "I'd rather you ask first. You are an unusual one. Have you no fear of anything?"

"Is there something to be afraid of?"

Mrs. Wilkes laughed. "You aren't afraid of me, are you?"

"No. I see no reason to be."

Mrs. Wilkes shook her head. "I admire your strength, Sara."

Sara shrugged. "Thank you."

"You're welcome. I think we will get along just fine as long as you can tolerate my moods."

"I think I'm able to do that, Mrs. Wilkes."

"Why don't you call me Mattie when it's just the two of us? I wouldn't want to ruin my reputation if word gets out that I might have a pleasant streak." She laughed.

Sara didn't want to spoil this unexpected moment, so she kept her questions about Mrs. Wilkes's mother Henrietta, the saddle, the horse, and the stable to herself. She'd wait for another time.

Sara couldn't explain what was going on in the house, but she didn't fear Mrs. Wilkes. Instead she felt sorry for her. It was evident Mrs. Wilkes was unhappy with her lot in life. Sara decided she would be, too, if she had lost a daughter and was an invalid unable to enjoy the things she used to. After breakfast one Sunday morning, Sara lingered in the kitchen to visit with Mrs. Burns.

"I would like to do something to brighten Mrs. Wilkes' days. I thought you might have some ideas how I could do that?"

Mrs. Burns dropped her dish towel on the table and stared at Sara. "You want to do something for Mrs. Wilkes?"

"Yes, is that so unusual?"

Mrs. Burns nodded. "You bet it is. All the girls assigned here couldn't wait to finish their internship and skedaddle. Some couldn't even finish and left without another look back."

"I have to admit my schedule is grueling, but I've been able to handle it."

"I had a feeling when I first met you that you would be different. So you want to do something to make Mrs. Wilkes happy?" Mrs. Burns lowered her voice to a whisper. "I don't know of anyone who can do that, except to be her granddaughter. She does seem to enjoy her."

"Have you ever seen her happy other than when she's with her granddaughter?"

"When I came to work for her she was just like she is today." Mrs. Burns resumed her chore of washing dishes, speaking with her back to Sara. "Maybe worse then. She was injured in the same accident that took her only daughter's life."

"What happened?"

Mrs. Burns handed Sara a dishtowel. "They were out riding one spring day. Both horses spooked and threw their riders. The daughter was killed and Mrs. Wilkes injured for life. She has never gotten over it."

"I can see why she's bitter." Sara stacked the dried plates on the table. "But I would like to try and make her days more pleasant."

"Her granddaughter Myra told me once that Mrs. Wilkes was an accomplished quilter. I've never seen any of the quilts she made. She must have put them away."

"So why doesn't she quilt anymore?"

"I suppose she doesn't have the passion she once did," Mrs. Burns said. "Besides, it must be hard on her to do such work, being an invalid and all."

"I've had some experience with quilting at the mission. I think I'll approach the subject with her and see what she says."

"She'll say no, for sure. I suggest you entice her."

"How do you mean?"

"Have a quilt started. Work on it when you are sitting with her. You might get her interested that way? I guarantee she'll put in her two cents."

"Good idea. Do you quilt?"

"No." Mrs. Burns pushed a strand of hair back behind her ear and cleared her throat. "I'd rather cook and clean, but I do admire the handiwork."

"Perhaps I should find a pattern she might enjoy. I would like to see some of her handiwork. You think she has stored her quilts somewhere?"

"I don't know for sure. Maybe she gave them away. Have you noticed there are no quilts on the beds?"

"I haven't seen any, but I haven't been in all the bedrooms. Some of the bedroom doors are closed on the second floor. Any reason?"

Mrs. Burns shrugged. "I'm not much for snooping around. I think it best you stay out of them. Mrs. Wilkes is a private person. Especially stay away from the third floor."

Sara drew in her breath. "Oh, I've already been up there,

but I just took a peek."

Mrs. Burns stared at her. "Mrs. Wilkes doesn't want anyone up there. Maybe it's unsafe. The floors, I mean."

"I kind of got that feeling when I asked her if it ever was a ballroom."

"Thanks for drying the dishes. Now, go rest while Mrs. Wilkes is napping. I'll finish up and leave for the day. There are fixings for lunch in the ice box. As you know, you will be in charge of lunch and the evening meal today."

Sara nodded. "Have a good day, then."

"I'll be back Monday morning to fix breakfast."

Sara left Mrs. Burns to tidy up her kitchen. She didn't feel like resting, so instead she climbed the stairs to the second floor. There were three rooms that she hadn't seen inside. Perhaps, Mrs. Wilkes had stored the quilts she had made in one of the rooms. Disregarding Mrs. Burn's advice, she quietly pushed open the door of one of the rooms farther down the hall on the north side of the house. A heavy musty smell rushed through the doorway, assaulting her senses.

This room hasn't been cleaned or used for ages, she thought to herself, wrinkling her nose.

Heavy drapes blocked out all vestiges of sunlight, except for a slight opening between the two burgundy drape panels. A shiver of expectation overcame her as she edged toward the room's interior. When her eyes adjusted to the lack of light, she determined the room was used for storage rather than as a bedroom. Instead of a bed, two large armoires occupied the space along two walls with a few cast off chairs. Her heart beat a little faster as she pulled the drapes apart to let in more light. A scraping sound caused her to whirl around and face the doorway. Her hand flew to her heart, and her pulse quickened. When she realized it was only the wind, she closed her eyes and exhaled with relief.

I don't believe in spirits, she reminded herself. *I don't believe in spirits.*

The extra light flooding through the window pane annihilated any imaginary ghosts that she had conjured. She straightened her dress, lifted her head and approached the first armoire. She tugged at the doors sealed shut with disuse. Several more pulls yielded to her grasp and opened. Inside were clothes, dresses mostly, hanging neatly side by side. She reached in and lightly touched them, moving youthful, expensive looking dresses aside one by one. Whose dresses were they? Did they belong to Mrs. Wilkes dead daughter? A prickle of sympathy enveloped her.

Standing on her tiptoes, Sara opened a drawer of an armoire overflowing with hats, matching hats for the dresses she had just seen. A thought caused Sara to quickly scan the walls in search of a portrait, a picture, of what the daughter looked like. There were none though, only a painting of the Victorian house.

The remaining armoire stood on the opposite wall. More of her things, Sara thought as she drew the doors open. Instead of clothes, she gasped in delight. Quilts. "Here are the quilts," she whispered aloud. The cedar lined armoire released a woodsy scent, penetrating the carefully stored quilts. She drew in a breath of the pleasing cedar aroma, and then reached for the top quilt. Her fingers lingered near its edge, and she drew her pointer finger down, counting about ten folded quilts.

I shouldn't be looking at Mrs. Wilkes memories without her being here with me, she admonished herself.

Resisting the temptation to pull the quilts out to see them, she abruptly closed the armoire doors. Her heart thumped against her chest. Suddenly feeling like a thief, she tip-toed from the room just in time to hear Mrs. Wilkes calling her on the tube.

— — — — —

Sara had been ignoring the two remaining unexplored rooms on the second floor for weeks. No amount of rationalizing could cover up the fact that she was intruding in Mrs. Wilkes' private life. Mrs. Wilkes hadn't made any gesture to share any part of her life with Sara. In fact, Mrs. Wilkes discouraged her questions. She knew she shouldn't be sneaking around the house and just accept the fact that Mrs. Wilkes wanted to remain private, but how was she going to help without knowing something about her life.

The house was quiet this Sunday afternoon. Mrs. Wilkes was resting and Sara had gathered courage to investigate. She tip-toed down the long hallway to the other room at the end of the hall. The door had been closed since she first arrived at the Victorian house. She turned the doorknob and pushed against it, but the door didn't budge. Locked! What could be in the room that Mrs. Wilkes didn't want anyone to see?

She turned toward the door to the room across the hall from hers. It was closed also. A tingle of excitement zinged through her as she tried the door. It opened with no trouble. To her relief the room wasn't nearly as dark as the room with the armoires she had visited weeks ago. This room, she concluded, wasn't used for storage. A bed angled into a corner was made up with a deep rose spread as if expecting company at any moment. The furniture appeared as if it had been recently dusted. A slight scent of lemon oil lingered. Two large rose and green flowered area rugs covered the board floors.

The glinting light streamed in the windows through ivory lace curtains, obscuring several pictures decorating the walls. Sara edged closer to them for a better view. One was a portrait of a young woman. Pretty but not beautiful, she decided. A sensation of familiarity washed over Sara. She pressed herself closer to the portrait and studied it for a few moments. Could it be Mrs. Wilkes when she was younger or perhaps it was her daughter? Next to it, a framed photograph occupied the space. This one was of an identifiable Mrs. Wilkes and a girl in her teens. She would have to get up enough nerve to ask someone who this girl was.

Mrs. Wilkes's daughter, she guessed.

There didn't appear to be anything in the room that seemed out of place or unusual. Sara shrugged at the thought it was just an extra guestroom. Satisfied she had seen everything except the locked room, she crossed the hall to her own room to lay out the material and pattern she had bought after school yesterday afternoon.

The quilt she had chosen to begin was suggested to her by a clerk at the fabric store. "Puffed quilts are the rage," she had told Sara. The clerk briefly had told Sara how to make one.

Repeating the instructions to herself, Sara cut out the large squares from an assortment of fabric. Remembering the clerk's warning, she cut half the squares one inch smaller than the others to give room for stuffing each square. She meticulously sewed two squares together and then stuffed it with batting for the puffed look. Sara hurried and completed several squares so that when she and Mrs. Wilkes had their tea after the evening meal, Sara could spring the project on her and hopefully piqué her interest. She heard Mrs. Wilkes stir just as she was finishing her fourth square. Predictably Mrs. Wilkes called for her. Sara put down her needle, tidied up a bit, and hurried downstairs to Mrs. Wilkes room.

The evening shadows of darkness had already infiltrated Mrs. Wilkes bedroom. Sara lit the lamp and helped her to the sitting position.

"It's cold in here. Throw another log on the fire." Mrs. Wilkes insisted.

Sara stoked up the fire as she was instructed, and soon the room took on a rosy glow. When the room warmed, Sara helped Mrs. Wilkes to a chair, and then went to fetch her a cup of tea. While Sara was in the kitchen heating the water, she thought about asking her about the photographs. How Mrs. Wilkes would respond was anybody's guess, but Sara needed to know. She threw caution to the wind, and as soon as she delivered the tea and made Mrs. Wilkes as comfortable as she could she asked, "I was curious about the unused rooms down the hall from mine and I went in to look around." Sara studied the expression on Mrs. Wilkes face, but it hadn't changed. "I hope you don't mind."

Mrs. Wilkes sipped her tea. "I suppose I should mind. If it was someone other than you, I might, but I know you did it out of curiosity not personal gain. Mrs. Burns probably told you about my daughter?"

Sara nodded and lowered her head. "I don't mean to be disrespectful, but I would like to know more about her. I'd understand though if it is too difficult for you."

"It continues to be painful." Mrs. Wilkes paused. "There's a portrait of a young woman in a bedroom on the second floor. That is…was my Isabel. The other photograph is of me and of her before she married. It may be hard for you to imagine, but we were quite close."

Sara waited for her to say more, but Mrs. Wilkes lapsed into silence. Sara wanted to know everything, but wasn't sure if she should press her.

Perhaps after supper would be better, she thought.

Fifteen minutes later, Sara wheeled Mrs. Wilkes into the dining room for a meal of baked fish and rice. Sara was famished and dug into her meal with gusto, but Mrs. Wilkes, she noticed, chased her food around the plate with her fork.

Oh, dear, Sara thought. *I upset her with the talk of her daughter.*

Both women ate in silence, apparently absorbed deep into their own thoughts. Sara was relieved when the meal concluded.

Once she wheeled Mrs. Wilkes from the table to the

parlor and served her the customary tea and dessert, Sara popped the puff quilt out of a large knitting bag that she had planted by her favorite chair.

"Sara, what do you have there?" Mrs. Wilkes asked.

"I'm working on a quilt. Have you heard of the puff design? It's the rage now."

Mrs. Wilkes sighed deeply. "I don't really pay attention to such things anymore."

"Have you quilted before?" Sara asked already knowing the answer.

"I have. In fact, I made many quilts and considered myself quite accomplished."

"You lost interest?"

"I did, besides it's too hard on my back to work on quilts."

Sara stitched a square and began to stuff it. "Do you think you could help me stuff the squares while I sew?" She gave the half-stuffed square to her along with the batting.

Mrs. Wilkes held it in her hand and shoved the batting into the square to give it the puffed appearance. "I might as well help you out for a while."

"Thanks. It will make my project go faster." Sara cleared her throat. "Would it be possible to see the quilts you made someday?"

"Some are stored away. Others I gave away."

"You don't use them anymore?"

"I...I don't for a very good reason. Isabel helped with most of them. She was a better quilter than I was."

Sara hoped that Mrs. Wilkes would offer to show them to her, but she didn't. Obviously, the quilts reminded her too much of her daughter and the time they shared together.

CHAPTER 5

Tex spent Christmas in Texas with Netty as he had planned, but time began to wear heavy while he was there. He missed his South Dakota ranch and made plans to get back before the winter storms began their fury. Besides, he kept thinking about the woman he met at the Christmas dance. He had enjoyed visiting with her at the refreshment table, and he had even danced with her, but had realized too late that he didn't even know Louisa's last name.

It was in February when Tex leaned against the counter of Tater's mission store. "Are you still sore at me?"

Without politely turning toward him, Tater answered over his shoulder. "It's going to take some time to forget how you used me. I didn't like having them perjury charges brought against me."

"But I paid your fine and the others, too."

"I know that, but I don't want my customers to think me a bad fellow."

"Nah, they'll forget all about it in a few months. Somebody doing something worse will come along and make them forget about us." He paused. "I won't bother you with my schemes anymore."

"That's just fine with me."

Tex watched as Tater unpacked a box of canned goods. "You like being a storekeeper?"

"It beats waitin' on a bunch of rowdy cowhands."

"You're still mad at me, aren't you, Tater."

"Yeah, some."

"I expect to be around here more now that the reservation is opened for lease."

"You plannin' on getting a share of it?"

"I hope so. The competition is awful stiff. All the big outfits are eyeing the reservation. I'm thinking of forming a partnership with the Bar Double B. It'd give us an edge."

"Ed would go for that?"

"You mean hook up with the likes of me?" Tex smiled.

Tater nodded.

Curt clamored into the store, his spurs jingling. "Hey, Tater, the mail come yet?"

"Yeah. It's sorted. Are you 'spectin' something important?"

"No, just a letter from his girl," Tex teased.

"I don't have a girl." Curt snapped his response.

"What about Sara?"

"Oh, she said she'd write, but I ain't goin' hold my breath. I bet she wrote Doc," he said, looking at Tater for confirmation.

"I'm not supposed to tell those things."

"You think Doc's your competition?" Tex asked. "Why he's just a skinny runt with glasses.

"You never know what women want," Curt said. "Tater, you ever had a girl?"

"Me? Why it's none of your business."

"Oh come on Tater," Curt coaxed. "We won't make fun of

you. We promise," he said grinning at Tex.

"Like I trust you two." He paused. "Oh, maybe once when I was young, but I couldn't see myself settlin' down and raisin' a passel of young un's. I like peace and quiet."

"But don't you get lonely?" Curt pressed.

"Nope." Tater handed Curt a couple of letters.

Curt shuffled through his mail. A downcast expression appeared on his face.

"Better luck next time," Tex said, consoling his son.

Tater turned to stock his shelves with the remaining canned goods. "Tex, I heard you were prancin' around with a woman at the Christmas dance?"

"You think I'd admit that to you?"

"Thought it was worth a try."

"Only thing, I don't know her last name or where to find her."

"That wasn't too smart. You must have lost your head."

Tex reached into the packing box and handed Tater a few cans. "I must have. Maybe she comes into your store?"

"What she look like?"

"Oh, I suppose in her fifties. I'm not good at guessing age. Dark skin, dark hair, and dark eyes. Told me she had two sons in about their twenties."

"A Lakota woman?"

"No, I don't think so. Her name is Louisa."

Tater placed the last can of peaches on the shelf and turned toward Tex. "I think I've seen her a time or two."

"Are you joshing me?"

"She lives on a ranch," Tater said. "Buys supplies to last for months."

"Know where her ranch is?"

"Never asked," Tater replied.

"Would you ask next time she comes in?" Tex asked.

"I'll think about it."

Tex sighed in disgust. "You want me to pay you something for the information?"

"Nah. It'll be a while before I see her again."

"Me, too. If the winter's a bad one, I won't get here very often. Still, I'd like to know more about her."

"I'll see what I can do."

"Appreciate it," Tex said.

"Want some coffee?'

"Yeah, a cup would be good. I plan to riding out to the Bar Double B. See what Ed has to say about the leases."

"You'd better get started pretty soon. Those clouds in the west look mean," Tater warned as he poured them both a cup of coffee.

Tex had arrived at the ranch just before the blizzard hit. The men watched helplessly while the wind shook the house and drove the snow into drifts. They didn't dare venture out into the swirling confusion to care for the livestock. They couldn't even see across to the corrals.

Days later, the heavy wet snow banks left over from the recent blizzard had melted down due to a warm spell. Rivulets of water trickled out from underneath the snow by the time Tex, Curt, Jet, and Ed rode southeast on the high ridges where the snow had been swept clean to inspect the damages from the blizzard.

"Maybe, we all will be lucky. The cattle could have drifted ahead of the storm," Tex commented as they approached the first ravine. Peering over the edge, he spotted several brown patches protruding from the snow pack.

Jet dismounted and waded through the knee high snow and scooped away its slushy consistency to uncover the soft nose of a dead calf. He pointed out several more dead calves and cows that had collected there during the storm.

Tex shook his head, "Dumb critters, thought they'd be

safe." No matter how many times he dealt with the dead crit-ters, the sight of their bloating carcasses sickened him. Not only because of investment loss, but the ugly contortion of death itself.

The men rode on, trailing cattle for a number of miles, and stopping to count the dead ones either overcome by the crusting snow, buried in the deep ravines, or driven off steep embankments. Finally, they gave up counting. Not all the cattle belonged to the Bar Double B anyway. Others with different brands from other ranches had drifted along with the storm, also.

The day warmed as they rode, Tex peeled off his vest, reached into its pocket, pulled out a Bull Durham sack and filled a cigarette paper with tobacco, rolled it, placed it in his mouth and lit it. He closed his eyes and inhaled, enjoying its intoxicating effect. "Dang," he muttered. "There's going to be a lot more."

After several more hours, Tex reined his horse to an abrupt stop. "I've seen enough."

His son Curt rode up beside him. "The dead ones have thinned out. We'll find the survivors during roundup."

"A little farther is the widow Louisa's ranch," Ed said. "She might have a cup of coffee for us."

Tex stirred in his saddle. "You know Louisa?"

"Yeah. She's widely known in these parts, especially for her pies. You know her, too?"

"If it's the same one, I met her at last year's Christmas dance."

"Ah, Tex, you scoundrel."

"Now hold on." Tex held up a gloved hand. "Haven't seen her since."

"Well, you will shortly."

"What's her last name?"

"Bissette."

The number of dead cattle dwindled by the time they

reached Louisa's ranch. A two story log ranch house and other log buildings became visible along a river bottom. Tex let out a low whistle. "Pretty fancy for these parts."

A smirk spread across Curt's face. "Getting ideas?"

Tex flashed him a warning glance. "Just curious. Ed, what do you know about her?"

"Not much. Her husband was Lakota and French. Dead now. They have two grown sons."

"Yeah, I know that. She pointed them out at the dance. Lean and tall and not too friendly."

Ed laughed. "Just being protective of their ranch and their mother."

Ed's ominous words sent a prickle of apprehension through Tex. *An odd reaction,* he thought to himself. Was he really interested in Louisa? Soon he would know. She was outside her ranch house feeding two wolf hounds as they rode up.

"Howdy." Ed tipped his hat to her.

She finished doling out the dog scraps. "Inspecting the losses?"

"Yeah. Looks like quite a death toll. Dead carcasses all over the place."

"Come on in. I got coffee on." She flashed a glance toward Tex. "Might even have something to go with it. You must be hungry."

Louisa ushered them into the large kitchen. An aroma of roasting meat pervaded the space. She motioned for them to sit at the large oak table while she opened a cupboard and removed several cups.

"So how much of your herd did you lose?" She filled the cups and passed them around.

"It's hard to tell. There's so many other drifted cattle mixed in." Ed slouched in the kitchen chair. "And you?"

"Don't know yet. The boys are still out." She sliced a loaf of bread and placed in on the table along with butter and plum jelly. "The boys will be back about dark. Will you stay the night?"

Ed shrugged and glanced at the men. "We weren't planning on it, but guess we could." He winked at Tex.

Tex's neck warmed under his collar. He rubbed his whisker stubble to hide his reddening face.

"Put your horses in the corral after you finish your coffee. Supper will be ready in about an hour. Boys should be here by then."

Tex and the fellas took Louisa up on her invitation and after carrying their empty coffee cups to the dishpan, they left for the corral with their horses. They had just removed the saddles when Louisa's sons rode up, their faces full of questions.

"We're from the Bar Double B." Tex extended his hand when the first son stepped down from the saddle.

"Name's Tric," The oldest said. "Figure on staying awhile?"

Tex straightened himself to his full height. "Your mother invited us to spend the night. Name's Tex, Curt, Jet, and Ed." He pointed to each one.

Tric waved his thumb toward his companion. "This here's my brother Wade."

"We've been out looking over the losses. Stopped here for coffee," Ed explained.

"Same here. Not a pretty sight."

The men slogged in silence through the slushy snow on their way back to the ranch house. The aroma of supper and soft light met them at the door.

Louisa's dinner ware gleamed white on a red and white checkered tablecloth. She was slicing a steaming roast onto a platter. Tex removed his hat, crossed his hands over the brim of his hat and watched her. A sense of hominess and warmth wrapped him in content. She mashed the potatoes, stirred the gravy, and then seated them, after her sons chose their usual places.

Ed filled his plate with the steaming food and then spoke. "So nice of you to invite us to stay, Louisa."

"My pleasure. Always like to hear the area news. We have to be good neighbors out here so far from everyone." Her dark eyes focused on her sons momentarily.

Tric and Wade remained silent, eyes on their plates during discussion about the recent blizzard and cattle losses. Tex noticed they wore wary and unwelcome expressions on their dark, chiseled faces.

So unlike their mother, he mused.

Relieved when the meal concluded, Tex stayed behind to assist Louisa with the clean-up. He knew he wasn't very handy in the kitchen, but he thought it might be the only way to spend time with her. He fidgeted at the table not knowing what to do.

Louisa smiled. "If you like, bring the dishes over here to the dishpan."

Grateful for the suggestion, Tex did as she said. Louisa had already poured hot water in the pan from the teakettle. After she added some cold water and soap, she began scrubbing the plates. "So glad you came by, Tex. Did you go to Texas for Christmas as you planned?"

"I did. Got a hankering for South Dakota so I came back early."

"In time for the blizzards."

"Yeah. Sure hate to see the cattle losses. Going to have to do some re-stocking of the range."

"And where is your ranch?" She asked, handing him a dish towel.

He took it, slightly embarrassed of his huge hands. "I've consolidated with Ed and the Bar Double B in order to get a lease."

"You got one?"

"We did." He paused. "That was my main goal since I've been in South Dakota, but I got a notion your sons aren't too keen on the idea of the leases?"

"They're like their father. Very protective of our land."

Tex realized that he had never thought about the ranchers who were here before the big cattle outfits moved in on the reservation lands. Certainly they would feel resentful. Typically he had always thought about himself first. Odd that a stranger would make him admit it.

"You keep a nice kitchen."

"Thanks. I like to cook and bake." She chuckled. "If I knew you were coming, I'd baked you a spice cake."

"You remembered?" He thought he saw a slight blush on her cheeks.

After Tex placed the last dish in the cupboard, he and Louisa sat at the table visiting, oblivious to the others in the adjoining room. Tex couldn't help but admire her dark skin and flashing intelligent eyes, her faint floral scent, and the dark print dress she wore with a thick leather belt, encircling her thin waist. He wondered where she got her quiet beauty.

"Will you be stopping by the mission soon?" she asked.

"I can on my way to the ranch."

"I promised Minnie a quilt pattern from the south, close to where I grew up. We actually didn't make quilts like they do here. Wonder if you could deliver it?"

"You're not from around here?" Tex's eyes sparkled with interest.

"My father ranches on land from the Spanish Land Grants."

"He still ranches?"

"Yes, with my brother Carlos."

"You're a longs ways from home. How'd you get here?"

"My husband Victor came to our ranch one day looking to buy cattle for one of his drives north to the reservations. Love at first sight. Went with him against my father's wishes at the age of eighteen. Victor was French and Sioux. He had enough Indian blood in him to qualify for reservation land. We stayed here and established a ranch after he finished the drive."

An imaginary young Louisa flashed before him. *She must have been incredibly beautiful,* he mused. Tric and Wade disturbed his thoughts by announcing they were turning in for the night and abruptly left the kitchen. He had to admit Louisa's sons were striking even if they were standoffish.

"Didn't realize it was so late. I should have had the fire started for you in the bunkhouse," Louisa apologized.

"We can do it ourselves," Tex said, leaving the coziness of her kitchen with Ed and the men.

Ed slapped him on the back once they stepped outdoors. "Have a good visit with Louisa?"

"Yeah. She's quite a lady, but then there are her sons." He shook his head. "I don't think they like us very much."

— — — — —

Within the June month, purple and white wildflowers bloomed beside the stench of rotting carcasses. Cattlemen recorded their losses and some made plans to re-stock the range. Ed and Tex had placed an order for cattle and planned a drive to bring them from a railhead on the Missouri River. They arrived in time to see the railroad cars filled with cattle pull into the busy cattle town. But before they could drive the cattle to their home range, the men herded them into foul smelling dipping vats to rid them of lice, ticks, and scabies. Bawling cattle, clouds of dust, and the smell similar to rotten eggs filtered through the town.

Unknown to Tex, Louisa and her sons had also ridden to Evarts for cattle. He caught a glimpse of her at the corrals dressed in a dark riding outfit, a Spanish style hat swinging on a cord behind her neck.

He edged toward her. "Didn't know you'd be here." He

shouted above the bellowing cattle.

She turned with a smile. "Why, Tex, what a pleasant surprise?"

"You waiting for cattle, too?"

She nodded. "We've been here since yesterday."

"We're waiting on cattle, too. It'll be awhile before we gather them and head out. Would you join me for a cup of coffee and something to eat?"

"Sure. Let me tell the boys where I'll be." Tex waited for her, but when she returned he thought she appeared disturbed. He didn't say anything. *Her sons are probably unhappy about her hanging out with me,* he thought. Too bad, he had just invited her for coffee.

"Any suggestions where to eat?" He asked.

"There's a café over here that serves decent food," she said, seemingly forcing a smile.

He gestured for her to go on ahead, wondering if he should have let her be. Once they were settled, they ordered the daily special with coffee.

"I gave the quilt pattern to Minnie," Tex said grateful he had something to talk about. "She liked it and said something about making one."

"Good. I hope to get to the mission this summer. We exchange patterns for our winter quilting projects. If I didn't live so far away, I'd join them for their sewing sessions."

"You must get lonely being so far from anywhere."

"Not really. I have my sons to care for. Cooking, washing, cleaning, and ironing keep me plenty busy."

While sipping his coffee, he studied her, admiring everything about her, how she looked, the way she moved, her determination. *A dedicated woman,* he thought. *But very attached to her sons.*

They had just finished their meal when Tric came into the café. "Ready to move 'em out," he said.

"I'll be right there." She patted Tex's hand. "Thanks for

the meal and your company."

Tex uncharacteristically panicked. "How about I ride with ya'll for a ways? Seems like you're a little short on help."

She pulled on her gloves. "I'd like that, but don't your men need you?"

"They'll get by for a few hours."

"Alright then. I usually ride swing," she told him.

"I rode them all during my trail days, was the best time of my life."

"Suppose you were young?" She smiled.

Tex chuckled. "You notice I've aged some?"

"You've aged well. I especially like your new moustache."

"Thanks. Thought I'd try one for a while." It had been sometime before anyone had complimented him, especially a woman. He liked it.

"I'm anxious to hear of your trail driving days," she said, mounting her horse once they arrived at the corral.

"Well, I do have a story or two, right after I talk to Ed." He left her momentarily to explain his plans to accompany Louisa on the trail for a few hours. Riding back to her, he felt giddy. He admired the way she looked at ease in the saddle, adventure flicking across her eyes.

"Go on, Tex, tell me about the cattle drives."

Tex settled in his saddle, wishing for a smoke, but thought he should wait. "I was about nineteen. Wet behind the ears. Thought I knew it all."

"Sounds like my sons. They don't heed my advice."

"Sons can be tough to handle." He sensed her relationship with her sons was strained. Only a father would understand their need to prove themselves. "Curt and I have had some tussles along the way, but he has learned. It's my daughter Netty who I don't understand. She seems to get along with her aunt though."

"I would have liked a daughter, but it wasn't meant to be. I know Tric and Wade miss their father, especially his guidance."

"They've kept your ranch together. Got to give them credit for that."

"I tend to forget."

They quickened the pace of their horses to drive a few strays back into the herd. Louisa rejoined Tex laughing.

"I enjoy a good ride," she shouted above the din of bawling cattle.

"You ride well." He told her when once again they rode side-by-side.

"I rode as a child on our rancho. My father insisted I'd be an accomplished horsewoman."

"Do you miss your life back there?" he asked.

"Do you miss Texas?"

Tex nodded. "I see what you mean. A person never forgets the childhood home, but sometimes we have to leave and make our own way."

"Exactly."

The drive continued to twilight when Tric and Wade selected the spot to camp.

"I guess this is it," Tex tipped his hat. "Goodbye, Louisa."

"When will we see each other again?"

"I don't know. Do you ever go to the mission church?"

She shook her head. "I'm Catholic. There's a church not far from my ranch. I go there when the weather permits."

"I see, but y'all buy supplies at Tater's store?"

"From time to time." Her face brightened. "We could establish a day to meet."

"Let's do that. Any ideas?"

"I do. How about the Fourth of July? I'll bring the fixings for a picnic."

"Sounds good to me. Meet you at the mission on July fourth." Under the faint glimmer of stars, he turned his horse and rode back toward his own herd. She liked him, too, he realized. He had to admit he was fascinated with Louisa, but it was her sons who bothered him. They could be a major obstacle. Did he like her enough to face the confrontations that surely lay ahead?

——————

The thick dust from the cattle drive floated in the air as dusk settled over the camp. The cattle were still milling, stirring up more dusty powder. As soon as they made camp, Louisa gathered kindling wood and started the night fire.

Louisa was filling the coffee pot with water when Tric tossed the firewood he had gathered from the creek bank on the ground, startling her. Even the frogs stopped their croaking, she noticed.

"Why is that cowboy hanging around here?" His voice boomed over the clamor of bawling cattle.

"Are you referring to Tex?" She asked with an irritated edge to her voice.

"Yeah, that guy."

She turned her back to him while making preparations for their supper. "Tex and I became acquainted at the Christmas dance last year. I guess he took an interest in me, and I in him."

"It's just going to complicate matters. We don't need him here. Did he ask you where the cattle came from?"

"No, he didn't."

"I find that odd that he didn't ask. Most cattlemen want to know where the stock comes from."

"I imagine he knew they're from Texas. As to the exact ranch, I guess he didn't need to know that they're from my father's ranch in Texas." She opened a can of beans and poured them in a skillet and placed it on the fire.

"I don't like it. Is it necessary for you to see him?"

She wheeled around toward him. "Don't worry. The ranch will be yours." Louisa braced herself against his comments. "I have a life of my own to lead. He's a nice man, and as of right now we're good friends."

"I still don't like it." He slapped his thigh with his hat. "He's bound to find out you have money, lots of money. He's the kind of guy that wants to get ahead. How do you know if he likes you for who you are or for your money?" He stooped toward the fire and poured himself a cup of coffee. "You haven't told him anything, have you?"

"We haven't discussed money. Like I said, we're friends nothing more. Don't worry. I'm not about to tell him my family history."

"Good, I just don't trust him. To my way of thinking, he's the ambitious sort."

"You're afraid he's after your ranch?"

"I'm just suspicious, that's all. What's wrong with protecting what's yours?" He stomped off toward the remuda, leaving her alone.

She tossed bacon in another pan and set it on the fire beside the beans. Tex had brought a ray of sunshine into her ordinary lonely life. Lately, she had felt that her sons were taking her for granted. They didn't seem to appreciate all she was doing for them, her cooking and washing, and taking care of them like she did when they were little boys. Tric had just proven he was more concerned about his own interests rather than what she desired.

Loneliness was something she dealt with every day since her husband died. She had tried to subdue it with work. Sometimes it eased the pain, especially when she fell into bed too tired to think. She knew she had spoiled her sons, but something had to change. She stirred the beans vigorously, contemplating throwing the beans and bacon in the fire, leaving them fend for themselves, but she was hungry and there was no need to waste good food.

The aroma of bacon permeated the camp and brought her sons to the campfire. They dished up their plates without saying a word. Louisa suspected Tric had been discussing Tex with Wade, too, as he had been eyeing her over his plate of beans.

"I see the discussion about Tex isn't over," she blurted.

"We've heard things about him," Wade defended himself.

"Like what?" She spat the words out of her mouth.

"He got in trouble for buying up relinquishments under false pretenses," Wade said. "His cook was showing homesteads near Tex's ranch to people who had no intention of staying on them. Then when they wanted out, Tex bought the relinquishment to his own advantage."

"Yeah, that's against the law," Tric joined in. "He wasn't going to homestead.

"I see, so you're trying to discredit him."

Tric helped himself to more beans. "Well, he isn't honest."

"Yeah, and the law came down hard on poor ol' Tater, not Tex," Wade added.

"Why don't you let me worry about that?"

"Ah, Ma, haven't you heard that love is blind," Wade reminded her.

"I'm not stupid. We wouldn't be where we are today if I was incompetent, besides I think Tex is a good man. Sure he was tempted once. We don't always make the right decisions."

"I can see we're too late," Wade said frowning. "You're already smitten with him."

Louisa smirked. "Even if I was, I wouldn't let him have the ranch. It's yours, it will always be yours. I promise."

Her sons finished their meal and placed their tin plates in the dishwater. "Guess we'll turn in," Tric said. "I'm beat and we still have a ways to go tomorrow."

"Goodnight," she said grudgingly as she began scrubbing the dishes in the little water she had. She sighed deeply, replaying the conversation they just had. These were the times she missed Victor the most when her sons became difficult to handle. Deep in her heart she knew Tex was a good man. He like many others she knew sometimes stepped over the moral line, but she could forgive him.

－－－－－

Tex was pleased that Louisa had selected the Fourth of July for their next meeting. He had been looking forward to seeing her again. In fact it was all he could think about even though he had been busy with spring roundups. Now that they were over with, he and the rest of men could take a few days off and partake of the mission's celebration.

The mission had been preparing for weeks. Elijah and Jeremiah planned a special church service for the celebration to kick off the two day event. The women had been cooking and baking to feed the people who would be coming for miles for good food and fun.

Cassandra's sewing class made red, white, and blue banners, as well as a patriotic-colored star quilt which would be given away in a raffle drawing. The banners and quilt were displayed on the newly painted gazebo. Red and white geraniums bloomed in pots at the gazebo's base.

Tex, Ed, Jet, and Curt arrived as the church was filling with people. They scanned the pews and seeing no empty ones, they stood in the back against the wall. Tex craned his neck, looking for Louisa, but he couldn't find her seated. But he really didn't expect her until after the service.

Tex fidgeted during the service, which was a little too long for his impatience. As soon as it concluded, he practically bolted toward the entry way and then he saw her. His heart skipped with delight. Then he felt foolish for behaving so. She and her sons had brought the buggy. She had just gotten down and was dusting off her dark brown skirt and jacket as he approached them. He tipped his hat when she turned to face him. Her sons glowered and offered a curt greeting and then left them alone.

"Your sons brought you?" He tried not to sound surprised, but he was.

"Yes. I insisted. Could you help me with these pies?"

She had them in two baskets which he lifted from the back of the two seated buggy. A tantalizing aroma made his stomach rumble. "Hmmm, smells good," he said, lifting the basket up to his face.

"Rhubarb and last year's apples."

"I hear you're one good pie maker."

"I hope these measure up."

He carried the baskets over to the food table laden with roasted meats, potatoes, gravy, vegetables from the mission garden and baked goods. After a prayer, the crowd lined up to fill their plates. Tex led her to a pre-selected spot where they could sit in semi-seclusion.

After all, he thought. *We have little time to be together.*

Louisa peered over her shoulder. "Don't you think we should sit with the others? They might talk."

"Let them talk. I want to be alone with you."

She held her hand to her heart. "Why, Tex, are you making advances?"

"I certainly am. There's too much distance between us to go at this slowly. You do like me, don't you?"

"I do but—"

"But what?"

"It's complicated."

"How so?" he asked already knowing the answer.

"My ranch, my sons, your partnership."

"Yeah, I know. Been thinking about it."

She whispered, "I don't even know you that well. This is moving too fast."

That wasn't the response Tex was hoping for, but at least he knew she liked his company. She was right, it was complicated. There was no way her sons would accept him at their ranch, and he did have obligations to the Bar Double B. Worst of all, he had no idea how to resolve this dilemma.

They set their personal discussion aside and watched the sack races and all the other activities that the mission had planned for the afternoon festivities. When the horseshoe competition began, Curt wandered over and nabbed his father.

"Let me see if I can beat you," he said.

"How can I turn down an invitation like that," Tex said to Louisa. "Come closer so you can cheer me on."

Tex pitched a few rounds, scoring a couple ringers over Curt's. "Ready to give up?"

"How about another game?"

Tex didn't want to keep Louisa waiting, nor did he want to disappoint his son. He stroked his chin. "Just one more game." This time he gave his son the edge.

The evening concluded with music. Tex snatched Louisa's hand and pulled her discretely along with him for an evening stroll. The stars had just begun to twinkle and the prairie's night life began to join in with their own melodies. Coyotes howled from the distant hills, crickets chirped their night songs and frogs croaked from the river. It was a perfect night for spooning, he thought. He was as nervous as a school boy as he made his move and took her in his arms and kissed her. The moment she melted into him he knew that he had to find a way to win over her sons.

CHAPTER 6

Kat listened with pleasure to the first meadow lark, chirping his spring song. Kat heaved a sigh, closed her eyes and smiled, as she washed the breakfast dishes. The winter had been long and snowy, but it was gone. The best part was she had survived the loneliness and desolation. Spring thrilled her, made her bloom just like the first wildflower. She wanted to run outside under the bright blue sky and do cart wheels on the greening grass.

She had passed the gloomy days throughout the winter by sewing quilts, cooking, and baking bread while Jet tended the cattle on the Bar Double B Ranch. She loved her quilts, but she was itching to get back to Deadwood to see her sister Annabelle and the new business venture. The reports she had been receiving lately from Annabelle encouraged her. Transitioning from a saloon to a restaurant had been a risky endeavor, but she was seeing that perhaps she had made the right choice. Hiring Aggie as cook was definitely an asset even though her sons had attempted to kill Jet in her saloon nearly a year ago. Even though Aggie had nothing to do with it, Kat had a difficult time getting over the incident and had resisted the idea of hiring her when Jet had suggested it; but it seemed to be working. She was putting out good meals and the customers were coming back for more.

Just yesterday Kat had sketched out an interior design for her restaurant. She hadn't purchased anything different for her new business other than to add a kitchen. She still used the same tables and chairs when the Birdcage was a saloon, not knowing if the food business would be a success.

During the long winter, she had thumbed through the mail order catalogs looking for ideas. The railroad had reached Deadwood from the south several years ago, so ordering something and having it delivered was no problem. Annabelle assured her that she had made money on her new business venture within the last few months. So to Kat's way of thinking, she could invest money in her establishment. While lingering over the morning coffee, she paged through the catalog, white wicker furniture caught her attention. It was light and airy just like the meadow lark's song that she had just heard.

What will go with white wicker furniture? She mused. *Perhaps birdcages filled with ivy instead of birds?*

She had given her birds away before she left so that would be no problem and, of course, quilts decorating the walls would add that special touch her place needed.

A year ago, she had gathered a group of saloon women to help her sew a log cabin quilt for Jet while he was imprisoned. The ladies had so enjoyed making quilts that they continued sewing quilts, which they gave away to the needy. When Ling Li lived in Deadwood, they had made several Chinese patterns, also. The sewing ladies had given the Chinese Lantern as a wedding present to her and Jet when they were married in Deadwood. She had it on her bed right now. In turn, the ladies gifted the Chinese Coin quilt that they had made to

Ling Li as a wedding present.

Kat suspected the ladies had little time to quilt, since she had left for the ranch. She imagined it took all their energy to keep the restaurant going.

The one drawback to spring was that Kat hardly saw anything of Jet these days. After the spring blizzard and the restocking of the range, Ed and his hired hands worked around the clock to get the ranch into tip-top shape. She was anxious to get to Deadwood. In fact, she had her bags packed.

Kat had put her catalog away and just finished up frying bread dough, when Jet came in for mid morning coffee. "Got some news. The stockholders sent a telegram and said they'd be here in a few days," he told her while washing his hands in the wash basin.

"I suppose they're staying here at the ranch?"

"Yeah. Ed said there'd be room in the ranch house."

She lifted out the crisp brown fried bread from the boiling lard and rolled the lengths in sugar, put them on a plate and set six of them on the table. "How long they staying?"

"About two weeks."

She wrinkled her eyes. "That long?"

"They want to ride the range. Take a look at things and see how their investment is doing?"

"Bet Ed's a little nervous."

"There's not much he can do. It is what it is. We couldn't help the blizzard and the losses."

"Well, you men do a good job. Work too hard in my opinion."

Jet stuffed the fried bread in his mouth and washed it down with coffee. "Got something to ask you."

"Yeah, what?"

"We need your help."

She glanced at him warily. "With what?"

"The English like their tea and crumbles."

"You mean crumpets," she corrected. "And I thought just women ate them."

Jet shrugged. "There. Do you see what I mean? Us men know nothing about such stuff. We need a woman around to help us out."

"I have to cook and entertain them?"

"Not all the time. Maybe once or twice. Ed asked me to ask you."

She threw up her hands. "What about Ed's regular cook?"

"He had to leave. His brother's sick."

"Great. I can't serve them in this shack. Besides I know nothing about crumpets."

"Write to Minnie. Someone at the mission might know. I got to go. Ed's never been this crabby before."

"A few days doesn't give me much time to do anything."

Jet hunched in his chair. "You might have to get their beds ready, too. Maybe clean up the ranch house a little."

Kat pushed her chair back, placed her hands firmly on the table. "How many men are coming?"

Jet leaned into her and pecked her on the cheek. "Don't know. Won't know 'til they get here." His eyes pleaded with her.

"Fine. I guess I'll have to do it." She glared after him as he trotted off toward the corrals.

Crumpets indeed, she thought to herself. She wasn't about to make crumpets, but she could make biscuits.

Ed had given Kat permission to use the ranch house to entertain the stockholders, but still she couldn't sleep when she had learned what was expected of her. She dreaded the two weeks she would have to devote to cooking, cleaning, and entertaining, but Ed said he would pay her well.

"Once or twice indeed," she ranted out loud, remembering what Jet had said.

The next day when the men went riding, Kat scurried over to the ranch house to tidy up and make a list of supplies needed for meals. One of the ranch hands would go and get the supplies for her at Tater's store. She had to admit she wasn't the best cook around, but she was the best they had for now. Thankfully, Minnie had given her cooking lessons when she had spent time at the mission. She would prepare what she knew how to cook.

That's all I can do, she consoled herself. She would have liked to go along with the ranch hand and visit with the mission women, but she simply didn't have the time. *Oh, well,* she thought, *I'll be in Deadwood soon.*

Luckily, Ed kept a clean house and it didn't take long for her to spiff it up a bit. The cook had left a good supply of staples. Other than a few canned goods and a good quantity of tea, she thought she could get by. Ed had told her that breakfast and supper would be the two main meals she would have to prepare. He thought they would be out riding most of the day. She wondered if the English gentlemen were prepared for the rigorous schedule that Ed and the men had planned for them.

By the time the four stockholders arrived in a few days, she had cleaned the ranch house, washed the bedding, made the beds, and lined up enough meals for two weeks and even baked enough cookies and cakes to serve with coffee or tea if they preferred.

They'll just have to do without their crumpets, she decided.

When Kat saw the English stockholders for the first time at the evening meal, she doubted they knew much about open range cattle. They entered the house with rosy cheeks and eyes flashing with adventure and good manners. They were dressed in riding britches tucked into high boots and bulky tweed jackets. Each carried a riding quirt, which they left by the door. Laughing at a blunder one of them commit-

89

ted out with the cattle, they seated themselves at the table after Ed introduced them to her. They were most polite and did not want to be seated until she sat down first.

"Please take your seats. It's fine if I sit down last. I'm the only one here to wait on you," she insisted. Reluctantly, they did as she told them.

She served them roast beef, potatoes, and vegetables and one of her cakes. They seemed like a jovial group and dug into the food as if they hadn't eaten for quite a while. She listened as the English gentlemen talked about the vastness of the land and the long horn breed of cattle they weren't familiar with.

"Hard to imagine so many cattle roaming the plains of Texas," one of them said. "I'd like to see them arrive by train."

Ed forked the last piece of cake into his mouth. "That could be arranged. The cattle town isn't that far from here. We could take a day and visit if you wish."

"What you need are our Hereford bulls. Put some meat on those lanky longhorns," another one said.

Tex pushed back his chair and stretched. "That's what I've been saying for a long time, now."

When Kat left her chair to pour more coffee, the Englishmen stood up. Once again she asked them to sit. "I appreciate your gesture, but it isn't necessary." She filled their cups and cleared the table while the men talked cattle.

"Kat and me been wondering what the B in the Bar Double B stands for," Jet asked the stockholders.

The stockholders looked from one to the other before anyone spoke. "It stands for our anonymous stockholder," one of them explained. "There are five of us. The fifth one isn't here."

"Do you know who the fifth one is?" Jet asked.

"We do, but we have never met...the stockholder."

Ed became interested. "But you do correspond?"

"We do." The Englishman patted his chest. "In fact, I have

a letter from our fifth partner right here in my pocket.

"Will we be able to meet this secretive partner of yours?" Ed asked.

"I don't know if you will. For some reason our silent partner wants to remain anonymous."

"I see. I guess it isn't necessary we know the identity. We were curious," Jet said, letting the inquiry drop.

One of the English men passed out cigars and soon the kitchen filled with choking smoke. Kat excused herself and stepped outside into the warm still air. She could hear their loud voices discussing the cattle business through the open windows.

The sound of chirping crickets followed her to her house, eventually drowning out the voices. She was weary and needed to get away from the boisterous men for a while. She had planned that when they retired for the evening, she would go back and clean up the kitchen and decide what she would cook for breakfast. Since they were making a trip to Evarts, she imagined they would want to leave early. Meanwhile, she sat down on a bench outside her house and listened to the night sounds, her legs stretched out in front of her and her shoulders slumped.

Within the half hour, she heard Jet approaching. "Had a long day?" he asked.

She pulled her slouching shoulders up and yawned. "I sure have. Suppose you did, too?"

"Yeah, kind of nerve-racking. The stockholders make the decision if we continue our operation here."

"What impressions are they giving you?"

"They've let us restock the range, so guess that means they'll give it another go for a year at least. It seems they like the way we've been handling things. Ed's the best manager around."

"He is a fair man" Kat said.

CHAPTER 7

Two weeks with the Bar Double B stockholders was almost more than Kat had the patience for. She had cooked for them, served afternoon tea, cleaned, and listened politely to their discussion of the new cattle breeding program. As soon as they departed for England, she took up her packed bags and left for Deadwood. Instead of taking the stage, she finagled a roundabout rail trip to Deadwood from Pierre arriving from the south. She purchased the ticket with the money she had earned from Ed.

As she walked down Deadwood's Main Street, greeting a few acquaintances along the way, an aroma of frying meat drifted from the Birdcage. She waited her turn to enter the restaurant clogged with customers. She smiled to herself. Her idea of a restaurant was working.

Her employees bustled about, oblivious to her presence until Jennie passed her with an armload of dishes and nearly dropped them when she saw her. "Kat, I didn't expect to see you."

"Here, let me help you." Kat rescued a handful of dirty dishes from Jennie. "I couldn't wait to get back and see you all." She followed Jennie into the kitchen where smoke rose up above the stove in a greasy haze.

Aggie forked golden brown steaks onto a large platter. Brown gravy bubbled and green beans simmered. She and Leona nodded a greeting, barely looking up from the task at hand.

"Shall I dish you up a meal, Kat?" Aggie asked without looking up.

"Please do. Would someone like to join me? By the way, where's Annabelle?"

Jennie shrugged. "She…hasn't come into work yet."

"She hasn't come in?" Kat's eyes grew wide with concern.

"Leona, could you cover for me? Dish me up a plate, too." Jennie led Kat into the dining room. "We've got to talk."

"What's the matter?" Kat asked. "Oh, wait a minute, let me guess. Annabelle's not doing her job."

"You got it. She met a gambler fellow. Spends a lot of time with him."

"And Miranda?"

"Found an older woman to watch her."

Kat frowned. "How long's this been going on?"

"Several months now."

"And her letters were so encouraging. Said business has been great."

"It has," Jennie agreed. "She's not been here much. Comes in every once in a while. We never know when."

"It appears the business has been doing fine without her."

"Yeah, it's been mostly me, Aggie, and Leona. Cilla works occasionally to relieve us."

"You should have written me," Kat scolded while cutting her steak into bite size pieces.

"I knew you'd walk in one of these days."

"Did she pay you your wages?"

94

"She did."

"Do you know about the receipts?"

Jennie nodded. "Annabelle shoved the books onto me. According to them, you've been doing well. Not as good as a saloon, but you're holding your own."

Kat stiffened. "Annabelle still in my house?"

"As far as I know."

"That will have to change."

"How long you staying?"

"Jet said for me to stay as long as I needed to." Kat heaved a weary sigh. "Looks like I'll have to make some changes."

"You're not going to sell, are you?"

"No. I still want a connection to Deadwood."

"You...and Jet getting along?"

"Oh yes, but I can't say I love his ranch life the way he does."

"You are going back?"

"I'll go back, but not for a while. Jet's so busy, he'll hardly miss me."

Jennie picked up her empty plate. "Aggie's waving at me. Got to go." She patted Kat's arm. "We'll talk later."

Kat sat sipping the last of her coffee, contemplating what she should do. Clearly Annabelle wasn't working out, but why should it surprise her? She had her doubts when she left Deadwood. *How could my own sister let me down?* She grumbled to herself.

"I'm going out to find Annabelle," she called out to her ladies. "Be back later."

Kat whipped on down the street, up the steps to her little house perched on the hill, her anger mounting with each step she took. She knew she had taken a chance with Annabelle so maybe it was her own fault after all, but still, she trusted her. As she neared the top step, she saw her carefully tended flower beds overgrown with weeds. She called to her cat that usually napped on the front porch, but it didn't appear. A tad disgusted, she pushed open the unlocked door to a kitchen filled with dirty dished piled high in several dishpans. The table was covered in dishes, too. A walk through of the house revealed more neglect. Beds unmade, the foul smell of garbage, clothes strewn about.

How am I going to spend the night in this mess? She wondered. Well, she wasn't. She'd sleep at the Birdcage, somewhere, anywhere until she found Annabelle and gave her a piece of her mind. She stormed back to the Birdcage and nearly knocked Aggie over when she barged through the door.

"Looks like you punched out your worst enemy," Aggie sputtered when she side-stepped out of the way.

"Annabelle is gone," Kat huffed. "She couldn't even take care of my cat. The place is a mess like she hasn't been around for a while."

"Now sit down. I'll bring you a cup of tea. It might not be as bad as you think," Aggie consoled.

"If it wasn't for you, Leona, and Jennie, I'd be ruined. I don't know how to thank you."

"Ah, it was nothing. We just wanted to prove it could work," Aggie said. "And it has."

"But it can't continue this way. I'll have to go back to the ranch eventually. Jet's happy there."

"We like our jobs," Jennie protested.

"Don't worry. Like I said I don't want to sell." Kat tapped her red fingernails on the table in thought. "You gals haven't had time to sew have you?"

Aggie set the cup of tea on the table. "No. It takes all our energy to keep this place going."

"Aggie, you're a fine seamstress. Leona makes quilts, and Jennie you have a good business head. How about we convert this restaurant into a sewing shop?"

"Oh, our customers will be devastated," Leona said.

"They'll just have to get over it," Kat fumed. "We've got to think of ourselves first. What do you think Aggie?"

"A sewing shop? That would be a dream come true. I can't believe you have that much faith in us?" Aggie said.

"You've proved yourself over and over. Leona what do you think?"

"Who's going to buy quilts or anything else for that matter?" Leona asked.

"I'm not sure. We'll just have to see what people want. Maybe it will be curtains, pillows, who knows. Jennie what do you think?" Kat looked to her friend.

"Whatever you think best," Jennie said. "As long as I can work for you."

"We could still serve tea and coffee, perhaps some pastries, cakes and such to go with it."

"A woman's shop," Jennie added.

"Exactly. A place they could come to look at patterns. Aggie could fit them for dresses. Leona could help them with fashions for their homes, quilts, pillows, curtains, tablecloths and such."

"I don't know much about them fancy things," Leona commented.

"You can learn," Kat said.

Jennie clapped her hands. "When do we start?"

"According to the bank account, I should have enough money to make the transition. It may take a while for the business to make a profit, but I guarantee you all a wage."

Anyway, I hope I can, she thought secretively.

— — — — — —

Kat woke from a nightmare in a cold sweat. She did her best to shake the searing images from her mind. When she finally erased the last haunting one from her head, she was relieved that it had been only a dream. It had been so real. Rio and Jed had been front and center, their guns blazing, and then she blacked out in the dream just like the night she fainted in the Birdcage.

She sat up in bed and swung her legs over the side and held her head in her hands. She realized now that she was putting too much faith in Rio and Jed's mother Aggie. What if Rio and Jed came back to Deadwood either looking for her or coming back to settle the grudge with Jet? What a dilemma she had gotten herself into. If only she had discussed this with Jet before she left the ranch. But no matter how she looked at the situation, she needed Aggie. She was the only one who could get this new venture off the ground. The business would be fine if she could stay here herself, but she knew she would have to return to the ranch.

Kat padded to the kitchen to brew a pot of coffee. She drew the kitchen curtains aside to see Deadwood waking for the day. How she had missed the sounds of the town she had grown so fond. Could a sewing shop make it on its own? She knew there weren't enough seamstresses in Deadwood. She found this out when she went looking for someone to sew the dresses for her wedding. Leona had pretended to do the sewing, but it was actually Aggie who fashioned the dresses, much to everyone's surprise.

And then there was Leona, an unpolished gem, a very simple woman with no refinement at all. She could sew quilts, but Leona was right. What would be the demand for quilts? Most women made their own. It was doubtful if Leona had any ability to help design a room.

If only her sister Annabelle wouldn't have let her down, but if she took up with a man, there was no way she would be able to convince her to spend all her time in someone else's business. How was she going to approach her when she did catch up with her?

After coffee and a piece of bread for breakfast, Kat dressed for a visit to the Birdcage. Perhaps her mind would clear once she saw the operation at work. She had to make a decision soon before she was needed back at the ranch. She frowned, recalling her dream of white wicker furniture and birdcages filled with ivy in her restaurant. That silly notion would have to wait.

Kat heard Aggie snapping orders at Leona, when she entered the Birdcage. Jennie smiled at her as she glided out of the kitchen balancing a tray of steaming food. Kat noticed customers happily chatting with their friends and family over their morning coffee. An ambience of contentment permeated the establishment.

"What can I get you, Kat?" Jennie asked on her way back to the kitchen.

"Thanks, but nothing. I ate at home."

"Well, you should have waited. Aggie makes a scrumptious breakfast."

"I see that. It's a shame to ruin such a good business."

"Having second thoughts, are you?"

Kat nodded. "What do you think I should do?"

"That's a tough one to answer. I suppose it's got to be a business we can handle the best when you're away."

"And what would that be?"

Jennie glanced nervously toward the kitchen. "Leona's giving me the look. I better get back to the kitchen. We'll talk later. Promise."

How is Jennie going to help me? Kat thought. This was a decision she had to make herself.

Not able to sit any longer, Kat left the table and stepped outside the Birdcage. She breathed deeply of the mountain air, holding it in her lungs, and then slowly expelling.

"What's this?" she said out loud. She moved closer to the for sale sign on the window of the adjoining building that used to be a clock shop. She peered in the window at the empty interior. It wasn't a spacious building, but there was potential if one wanted to expand a business. A name to contact was scrawled across the for sale sign.

"I wonder," she said under her breath. Mr. Lockert's name was on the sign of the building next door to the Birdcage. She knew where to find him.

Kat wasted no time beating a path down the boardwalk to the Miner's Restaurant. Mr. Lockert was her competition now, and she had stolen his best cook. She prepared herself. He might not be too cordial. She could smell the stench of grease before she even stepped over the threshold of the Miner's Restaurant. She adjusted her eyes through the cooking smoke until she spotted Mr. Lockert with a waitress. She waited until he finished and then she approached him.

"Kat, you're back. Thought you were out east someplace."

"I was. I mean I am, but I came back to tend to business."

"Do I get my dishwasher and cook back?"

"I don't think so."

A glint appeared in his eyes. "Are you planning to sell?"

"No, I'm not. I probably should, but I like Deadwood and hope to come back some day."

"Hmmm, I see that you are running a busy restaurant over there."

"It's doing well according to my help."

"So what can I do for you today?" He asked.

"You own the shop next door to me. What you asking for it?" she asked without flinching.

Mr. Lockert quoted a price. Kat grimaced. "If I didn't know you any better, Mr. Lockert, I would think you were trying to fleece me."

His eyes narrowed. "Ah, I wouldn't do no such thing."

"I bet." She pulled a piece of paper out of her purse and wrote an amount and handed it to him. "This is what I'll pay."

"You've got to be kidding me. I can get more than that out of it."

"Go ahead and try. The building is too small for much of a business. You're not going to get many offers." She turned and walked out the door. Kat wasn't certain whether he would come around to her way of thinking, but she couldn't afford anymore. In fact, she wasn't sure where she was going to come up with the money she had offered.

Two weeks had passed since Kat had made an offer to buy Mr. Lockert's property next door to her business. She sat at the table in the Birdcage with her chin resting on her hands.

"What's the matter?" Jennie asked her.

"I haven't heard from Mr. Lockert. I doubt if he's going to take my offer."

"Can you afford to pay more?"

"I don't know. I would have to gamble on the restaurant to make the payments."

"I don't follow." She sat down with an empty tray.

"I realized that I can't discontinue the restaurant business right now. It's paying for itself and will have to pay for the building next door if Mr. Lockert and me can come to a deal."

Jennie squinted her eyes. "And what you going to do with the building if you buy it?"

"That's where we could set up a sewing shop. It would be quite small at first. You see, I decided to test the waters first."

"Okay, but when you're gone who's going to run two businesses?"

"I haven't figured that part out yet."

"I think you had better think on that one. Us women can hardly keep up with this business. And I thought Aggie and Leona were going to be a big part of the sewing shop."

"And you too," Kat reminded her.

A worried look played across Jennie's face. "Yeah, me, too. That's my point. How can we be in two places at once?"

"I don't rightly know. I thought maybe Aggie could train

someone else to cook. Teach a new cook her skills."

Jennie shook her head. "I don't think anyone could learn her skills. Aggie has a special way around food."

"Come on, now, Jennie. You're ruining my plan."

"I don't mean to. Just trying to be practical. If you were going to stay we could do it."

"I know, but I have to go back to the ranch. I wish Jet were here. He might have an idea."

"Yeah, I bet I know what it would be?"

"What?" Kat asked.

"Give up all these ideas of yours and come back to the ranch."

"I know in my heart that's what I should do, but I like it here. I like my own business."

Jennie looked at Kat intently. "You can't be in both places at once."

"I know, but if I sold everything, you gals would be out a job."

"I'm sure we could find work somewhere else. I love working for you, but I can adjust."

Kat frowned. "I guess I need to face facts."

"You know what? I think I have an idea." Jennie scooted to the edge of her chair. "You like running a business, right?"

"Yeah." Kat's face brightened at the thought of an idea.

"I've never been to that mission of yours, but you said it was growing into kind of a town."

"But it's a mission. I can't open a saloon."

"I wasn't thinking of a saloon."

"I can't have a restaurant either. The ladies at the dormitory feed everybody right now. And there's already a general store."

"A sewing shop then?"

"The women at the mission fulfill that need, too."

"Oh." Jennie's enthusiasm popped like a bubble.

Kat suspended her hand in the air. "Hold on a minute.

Jet wrote that there's a livery barn going up at the mission, so that means people must be traveling through the area and they might need a place to stay and a meal."

"Are you thinking of a hotel?"

"A small one. More like an inn."

"How you going to run that so far from the ranch."

"Most people will be traveling during the warm months. When winter sets in, I can hire someone to keep it open if need be."

"Won't be much of a money maker," Jennie predicted.

"Probably not. Just so I can earn back my investment. I can't give up my notion to buy the building next door to the Birdcage. It would make a fine sewing shop for you ladies." Kat tapped her chin in thought. "If I sell the Birdcage, I can use that money to maybe buy the building next door and set up an inn at the mission."

"But you still will be miles from the sewing shop. Unless—"

"Another idea?" Kat asked.

Jennie nodded. "Yeah, but I'm not sure if it will work."

"Want to share it?"

"I don't want to get your hopes up," Jennie said. "If I can get some ladies to go in with me, maybe we could buy the sewing shop from you. That would give us all a respectable place to work."

"Do you think you could?"

Jennie placed her elbow on the table, resting her hand on her chin. "I've some money put away. I doubt if Aggie and Leona have any. But I'm sure they'd want to work for us. Cilla might be interested. She's tired of being a bar maid."

Kat winked. "How about if I'm still part owner?"

"Sure, if you want. Actually, that would be great."

Kat rubbed her hands together. "Now to get the building bought, and I may have solved my problem."

"And how are we to do that?"

"We'll just have to offer more money," Kat said grimly. "Too bad, I couldn't depend on Annabelle. She could have helped us out."

"I thought she was down on her luck when she came here."

"She shouldn't have been. If she sold the family home before she left, she should have some money. In fact, some of that money should have been mine. I've been too good to her and look how she repaid me? Any idea where she might have gone?"

"She could have run off with her new man that came into the restaurant on a daily basis. If I remember correctly, he talked about Wyoming."

"Wyoming? I've never been there."

"It's a pretty big place. Don't know where they would have gone."

"What kind of man was he?" Kat asked.

"He was one of those flashy men. Dressed real nice and talked big. You'd thought he owned the world to listen to him."

"Yeah, one of those a woman shouldn't trust."

"That's how I would describe him," Jennie agreed.

"I wonder if she intends to ever come back."

"I imagine she's afraid to face you."

"I suppose she is, but maybe I'll try and find her." Kat said. "Know his name?"

"Bill...Bill Ammons," Jennie said.

"Think I'll go ask around a bit. Do you know where he stayed while he was in Deadwood?"

"I'm not sure. You might have to try all the hotels."

Kat stood. "I might as well start now. It's time I found my sister. I've been waiting for her to come back on her own, but it doesn't look like she will."

"Stop back and let me know if you have any luck."

Kat nodded, and then began her search at the hotel closest to the Birdcage. The clerk had no one registered under the name Bill Ammons. She continued on down the street and stopped at each hotel and boarding house. Finally, she found his name on the register at the Gold Strike hotel. The clerk was reticent about giving her any information.

"This man ran off with my sister and my niece," she told the clerk. "I want to make sure they're all right."

He held his head aloof. "It's none of my business. I respect the rights of my customers."

She frowned and dug in her purse for a bill to persuade him to spill what he knew. "Here, now let's try this again. Where do you think I might be able to find him?"

The clerk turned the money over in his hand. She sensed he was about to ask for more when she grabbed a hold of his vest. "I'm serious. I fear my sister might be in danger."

The clerk straightened his vest and glowered. "Alright, lady don't get upset. He registered as being from Sundance, Wyoming."

"Anything else I should know?"

"I did see him with a red headed lady and a little girl."

"That would be my sister and niece. Thanks for the information." She turned and left for the Birdcage where Jennie ran up to her as soon as she walked into the restaurant.

"Did you find something?" Jennie asked.

"I did. I had to bribe the low-down clerk, but he told me the man's from Sundance."

"That's the place the Sundance Kid got his name. He was jailed there over ten years ago for stealing a horse."

"Is that the one that rides with Butch Cassidy?"

"He's the one."

Kat laughed. "I doubt if we'll meet up with him there."

Jennie ignored her comment. "Kat, I think someone should go with you."

"Have you been to Sundance?"

"No. I'm not sure what you'll find there, but I'm willing to ride along."

"See if you can get someone to fill in for you. I have no idea how long I'll be gone."

"I'll go and talk with Aggie right now. Don't leave."

"I'll be right here." Kat sat down at an empty table and mulled over her trip to Wyoming. She hadn't told Jet anything about what she was planning to do. He would be miffed at her when he found out, but she decided she just didn't have the time to tell him.

She would check with the stage line today to see when it left for Sundance. She hoped she could find Annabelle there or else she would have no idea where to look. Like Jennie said, Wyoming was a big state.

CHAPTER 8

Three days later, Kat and Jennie stopped by the Birdcage for breakfast before they boarded the mid-morning stage to Sundance. Both were dressed in their best traveling suits and hats. Kat had chosen a deep apricot ensemble and an apricot and white hat to compliment her red hair. Jennie wore a light grey traveling dress, trimmed in red with a red hat to complete the outfit.

Aggie sauntered over to their table with a smirk on her face. "You ladies had better watch out. Someone's going to think you're there to open a saloon. The competition might not be too happy."

Kat stiffened. "You saying we look like saloon girls?"

"Maybe a might. Anyway you're liable to get plenty of stares," Aggie said with a grin and then scuttled toward the kitchen.

Jennie's eyes grew wide with concern and her hand flew to her throat. "Do you think we should change?"

"No." Kat waved away the notion with her hand. "Aggie's

just jealous. We're fine the way we are."

Casting Aggie a sideways glance, Kat and Jennie left the restaurant for the Deadwood stage.

"I'm not looking forward to the trip, but I have a feeling this is something I have to do," Kat commented before she climbed into the coach where a man and a woman were already seated. Kat introduced herself and Jennie to the middle aged couple.

"Pleased to meet you," the man said. "This is my wife Beatrice, and you can call me Glenn."

"On your way to Sundance, too?" Kat asked.

"We're hoping to open a business there. And you ladies?"

"We're...going to visit my sister."

"Oh, I see."

Kat felt self-conscious about Aggie's remark and wondered what was going through his mind. His wife Beatrice was dressed rather plainly.

"You ladies from Deadwood?"

"We are."

"Have a business there?"

"I own the Birdcage Restaurant."

He narrowed his eyes. "Didn't that used to be a saloon?"

Kat bristled. "It did, but I thought a restaurant would serve the needs of Deadwood better." She noticed Beatrice tug at her husband's arm. What was Glenn trying to prove anyway? She wasn't about to let him get the upper hand. She would ask some questions herself. "What business are you going to establish in Sundance?"

"A dry goods store." He patted his wife's hand. "Beatrice's idea."

"I don't remember seeing you around Deadwood," Kat said.

"No. We wouldn't live in Deadwood. Too immoral for us. We lived in the southern hills."

"Good luck, then." Kat ended the conversation and

opened up a deck of cards. She thought she heard Beatrice gasp. "Jennie, what's your pleasure," Kat snapped the cards in defiance.

Taking Kat's cue, Jennie named a poker game. The couple across from them whispered back and forth between themselves during the jaunt to Spearfish, where they would change stages for the remainder of the trip to Sundance.

At Spearfish the passengers stretched their legs before they changed to another stage. Wearily Kat and Jennie climbed aboard. Toward dusk, the stage stopped at a relay station, budding into a town, to change horses and stop for the night. Here the passengers were offered a meal, and a room for the night. The women noted that this relay station just across the Wyoming border offered more accommodations that most, including several saloons and a dance hall.

"A real hotel," Jennie said with enthusiasm. "I thought we'd be sleeping on a dirty cot in a corner somewhere."

"Now, don't get your hopes up just yet. Hotels have surprises, too," Kat cautioned.

"Will yours?"

"I intend to have a clean hotel with the best accommodations I can afford."

"Handmade quilts on the bed?" Jennie suggested

"Good idea. The mission can help me with that."

"I'll have to come and visit."

Kat smiled. "I hope you do. One of these days the railroad will come through. Travel to and from will be so much easier."

"It'd help if the railroad came near to the mission, then you'd really get the business."

"That would certainly help. Without the railroad most towns die away. I hope it won't happen to the mission."

Kat and Jennie checked in at the hotel, took their bags to the room, and then went to the dining room for supper. Kat took notice of everything, making mental notes of what she could incorporate into her own future plans of a hotel. Happily, the hotel appeared relatively clean to both woman's satisfaction. They bumped into Glenn and Beatrice at the door who barely acknowledged them and hurriedly selected a different table.

"Now how's that for a slap in the face?" Jennie grumbled.

"Ah, don't pay them no mind. I guess they think they're better than us."

"I just bet Beatrice would love to have some pretty clothes. Seems to me she's brow beat by her husband."

"I'd agree to that. But they're not our concern." Kat told her, picking up a menu.

Kat ordered a hearty meal, but Jennie complained about an upset stomach.

"Stage rides have a habit of doing that to a person," Kat said. "You should order something though."

Jennie took Kat's suggestion but when the meal arrived she grumbled. "Sure doesn't taste like Aggie's cooking," Jennie said, tasting the meal the waitress delivered.

Kat stirred the contents on her plate. "I agree to that, but it's still better than most."

"Kind of sad you won't have the restaurant anymore."

"In a way it is, but cooking and waiting tables is a lot of hard work."

"It is, but still better than being a barmaid."

After supper Kat and Jennie strolled about the town, stretching their legs from the confinement of the stage. Music blared from the dance hall.

Kat smiled. "Want to go dancing?"

"I don't think so," Jennie laughed, pointing to a couple inebriated men leaving the hall.

"Tomorrow, we'll be in Sundance," Kat commented.

"Where do we begin once we get there?"

"I'm not sure. It'll take a few days to find her if she's there. I just hope we're on the right trail."

— — — — — —

The next day, after lunch, the stage arrived in Sundance, a town dwarfed by a picturesque mountain. While Kat and Jennie admired the surrounding pine covered hills from the stage station, a man scurried past them to greet Glenn and Beatrice. He placed the couple's bags in his hack and drove them away without even a wave.

"We should have been plain, and we probably could have gotten a ride to a hotel," Jennie commented, looking after them.

Kat shrugged and pointed down the street. "I think I see a hotel about a block away. Think you can walk it?"

"Sure I can. Luckily, I didn't pack too much."

The ladies hefted their bags and paced the level ground to the closest hotel. "At least it isn't raining or the wind blowing like fury," Kat said. "I think we'll change clothes once we check in, eat, and then tour the town."

"You mean put on something that won't attract a lot of attention?"

"Yeah, I suppose we don't want everyone staring."

"That's going to be hard to do with your gorgeous red hair."

"I'll wear a hat," Kat muttered.

The ladies found the hotel to their satisfaction, changed clothes, and checked on the lunch menu in the dining room.

"Beans and cornbread," The waitress told them.

"Thanks, we might try supper." Kat spoke for Jennie, too. "Let's look around town. Find something with fresh vegetables. Someone must raise a garden around here."

The women explored the town, taking note of the businesses, hotels, and eateries. After checking out several, they decided on one that was serving something to their liking, which included fresh vegetables. The waitress seated them by the window at a table covered with a blue print tablecloth. A slight breeze blew in through an open window, ruffling wisps of Kat's red hair. The women gazed upon the street.

"Kat, look over there. Isn't that Beatrice and Glenn standing in the doorway of the building across from us?"

"I suppose that's the dry goods store they were talking about."

"Odd people, I would say," Jennie mused. "I wonder how they're going to get on with new customers."

The waitress placed two plates of meat, potatoes, and green beans on their table, interrupting their conversation for the moment. She poured two cups of coffee and left them to their meal.

After relishing several bites of the well prepared food, Kat discussed their plan. "I do have a picture of Annabelle in my compact. If I have to, we'll ask some of the business people if they have seen her. But first we'll just walk around the town, maybe sun ourselves on a bench for a while. Simply observe the town and its people."

Jennie buttered a fresh baked bun. "How many days are we going to look around here?"

"I don't know for sure. I would think we should find out something within two or three days." She waved her fork. "In the meantime pretend you're on vacation. Maybe we can find a dress shop."

"Now you're talking. I could use a new one."

Kat placed the napkin across her lap. "Then let's get to looking after we finish eating."

To Jennie's delight, they found a small dress shop on the edge of town run by a friendly middle-aged woman. The scent of new materials and fabric dyes allured the two customers inside. A few dresses hung on a rack, bolts of material were stacked on a couple of oak tables, and a sewing machine sat in the corner with a partially completed dress across it. Apparently, the woman sewed most of the dresses she had for sale.

Immediately the bright array of dresses drew Jennie to them. She searched through them and found several. "Could I try these on?" she asked the woman.

"Sure." The woman pointed to a curtained room. "You ladies from around here," the proprietor of the shop asked.

"We're from Deadwood," Kat answered. "I'm planning on opening a shop similar to this one. Except we'll make a few quilts, too. Do you find yourself busy?"

"Oh yes. Some women just don't have the time to sew for themselves not after they make all their children's clothes and shirts for their husbands. I have a lady who comes in occasionally and makes hats. She has a knack for it."

"I never thought about hats. That's an idea," Kat said. "Do they sell well, too?"

"Surprisingly, they do."

Jennie flounced out of the dressing cubical, wearing a new rose colored print. "What do you think of this one?" she asked twirling around to present a complete view.

"You look pretty. Is it comfortable?" Kat asked.

"It is, but I'll try on the lavender one, too."

Kat turned her attention back to browsing. She searched through the dresses and talked herself out of buying one. Instead, she rummaged through materials with quilting on her mind. If she did hire someone to build an inn or a hotel at the mission, she would want quilts for the beds. The mission ladies probably bought all their materials at Tater's store, but she found a few prints she thought were quite unique. She asked the proprietor to cut her a quarter yard of each.

Jennie appeared in the lavender print, which looked as equally well as the rose print. Jennie appeared in a quandary. "Which one? I like them both."

"You look gorgeous in both." Kat said. "Which color don't you have in your wardrobe?"

"Lavender, but I don't have a hat to match."

"I have some hats over here. By the way, call me Madge." She led them to a hat display toward the back of the shop. "Want to try one on?"

Jennie chose a straw hat and placed it on her head, and then looked in an oval oak- framed mirror. "Nice looking hat, but it has no color."

"You might be right." Madge placed her finger tip to her cheek. "I have an idea. The lady who does my hats will be here tomorrow. Stop by and she can add some lavender ribbon or flowers."

Madge wrapped up the purchase in brown paper, and the ladies left to continue their search.

"Let's take our packages to the hotel and visit the businesses," Kat said.

The women left their packages in their room and continued the search for Annabelle.

"Where shall we start?" Jennie said as she followed Kat down the hotel stairs.

"Let's just begin with the first business on the street."

"Even the saloon?"

Kat squared her shoulders. "I'm not afraid of saloons. They might ask us to leave, but at least I'll have a look."

"Annabelle wouldn't work in a saloon," Jennie protested.

"Probably not, but I have to make sure."

Kat and Jennie visited every business in town, including the saloons where they both met with stares. "Funny," Kat commented. "I never noticed stares when I owned the Birdcage Saloon, but these looks we're getting now bother me."

"I know what you mean. I feel the same way."

"Are you certain you haven't seen Bill Ammons in any of the saloons?"

"I'm certain. It's impossible to miss his flashy duds."

After checking all the businesses Kat was satisfied that Annabelle or her man weren't anywhere to be found. As their last resort, they even walked among the homes and rooming houses to no avail. Kat was hoping to see Miranda playing in a yard, nearby.

Jennie began to lag behind Kat, stopping occasionally to massage her foot. "Kat, I hate to complain but my feet are beginning to hurt."

"Yeah, mine, too." Kat slumped in frustration. "Tomorrow, I'll show Annabelle's picture around. If no one recognizes her, I'll just have to give up."

"Maybe she and Miranda weren't out today," Jennie speculated.

"Maybe not." Kat placed her hand on Jennie's shoulder. "Let's see what the hotel's serving for supper. We'll try again tomorrow."

The following morning, Kat and Jennie ate an early breakfast of eggs and toast and inquired about the stage departure to Spearfish. "Good, we have a few hours until we board the afternoon stage," Kat said. "I should be able to show Annabelle's picture about town before then."

"How about we stop and get my hat first? I want to make sure it's finished before we leave town."

"Good idea. Hope the milliner's there."

An open sign on the sewing shop's door encouraged the two women inside. Madge was busy at the machine finishing the dress Kat had seen yesterday.

Kat smiled. "Good morning Madge."

"Ah, ladies, you're a bit early, but my milliner is here. Let me take you to her." Madge left her chair and led Kat and Jennie to a backroom where a lady with red hair was working with lavender ribbon. "Your customer is here," she told the woman.

Just as she turned, Kat caught a glimpse of her and gasped. "Annabelle!"

"Kat, what you doing here?" She immediately let the ribbon slip from her fingers.

"Looking for you."

Madge popped her hand against her mouth in astonishment. "You know one another?"

"We do." Kat's voice cracked with emotion. "We have some business to settle."

"I'll leave you alone then," Madge said and scuttled from the room. Jennie followed close behind.

"You ran out on me, Annabelle." Kat's face grew red. "I thought I could trust you. If it wasn't for Jennie, Aggie, and Leona, my business would've gone under."

"I didn't mean to leave you like that." Annabelle's eyes seemed earnest. "It's just that Bill, well he just swept me off my feet. No man has ever paid attention to me like that for a long time. He promised me all sorts of things."

"I bet he did. Where's Miranda?"

"She's with the woman I rent a room from. I help her out with housework and errands; in turn she watches her for me."

"And Bill?"

"He...ran out on me."

"He got tired of you?"

"More than likely it had to do with money. He got the idea I was loaded. When he discovered otherwise, he dropped me, and left town."

"You should have come back to Deadwood and the Birdcage."

"I couldn't face you. I'm sorry Kat."

Kat stood defiantly even though her sister's apology seemed genuine. "I was mad. You left my house in a mess. You left my gals high and dry. I was depending on you. And I can't even find my cat."

"I know. I did a stupid thing."

Kat's tone softened a little. "I'm glad I found you, and

you're safe. Jennie and I are leaving on the afternoon stage. I'd like you and Miranda to come with us."

"I can't just up and leave. I have a few more hats to finish for Madge's customers." Jennie picked up the lavender ribbon and began to remake the bow. "Including this one for Jennie."

"I see you have commitments, but can I trust you to come back to Deadwood and not take up with some other man that flatters you?"

"Are you sure you want me back?"

"I have another proposition for you. An investment."

Annabelle threaded a needle and poked it through the bow. "An investment takes money."

"And I think you have it. I've an idea that you may have told your Bill that you sold some property in Cleveland. Our parent's property."

"But Daddy and Mama gave it to me."

"I figured they cut me out, since I left against their wishes. I guess it was my fault."

Annabelle's face tightened. "Are you asking me for your share?"

"No, but I want you to invest in a shop next door to the Birdcage. I think I may sell the Birdcage and try to buy the smaller shop next door. Turn it into a sewing shop, something like what Madge has here."

"I can't afford to buy a building."

"Jennie would go in on it with you. Maybe Cilla, too. I could invest some if I had to."

"Do you think we could make it work?"

"Now that I see you can make hats, I'm sure you will do well. Aggie and Leona can sew, you make hats, and Jennie is a good manager. That's quite a number to split the pie, so I don't know how well off anyone will be, but it might be easier than running a restaurant."

"So you're not going to be involved in the business?"

"No, not any more. Does that relieve you?"

"Some."

Kat ignored her remark. "My place is with Jet, and besides I have an idea for a business at the mission."

"You're not satisfied until you're running something, are you?"

Kat laughed. "You mean your life?"

Annabelle held her head defiantly. "Sometimes you try to. Remember I'm fully grown."

"I've taken control all my life. If I listened to Mama and Pa I would be married to a twerp. How can I quit being controlling now?""

"He wasn't that bad."

Kat's eyes snapped. "I beg to differ."

"So what's your business plans for the mission?"

"A hotel or an inn. Haven't talked to Jet about it yet."

"That figures."

Kat frowned. "So what do you think of the business offer? I'll be out of your way. You only have to answer to your partners, not to me anymore. Are you in?"

"I don't know. I'd have to see the building and see what it's going to cost. What about your house? Are you going to sell it, too?"

"I'll give you a deal on the house. Depends what I can get out of the Birdcage."

"Hmmm, everything depends on something else. I'll have to think on it awhile."

"That's fair enough. Promise me you won't run off without telling me where you're going?"

"I'm not a child anymore," Annabelle reminded her.

"I know you're not, but all we have is each other. I'd like to know where you are."

"You have Jet."

"I do, and I'm grateful. Some day you'll find someone, too."

"Maybe. It's hard to find a man when there's a child involved." Annabelle finished sewing the lavender bow and band on Jennie's hat and held it up to inspect. "Ever plan on having a baby?"

"Me?" Kat shook her head. "I think I'm too old for a baby, but Jet says it's up to me."

"Too, bad. I think you'll regret it."

"Why do say that?"

"I'd be alone if it wasn't for Miranda. Besides, I have someone to think about other than myself."

"What about finding a man?"

"If he doesn't want Miranda, then he isn't worth my time."

"You're becoming wise, baby sister. You will come to Deadwood when you finish your projects for Madge?"

"I won't let you down this time," Annabelle crossed her heart and promised.

CHAPTER 9

Several weeks had passed, and still Kat heard nothing from Annabelle. She was sure when she left Sundance, Annabelle would keep her word and return to Deadwood. Kat wouldn't be able to sell the Birdcage until she knew if Annabelle was going to invest in purchasing the building next door. As each day passed Kat became distraught. She confided her frustration to Jennie one day in the Birdcage.

"Mr. Lockert might sell the building next door to someone else before I even hear from Annabelle," Kat told Jennie. "I don't know what to do."

"Have you visited with him lately?"

"I haven't."

"Maybe you should," Jennie said. "Let him know you're still interested."

"I've been thinking the same thing." Kat drummed her fingers on the table. "I should offer him a little more money this time. Even if Annabelle doesn't come through, I think we can swing it, especially if I sell my house, too."

"Oh, Kat it sounds all too final."

"It has to be this way. I have to face facts. You do, too." Kat met her gaze.

"What has Jet to say about this, surely you've written him."

"He isn't much of a business man, but he says to do what will make me happy as long as I come home soon."

"And what about the idea of a hotel?"

"He's not too crazy about us being separated even for a week, but he says he can adjust if that will keep me near," Kat said. "He also predicts that the days of the open range and the big cattle empires are about over. With the railroad comes the homesteaders, who want the land for farming."

"So what would Jet do?"

"I don't know. It remains to be seen. No one can predict how the country will change. I don't even know if it's a good idea to build a hotel."

"What about Deadwood?"

"Deadwood will remain, but it will change, too. I'm not sure how, but it won't be the same."

Jennie glanced toward the door. "I see the customers are pouring in. Better get back to work. Want some lunch?"

"No, I think I'll dine at the Miner's Restaurant and have a visit with Mr. Lockert. I can't wait on Annabelle any longer. I was hoping she'd change, but I'm afraid I put too much faith in her again."

"She might come through yet," Jennie assured her.

Kat smiled at her best friend. "Thanks, Jennie, for being there for me."

"Anytime, Kat. Stop back this afternoon."

Kat nodded and left the Birdcage for the Miner's Restaurant. Relieved to see Mr. Lockert when she entered the smoky establishment, reeking of onions, she seated herself at a small corner table. The haggard looking waitress took her order of the special, liver and onions, and agreed to tell

Mr. Lockert that Kat wanted to speak to him.

Kat finished half her meal, before Mr. Lockert sauntered over to her table wearing a grimy apron. She asked him to sit. Mr. Lockert flagged over the waitress, who poured him a cup of coffee.

"Looks like you're working today," she commented.

"Yeah, we're short on kitchen help. What can I do for you?" he said, wiping his forehead with his apron.

"Is the building next to the Birdcage still for sale?"

"It's at the same price I quoted last time. Thought maybe you gave up."

She looked over the rim of the coffee cup. "I am able to offer you a little more."

He lifted his brow. "You are?"

"Yes."

"Perhaps we can work out a deal," he said and then grinned.

"Depends if you're willing to work with me."

"So what's your offer?" He asked.

"One hundred dollars more than I offered last time."

Mr. Lockert stroked his chin. "I tell you what. There's something you don't know. Since I'm selling the Miner, too, I might just take that offer."

"You're selling the Miner?"

He nodded. "I'm leaving Deadwood. Tired of this greasy spoon. Got some prospects in Denver."

So he is selling too, Kat thought to herself. She hadn't told Mr. Lockert that she was thinking of selling the Birdcage. Now there would be two restaurants for sale.

"Do you think you'll have any trouble getting rid of your restaurant?" She asked offhandedly.

"There's plenty of people wanting to go out and eat. I can wait a while before the right person comes along."

Kat was in a hurry to sell. Now that she had made the decision, she was ready to put her plan into motion. "Then, it's a deal? I can buy the building next door to me?"

He laughed. "Yeah, you won't be my competition any-more. And I can forgive you for stealing Aggie away from me."

Kat smirked. "I'd like to close the deal as soon as possible."

"Sure, no problem. I'll meet you at the bank tomorrow morning about ten." Mr. Lockert finished his coffee and left her table.

Kat's mind whirled with excitement. She had a lot to do before the building would become theirs.

—————

Several days after Kat bought the shop, she, Jennie, Cilla, Aggie, and Leona trouped over to the little building before they opened the Birdcage Restaurant for the day. Kat turned the key in the lock, and they entered the small building smelling of stale cigars.

"Pugh, this smells like a cigar store instead of a clock shop," Leona said in disgust.

Jennie pinched her nose. "I bet the owner sold cigars on the side."

It became quite evident to them that Mr. Lockert hadn't cleaned the interior. Discarded boxes and debris littered the dingy wood floor. The walls had been painted a dirty gray, which had been marred by years of use. A wood stove oc-cupied the corner and needed a good cleaning and shining.

"Looks like we got our work cut out for us girls," Kat commented with her hands on her hips. "But I can envision it as a sewing shop."

"Yeah, when are we going to find the time?" Aggie scowled.

"I'll put a for sale sign in the window of the Birdcage to-day," Kat said. "I hope I can find a buyer soon. Then we'll have time to fix this building up a little." She had never let on that finding a buyer had haunted her since she had talked with Mr. Lockert. Two restaurants for sale in town were two too many. She honestly felt that her establishment had more to offer, but it depended on what Mr. Lockert was asking for his restaurant.

After looking around for awhile and discussing the layout for a sewing shop, Aggie, Leona, and Cilla left for the Birdcage to begin breakfast. Kat and Jennie remained, piling boxes together and picking up trash.

"Jennie, you're the manager. Where do we start?"

"I...thought you would have the ideas."

"Like I said, I don't plan to be involved in the decision making. I did put up some money, but you all will pay me back in time."

"Okay." Jennie pursed her lips in thought. "Guess we got to clean up the junk, wash down the walls, and paint them a cheery color. Aggie or Leona can make new curtains for the window." She scuffed at the floor. "Not sure what to do with the floors. Maybe oil them or something."

"I'll volunteer to clean out the junk today and find someone to haul it away for us," Kat said. "I can wash walls and paint, too."

"You'd do that for us?"

"Of course. I need the practice for my hotel."

Jennie smiled. "You've been too good to us."

"What are friends for?" Kat turned quickly to hide her quivering lips. She chided herself for becoming sentimental. She would miss her friends and Deadwood. "Go on back to the Birdcage. By this afternoon, I'll have this place looking better. Don't tell the girls what I'm up to." She winked. "It will be a surprise. Oh, and put the mop, a rag, and scrub bucket by the back door. I'll sneak by and get them."

Kat picked up the piled boxes and threw them out the back door of the sewing shop along with the litter that had been scattered about. She found an old broom and a dust pan in a closet and swept the floor as clean as she could. Then she swept the cob webs off the walls. A cloud of dust mushroomed around her. She sneezed more than once, sending her out the back door for a breath of air, and then she tackled the task again. When she had conquered most of the dirt, she sneaked to the Birdcage's back door, grabbed the bucket and mop and filled the pail with water. Next, she tackled the walls and scrubbed them clean.

Jennie walked in the front door with lunch. "Here Kat, brought you Aggie's famous fried chicken."

Kat flopped down on a crate that she hadn't thrown out yet. "Ah, just what I needed."

Jennie's gaze swept the room. "Looks better already, but I think you had better quit for the day."

"Not until the floor's scrubbed. Mmm, this chicken is good." Kat wiped the crumbs off her chin. "How's business?"

"People are flocking in by the droves. They're really going to miss the food when you sell out."

"I know. But you won't miss the hard work, will you?"

"It's not any worse than being a barmaid. Do you think a sewing shop will make it in this town?"

"I do," Kat said.

"Hope you're right. Better get back before they miss me." Jennie waved and scooted out the door.

"Thanks for lunch," Kat called after her. She thought about Jennie's concerns. She knew better than to count on anything, but she had a definite hunch a sewing shop would work. Anyways, she hoped it would or she would be letting her friends down. She promised herself she would come back and check on them from time to time.

As soon as Kat finished lunch, she gingerly lifted herself off the crate and plopped the mop in the bucket of water, thinking she'd have to buy a new mop when she finished the long neglected floor.

The first mopping removed most of the dirt, but another mopping was needed. Her back was aching by the time she finished the second round. She was surprised how good the floor actually looked. *A good oiling will restore the wood,* she thought.

Kat wearily sat on the crate and admired her handiwork. She poured herself some cold coffee and let her mind visualize what the sewing shop could look like. She planned that they'd move the sewing machine over from the Birdcage as soon as the floor was done and place it toward the back of the room. Eventually a second sewing machine might be needed, but there would be room. She had several tables and chairs that could also be moved from the Birdcage. The fabric bolts would occupy one table. She could almost smell the newness.

The girls from the Birdcage burst through the door, jarring her out of her musings.

"Wow, this looks great," Jennie practically shouted.

"Kat, you're amazing. You must be exhausted," Cilla said.

Kat had regained her energy and popped off the crate. "I am at that, but I wanted you gals to see the potential of a sewing shop."

"We do, we do," Jennie agreed.

"Now for paint and new curtains. Any ideas?" Kat searched them for suggestions.

"Leona is good with color." Aggie informed them.

Leona appeared surprised. All eyes were staring at her. "Let's...choose the curtain material first. Pick out a color from that."

Jennie smiled. "I like that idea. Why don't you and Kat go pick out something."

"That means a trip to that uppity woman?" Leona scowled.

"You referring to Corella?" Kat laughed.

"Yeah."

"We know how to deal with her and her questions."

"We do?" Leona asked.

"Remember? We just don't tell her anything," Kat said with a laugh.

Leona nodded. "Let's go then."

"Lock up when you leave," Kat reminded the gals when she and Leona stepped out the door on their way to the mercantile.

"She might not be there," Leona said.

"You're right. She might not."

As they entered the store, Corella stared at them without even cracking a smile. "May I help you?"

Kat brushed past the counter with Leona following until they came to the material. "No, I think we can manage."

Kat let Leona take the lead in selecting a print for the curtains. Kat found one that she liked, but she kept quiet.

After scrutinizing several bolts of material, Leona settled on a print with cool greens. "Do you like this one?"

"I do. Good choice." Kat took the material to the counter. "We'll need four yards."

"Are you sure?" Corella asked. "Four yards doesn't seem like enough for the Birdcage? But I see you're selling your business."

Kat's jaw tightened. "It isn't for the Birdcage."

"Oh, then it's for your house?"

"It's for neither. Four yards, please."

Corella cut the yardage and bundled it in brown paper. Kat paid the bill and left. Corella stared after them.

Leona broke into side splitting laughter once they were outside the store. "It just kills her when she doesn't know what's going on."

"Yeah, it's probably not nice to goad her like we do."

"Well, she shouldn't look down her nose at us the way she does," Leona countered.

Kat remembered Elijah's sermons at the mission— to treat others as you would like to be treated.

CHAPTER 10

Tex hadn't seen Louisa since the Fourth of July celebration. Four weeks was a long time without her. An empty feeling that he hadn't experienced for quite some time nagged him. There wasn't a day that didn't go by that he didn't think of her. He had been so busy that he hadn't even been to the mission in months. There was just too much distance between them, and he didn't know how to fix it except to just get on his horse and ride.

The August heat was baking the prairie when he decided to make the trip and surprise Louisa. He calculated that he would stop at the mission and visit Tater, spend a night and then continue on to Louisa's ranch. Ed gave the go ahead, assuring Tex that they could get along without him for a week or so.

A mirage of heat waves shimmered in the distance as he approached the mission. He blinked once and then twice. Was he seeing things? The mission seemed to be growing more into a town each time he came by for a visit. Tater had even expanded his store. Riding up to Tater's establishment, Tex dismounted and entered the crowded store. Someone else was behind the counter with Tater waiting on customers. Tex removed his hat and untied the navy blue kerchief from his neck, jerked it free and wiped the sweat from his brow. His thoughts drifted to a cold beer, but he knew Tater didn't sell beer in his store. Alcohol was off limits on the reservation, but he had to have something to quench his thirst.

"Hey, Tater, what you got to cool a man's thirst?"

Tater waved a greeting. "Come over here, got just the thing."

Tex stirred his stiff, tired body into action and approached the counter. Tater reached in the ice box and produced a brown bottle. He popped off the cap.

"What's this?" Tex asked as he took the chilled bottle and held it against his sun parched face.

"Just what it says."

Tex lowered the bottle and read the label. "Root beer. I thought you couldn't sell alcohol?"

"I can't. Haven't you heard of root beer? It ain't alcohol. Take a drink."

Tex lifted the suspicious liquid to his nose, and then tipped the bottle to his lips. A sweet, nippy flavor awakened his taste buds. "So this is what they call root beer." He ran his tongue over his lips not quite deciding if he liked this new sensation. "Kind of sweet. What do I owe you?"

"On the house this time." Tater edged toward the other end of the counter. "Got to wait on my customers."

Tex lifted his brow and swigged from the bottle, wrinkling his nose with each taste. He held the bottle up to eye level. "They call this beer?" he said to no one in particular. He shrugged when his own voice bounced back to him.

Since Tater was too busy to chat, he roamed around the store looking at what Tater had to offer. He discovered that Tater stocked every niche of the store to full capacity, and it appeared nothing was gathering dust. He had to hand it to his former cook. He had a knack for business.

Tex stumbled across a table in the corner of the store, where he sat to watch business in bloom and to cool himself from the heat. He no more then finished his root beer when a tall stranger approached the table, his spurs jingling with each purposeful step. The man pushed his black hat from his forehead exposing a dark complexion.

"You Tex? Tex McMurray, manager of the Bar Double B Ranch?"

Tex rose from his chair. "I'm one of the managers. Who's asking?" He frantically searched his memory for a man who dressed in black heavily embellished with embroidery. He was Spanish, no doubt in Tex's mind, but who was he?

"You don't know me. My name's Juan Diaz." He motioned toward an empty chair. "Could I sit a spell?"

Tex nodded without removing his eyes from the stranger.

"I'm looking for a job."

Tex laughed. "Is that all?"

"Didn't mean to rile you."

"Not to worry. Just haven't seen you around these parts."

"I used to work for Louisa Bissette.

Tex shifted in his chair and propped his elbows on the table, his interest piqued. "When?"

"Several years ago."

Louisa had never mentioned having a vaquero working for her. "You don't now?"

"No, after I quit a couple of years ago, I drifted to Montana. Didn't like it there so I came back."

"Mind if I ask why you quit working for Louisa?"

"She's a fine woman, but it just didn't work out. Don't get me wrong. I'm a good vaquero."

"There must have been something?" Tex pressed.

"Her sons resented me being there. So I left."

Tex understood. He noticed their resentment toward him, too. He regretted this volatile situation with a woman he was interested in. He liked Louisa too well to let her sons get the best of him. "This is quite a coincidence. I was planning on riding out to Louisa's Ranch."

"You know her then?"

"Met her at a dance."

Juan smiled. "I see."

Tex saw no need to explain his motives and just left the matter where it stood.

"Do you have a ranch job for me?"

"There's three other men that have a say. We merged our ranches. You staying at the mission a while?"

"I can if there's a chance for a job."

"I plan on visiting Louisa for a day and then I'll ride back to the ranch and talk to my son Curt, and the others, Ed, and Jet. Come out to the ranch in about three days."

"Sounds fair enough."

Tex stroked his chin. "I'm curious. Where did you meet up with Louisa?"

Juan laughed. "Not to worry. I'm her cousin."

"I didn't mean that. It's just that she never mentioned you."

"I rode up with her and her husband Victor from Texas. Stayed on a while until the ranch was established, and then I wore out my welcome and left."

"Families tend to do that. Louisa told me that her brother and father have a rancho in Texas."

"A big rancho from a Spanish Land Grant." Juan shook his head. "These ranches around here don't compare. I don't know why she stays here when she could go back home to comfort and luxury."

Tex scratched his head realizing there was more to Louisa than she had let on. "Luxury you say?"

Juan smirked. "Oh, yes, the hacienda is filled with the

finest furniture, carpets, and tapestries that you could find anywhere. Acres and acres of grasslands for cattle, no blizzards to worry about."

Clearly, Tex realized there was much about Louisa he didn't know. But how could he? He just met the woman. In his opinion, she was out of the ordinary. He knew this when he first laid eyes on her. If he had his right sense he would leave her alone, but he couldn't help himself. He simply had to know more.

— — — — — —

Early the next morning, Tex rode out toward Louisa's ranch. He knew he was taking a risk that she might not be home. He admonished himself for not writing her before his jaunt, but he simply didn't have the time.

The day grew warm but not as hot as the day before. Even though it was cooler, he stopped a few times to sit in the shade of a cottonwood tree and water his horse from a creek that hadn't dried up. He chewed on a piece of grass and thought about this lovely lady, her dark skin, and dark eyes, who had captivated him since last Christmas. He didn't know much about her, just bits and pieces of information, but he was enamored with her.

As he drew closer to the ranch, he became anxious. Perhaps he had made a poor choice surprising her. But he just had to see her. By late afternoon, he came within shouting distance. Louisa was taking clothes off the line when he rode in.

"Why, Tex. I didn't expect you." Her hands flew to her hair whipping in the wind.

"It was a spur of the moment decision." He rested his hands on the saddle horn and gazed down on her. "I should have wrote you, but there wasn't time."

She smiled. Her gaze met his. "Get down off your horse.

Bet you're ready to get out of the sun."

Once inside the house, she untied her apron and replaced it with another. "You'll have to excuse me. I've been busy all day." She poured him a glass of water.

"Have I come at a bad time?"

Louisa motioned for him to sit. She sat across from him and placed her hands on the table. "I got word the other day that my father's quite ill." Her voice broke. "I'm planning to visit him in Texas. I've been washing and cooking for the boys. I don't know how long I'll be gone."

His eyes lingered on her hands. He wanted to take them in his but resisted. "When do you leave?"

"In about a week."

He lifted his brows. "You going by yourself?"

"I am. The boys have to stay here."

His hands moved closer to hers. "I saw your cousin Juan yesterday."

"You did? I didn't know he was back."

"He's looking for a job with the Bar Double B."

"He is?"

"Said he worked for you for a time." Tex told her, watching her reaction.

"He did. He's a good worker, but most of the time business and family don't mix."

"Maybe he can go with you to Texas," Tex suggested.

"You think I need an escort?"

"I'd feel better if you did."

"Hmmm, I see."

"He'll be out to the ranch in a few days," Tex said. "I can tell him then what you told me about your father."

"Mention it, but I don't think he'll be interested. He didn't part from us on the best of terms."

"Got anyone who can help out at the Texas ranch?"

She withdrew her hands from the table. "My brother runs the operation along with help from my father."

"A big spread?" He asked the question already knowing the answer and placed his hands on his lap.

"Yes. My brother Carlos will be hard pressed to run it by himself, unless father gets better."

"All the more reason Juan should go with you."

"We'll see what Juan decides," she said. "I don't want to force him to do something he doesn't want to do."

"Fair enough."

She poured him another glass of water. "How long can you stay?"

He shuffled his feet under the table. "Tonight, then I better head back tomorrow some time."

"Good. Maybe after supper we can go for a buggy ride. I haven't been out to see the calves lately."

"The boys will be home for supper?" Tex asked casually.

"No. They're in Fort Pierre today. So it will be late."

"No need to make a big meal for me."

"Would sandwiches work?"

"You bet. That way we can spend more time out with the cattle."

She smoothed her hair. "I'll fold the clothes, make the sandwiches, and then we can go."

He stood holding his hat. "While you're doing that, I'll stable my horse and hitch up the buggy."

Tex took his time in the barn. He figured she needed a few moments to finish her household chores. He remembered his wife didn't like to be bothered when she had errands to complete. Later when he entered her kitchen, she had the sandwiches made and on the table. He noticed she had even changed her clothes and rearranged her hair. He had difficulty not to stare at her. Her dark hair and skin drew her to him like a magnet, tightening his chest and taking his breath away.

"Glad I had something for sandwiches," she said as she sat down across from Tex. "The boys complain if I don't have the fixings to put between two slices of bread. I bet you're hungry?" She looked up at him, their eyes meeting.

He nodded and dropped his gaze. "Much obliged for the meal."

Finished with the light supper, Tex helped Louisa into the buggy and following her directions, they headed across the pasture to the cattle. "I love to watch the calves grow, don't you?" she asked

"I do. That's what it's all about. Finding those dead calves after the blizzard was gut wrenching." His face grew grim.

She patted his arm. "Thank goodness every winter is not like that."

"We don't have that problem in Texas," he reminded her.

"No, but we had to battle tick fever."

"Always something, I guess." He caressed the stubble reappearing on his chin.

"Oh, look," she pointed to the calves with their mothers. "Growing good, don't you think?"

"Sure do. The grass is good, water too." He noticed her cattle grazing peacefully and branded with a large /B. He had seen that brand before, but he hadn't thought much about it. The ranch he merged with was the Bar Double B. He knew that stockholders from England had helped finance it. They had come out to the ranch for a visit this spring. When the managers had asked the stockholders where the B came from, they wouldn't say other than one stockholder was anonymous.

Anonymous didn't mean that the secret stockholder had to be English or even a man. Could it be? He thought.

For the remainder of his visit, he looked at Louisa in a different light. He realized she could be the anonymous stockholder. Here was a woman who could be extremely wealthy. Wealth complicated relationships and to top it off, she could be his boss. His heart sank to his feet. He knew her sons resented his intrusion into their life. Now she would be leaving for Texas. It was very possible she would remain there indefinitely. Behaving like a lovesick school boy that he was could not be an option for him anymore.

The next morning when he left Louisa Bissette's ranch, he wished her well and asked her to write. After kissing her lightly on her lips, he turned his back, swung his leg over the saddle and rode away.

— — — — — —

The thought of Louisa Bissette being the secret stockholder played on Tex's mind for weeks. Finally, he drew Ed aside when they were unsaddling their horses after a ride and told him about his suspicions.

"I've suspected it for some time," Ed said. "I knew Louisa and her husband long before you met her. Her husband was a fierce supporter of the open range. He abhorred the thought of farmers coming in and ripping the grass roots from the prairie. "The prairie was created for grazing," he always ranted.

"So what made you think that Louisa is the anonymous stockholder?"

"Think about it for a minute. Why would a stockholder want to remain secret?"

Tex scratched his ear. "Didn't want anyone to know he was rich. So maybe that means it's someone we know?"

"Exactly. And the stockholder doesn't have to be male, either. You know how men like to take orders from a woman?"

"Oh, I get your drift." Tex tilted his hat back on his head.

"Louisa may also be trying to perpetuate her husband's wish. She's funding the industry he supported."

"But where does she get the money?" Tex shook his head. "They have a nice ranch, but we're talking about a lot of dough."

Ed lugged his saddle into the low built barn, talking over his shoulder as he walked. "She might have property of her own in Texas or she's getting help from her Texas family."

"Hmmm, guess I was right then. What about those boys of hers?"

"What did you say?"

"What about those boys of hers?"

Ed came out smiling. "They've been giving you the cold shoulder?"

"Haven't been friendly," Tex admitted.

"I think they're harmless, but protective of their ranch. They keep to themselves and aren't much for talk."

"They hiding something?" Tex hefted his saddle.

Ed followed Tex into the barn. "I don't know unless it's the fact that their mother is the secret stockholder."

"Could be, I suppose."

"Tex, I don't know if you've thought about it much, but I think our way of life is doomed. The blizzard that wiped out lots of cattle has troubled stockholders everywhere." Ed turned to walk out of the barn. "We were lucky that our stockholders let us restock the range, but other outfits haven't been so fortunate. Unless we have an Indian connection or become a farmer, we won't be here much longer. What extra land is available on the reservation will be parceled out to the homesteaders."

Tex kicked at a clod of dirt. "Guess I haven't wanted to face that fact. So what will we all do?"

"Find another way of life. I don't like the law practice nearly as well as cattle, but it will make me a living. What about you?"

"Return to Texas and find something to do. My daughter Netty is still there. She's been wanting me to come back." Tex stuck his hands in his pockets. "I'll buy a small ranch somewhere."

"At least you have a plan in mind."

"Have you said anything to Jet and Curt?"

"I talked to Jet," Ed said. "Thought you could break the news to Curt. I'm not saying this is going to happen tomorrow, but it will happen within a few years."

The men led their horses out to the pasture and let them loose to graze. Ed rested his hand on a corral post, his gaze resting on the prairie. "I don't like the notion of this grassland being plowed up, either. It will never be the same again."

"Suppose not," Tex commented. Suddenly he felt disheartened. Driving cattle and ranching was all he knew. Perhaps, he shouldn't wait to find his ranch in Texas.

"After lunch, I'd like you to ride the south pasture. Saddle up a new mount when you're ready."

Tex nodded and both men strode to the ranch house where cook had a meal ready for them. After washing up, he sat down at the table. His mail was waiting for him beside his plate. He shuffled through the assortment, finding a letter from Louisa. He resisted the urge to rip the letter open right then and there, but since he wanted to keep his feelings for her a secret he reshuffled it back amongst the rest of the mail to read later.

Tex had difficulty keeping his focus on Ed and Jet who gathered for lunch. Their talk usually centered on the ranch operation but today conversation picked up where Tex and Ed had left off.

Jet seemed puzzled. "So you think Louisa Bissette is the anonymous stockholder?"

"That's what we're thinking," Ed confirmed.

"Guess it doesn't make any difference to me as long as she agrees with our British bosses," Jet said. "They're not ready to give up on us yet."

"Might make a difference to Tex." Ed nodded toward him.

Jet winked. "I thought you was interested in her."

"Well, maybe just a little."

"Ah, it's alright. Gets lonesome out here without a wife."

"And how about yours?" Tex asked, drawing the attention away from him. "When she coming back."

"Soon I hope."

As soon as Tex could leave the table, he excused himself and disappeared to the barn where he could be alone. He opened Louisa's floral scented letter. He read.

Dear Tex,

Juan and I arrived safely in Texas. I have to admit it was a good idea to ask Juan to come with me. Some desperate looking men sat across from us on the train. I felt much better when he was by my side. I think they would have robbed me if it wasn't for him.

I was surprised to find my father's ranch in disarray. My brother has too much to care for since my father became ill. I'm afraid his illness has affected his thinking. He is very forgetful and no help to my brother anymore.

For the time being at least, my brother can hire Juan to help him out and get things back in shape. But I will have to remain indefinitely to care for father and my brother and Juan as well. The place is a mess and definitely needs a woman's touch.

When we parted, you seemed troubled. I hope I didn't say or do something that disturbed you. Separation isn't good for us, but I have no choice in the matter.

If you don't mind, I'll write you from time to time and let you know what's happening here with us. Take care and if you have time, please write me, too.

Best regards

Louisa Bissette

Could he write to Louisa? There was nothing to say except that he was confused about his feelings for her. Maybe a separation was what they needed. It would give him time to think this through. There was just too much at stake to leap into the flames of love.

Besides his confusion with Louisa, Ed's prediction about the open range disturbed him. It might be a good idea to find a ranch for him, Curt, and Netty in Texas. The next chance he got, he would ask Ed for some time off.

He folded her letter and placed it in his pocket, saddled a horse, and rode to the south pasture, writing and rewriting his letter to Louisa in his mind.

CHAPTER 11

꞊ᵛᵢᵥᵉ꞊

"I'm ready to paint," Kat announced as she barged in the Birdcage carrying two gallon pails of green paint. Anyone able to help?" The aroma of frying bacon made her stomach rumble, reminding her she had forgotten to eat breakfast.

Jennie shook her head. "We're full up with customers. Don't think I can get away."

Kat peeked in the kitchen to see Aggie and Leona scrambling to keep up with the orders. Cilla brought in a tray full of dirty dishes, which she plunked in the dishpan and began washing.

"Guess I'll have to do it myself," Kat muttered. She poured herself a cup of coffee to take with her to the shop and swiped a piece of French toast off a plate.

Once inside the shop she set down her supplies, gulped the coffee, stuffed the remainder of the French toast into her mouth, and left for the Birdcage to find the ladder.

No one offered her any help or even commented on her hair tied up with a kerchief. Disappointed, she dragged the step ladder back to the shop where she positioned it against a wall. Painting wasn't something she enjoyed, but she had done some in her little house on the hill. After prying open the paint bucket, she dipped in her brush and stroked the color on the wall. When she saw the transformation from dingy gray to cool green, her spirits perked up. She had one wall nearly completed when she heard the door open. Expecting Jennie with her lunch, she turned toward the door.

"Annabelle." Her look of surprise changed to irritation. "It's about time." She stepped down the ladder and wiped her hands on a rag.

"I'm sorry. It seems like I'm always apologizing to you, but I just couldn't get away any sooner. Madge needed me."

"You could have written. I was waiting for you so I could make an offer on this building. But I finally gave up and bought it anyway."

"I didn't think about that."

"That's the problem. You don't think."

"I quit my job to come here. For nothing?"

"I don't know what to say." Kat threw up her hands. "I put in money for your share. Whether the gals want you as a partner is their decision. You're not exactly what I would call dependable."

"I am dependable. I stayed and finished my job with Madge."

"Jennie, Cilla, and I went together to buy this shop. I'm willing to sell my share if they okay you as a partner. Where's Miranda?"

"She's at the Birdcage eating lunch. Why don't you take a break and come with me and eat lunch? We can discuss the shop some more."

"Looking like this?" Kat pointed to her paint stained clothes.

"We could sit in the kitchen."

"I guess we could." Kat closed up the paint pail and

wrapped the brush in a cloth and followed Annabelle to the kitchen's back door.

It was then that Aggie really noticed her. She laughed and pointed. "I never seen you look so unraveled."

Kat feigned being offended. "What you expect a gal to look like when she's painting? I could use some help."

"Sorry, Kat, we're just too busy," Jennie said, defending them.

"I'll change clothes and help you," Annabelle offered. "I have some older clothes in my bag."

Leona set two plates of food in front of them. Kat dug in with gusto. One piece of French toast hadn't begun to satisfy her hunger.

"If the gals want you as a partner, I'd say come on and paint." Kat looked at Jennie and Cilla for confirmation. They nodded as if they never had any doubts. "Looks like it's a go. After lunch you can go upstairs and change and we'll get to work."

Miranda came running when she heard her mother's voice in the kitchen. Kat patted her on the head, a sudden maternal feeling overcoming her. She abruptly dismissed it as a sentiment of pity for a girl without a father or a true home.

"Come with me Miranda, we'll change you, too," Annabelle said. "Aunt Kat and I are going to do some painting. You can come and watch." Miranda's eyes glittered with excitement as she followed her mother upstairs.

"Looks like you have your help," Jennie commented.

"Yeah, don't know if it's good or bad."

"We really are grateful to you for helping us out," Jennie said. "I don't know how we'll ever repay you."

"No repayment necessary. I'm anxious to get this shop off the ground. Jet is getting impatient for me to come home. And I'm looking forward to begin building my hotel. Once we get the painting done and the curtains hung, I think you can open for business. I'll help out at either place for a while and then I'm heading back to the ranch."

"Annabelle's committed?"

"I hope so. She isn't always dependable, but her hat making skills will be a boon to the business. That's the only job I would give her. I'll talk her into buying me out, so I won't be involved anymore."

"We hate to see you go, but we understand," Jennie said.

"I know. Come over to the shop after you close and see what you think of the paint. Oh, and bring the curtains."

Kat and Annabelle painted all afternoon until the walls were shining like foliage in a forest glade. They were cleaning their paint brushes when the ladies arrived from the Birdcage. The look of surprise on their faces said it all.

"You like it?" Kat asked.

"I can't believe how good it looks," Cilla said.

"The walls by the windows are dry," Kat told Leona. "Let's hang the curtains." Kat pulled the crate under the window and handed Leona the first curtain. Leona climbed upon the crate and leaned into the window, threading the curtain through a rod secured by two brackets. The ladies clapped their approval. Leona stepped down and shoved the crate under the second window and put up the final curtain, adjusting the gathering with her fingers pressed against the curtain's heading.

"Have you brought along any milliner supplies, Annabelle?" Kat said.

"I do have some with me. Enough for a couple of hats."

"Good. I would advertise millinery on the window."

Jennie took her cue. "We'll make a temporary sign until I can find someone to make me a decent one. "What are we going to call this place?"

The ladies hunched their shoulders and rolled their eyes.

"By tomorrow, let's have a name," Kat declared.

They nodded in agreement.

"Have you thought about ordering material, patterns, and such?" Kat asked.

Jennie appeared concerned. "I don't know if we have enough money for all that."

"Perhaps we can tap into our restaurant funds. We can cut back on some of our restaurant expenses," Kat suggested.

Jennie's eyes grew wide with panic. "This sounded all so simple at first, but I have no idea what to order or how much."

"Let's see what the customers want first. Maybe, then we'll know how to go about this," Kat said, just as unsure of their new venture as Jennie.

A hand written sign on the sewing shop window announcing a new milliner brought about the interest the Birdcage ladies needed. Annabelle had ordered materials immediately and the few supplies she had brought with her were used up within a week. Along with the new hats the customers ordered, new dresses were desired. Aggie did her best to juggle her cooking with the sewing, but she grumbled she was being split in two.

Several interested parties had come by to look at the Birdcage Restaurant over the past few weeks. Most approved of what they had seen, but so far no one had made an offer. Kat became discouraged.

"I simply have to get back to the ranch before too long," Kat told Jennie while taking a break at the Birdcage. "With me gone, you'll be short handed. Five women can't run two businesses and do justice to both."

"We'll just have to stall the sewing until the Birdcage gets sold," Jennie said, balancing two plates of left over scrambled eggs, which she set on their table.

Kat peppered her eggs and smeared jelly on her toast.

"But I want you ladies to be successful in the sewing business. You can't put off customers for too long or else they'll go somewhere else."

"It'll work out." Jennie sipped her coffee. "We just have to be patient and hope we don't run out of energy."

"I'd like to get the hotel built before it snows."

Jennie sighed. "You might have to wait until spring."

"I can't do that." Kat's voice snapped. "I have to have something to do this winter."

"Kat, I hate to tell you this, but you're driving yourself crazy with everything." Jennie put down her fork, her gaze meeting Kat's. "And us as well."

"Sorry, guess I've been testy lately." Kat pushed her plate away. "I miss Jet. I thought this was home to me, but it isn't. My home is with Jet, no matter where he is."

"I'm glad you've come to your senses. I was afraid you'd leave Jet for Deadwood. You wouldn't have been happy here without him."

"You're absolutely right. I found it out in just a few weeks. It's not the same anymore. Hey, who's the man coming in?"

A sign painter plodded into the Birdcage carrying a painted board. "Where you want this?"

"Our sign, oh, don't it look good? We want it on the building next door." Jennie pointed.

Both women left the Birdcage to watch him nail the sign above the door. "*Deadwood Stitches.* I just love that name," Jennie gushed.

"Yeah, I just hope you'll remain in business until the paint dries at least." Kat sighed.

Jennie scowled. "Where's your confidence? This was your idea."

"Just kidding. I'm sure you will do well."

Jennie tapped Kat on the shoulder and gestured toward the Birdcage. "Say Kat, isn't that the couple who looked at the restaurant last week?"

"I think so. I better go see if they're still interested."

Kat's heart skipped a beat, hoping that this wasn't another dry run. "Good afternoon, may I help you?" she asked the couple, adding the best smile she could muster.

"We'd like to see the business again."

Kat spent the rest of the afternoon showing the interested couple every nook and cranny of the Birdcage. She explained how they managed to make it a successful business and assured them if run properly it would be a money maker. She pointed out the advantages of the upstairs rooms and the good location in Deadwood. By the end of the day she was exhausted, but she had struck a deal. After a visit to the bank, she was dancing on air.

When she entered the Birdcage for supper, she had good news for her ladies. "It's a done deal. They'll take possession in two weeks and they're going to keep the original name." Kat clapped her hands. "Now you all can concentrate on the sewing shop, and I can go home to Jet."

"And the Deadwood citizens will be begging Aggie to cook for them again." Leona frowned.

"That may be, but they'll get over it when they see what she can whip up on a sewing machine," Kat promised.

After supper was served and the place cleaned up, Kat brought them all together in the dining room. "I may not have another opportunity to thank you all for the great help you have been. I will miss you all terribly, but I have faith you can turn the sewing shop into a profitable venture and hopefully not work yourselves to death."

"And thanks for the chance you've given us," Aggie said. "Leona and me haven't had much in life except for cleaning and cooking. Sewing for people is a step up for us."

"Just let me know how it's going here. If I can help in any way just let me know. Annabelle will live in my house until she can afford to buy it someday. She will also buy out my interest in the shop. Jennie will be manager and of course work in the shop, too."

"When are you leaving?" Jennie asked, her voice thick with emotion.

"Within a few weeks. I have a lot to do when I get back to the mission." Kat noticed the sad faces staring at her. "I didn't say I would never come back here again. I'll try to visit and when the railroad comes through from the east to west, we can see each other more often."

CHAPTER 12

Once the weather warmed, Sara had difficulty remaining in the Victorian for the entire weekend. The outdoors called to her almost constantly these days. During Mrs. Wilkes's afternoon nap, Sara stepped outdoors to visit Simon in the paddock with a carrot in her pocket for him. She poked the carrot over the fence for him to munch while she enjoyed the bright sunshine. It was a rather warm day, but she didn't mind. Somehow, the warm sun and the summer breeze cleared her head of duties. After Simon finished his snack, Sara decided to explore the carriage house thoroughly. She stroked the horse's neck one more time and savored his horsey scent before she left him standing looking after her. She hadn't asked Mrs. Wilkes's permission to explore the carriage house, but she didn't think she would care. What secrets would she find anyway?

At first glance everything appeared to be just as it had when she first discovered the carriage building. She inched in farther than last time until she came to a door that opened into another room. She saw a lock on the door, but it was not engaged. Did someone forget to lock it? Why was it locked in the first place? She wondered. Sara looked over her shoulder and listened. She didn't hear anyone. Her pulse quickened, as she slowly unlatched the door and turned the knob. She listened again, but when she heard nothing, she pushed the door open into a room containing a bed, a bureau, and a heating stove. Sturdy boots stood by the bed.

This must be where the gardener lives, she thought. She had never concerned herself where he stayed, before. She just assumed he lived elsewhere.

The room had been swept clean and the bed was neatly made. She was about to close the door when she spied a picture on the bureau. She leaned in closer for a better look at a young smiling couple dressed in what looked like wedding dress and a suit. The woman in the picture looked familiar as Sara studied it from a distance.

Her concentration was broken by the horse whinnying and a man's voice. Quickly she shut the door. There was no way she could exit the carriage house without being discovered. She hunkered down behind the carriage and waited, afraid to even breathe.

After a time the man she assumed to be the gardener entered the carriage house and walked toward the room she had discovered. She heard him mumbling about the lock before he shut the door after him. Edging closer to the outside door, she listened and peeked at the closed door. When she thought all was clear, she bolted to the doorway and left the building.

Sara practically ran Mrs. Burns over when she came in the back door.

"Whoa, slow down. Where have you been?" Mrs. Burns demanded while shaking the rug.

"I...went for a walk. Ran into a snake."

"What kind of snake?"

"I...don't know. Didn't stop to look."

Mrs. Burns eyed her warily. "I heard Mrs. Wilkes calling. I think you take too many walks, young lady."

"Yes, ma'am. I'll attend to Mrs. Wilkes. It's time for our quilting session."

Sara breathed deeply in an attempt to quiet her nervousness. Clearly, Mrs. Burns didn't approve of her snooping around. She would have to be more careful.

Sara wheeled Mrs. Wilkes to the parlor where she plied her with tea and cookies, and then brought out the quilting pieces for them to stuff and sew. Mrs. Wilkes seemed more talkative than usual, so Sara attempted a few questions.

"Every once in a while I come across the gardener, but I don't know his name." Sara inquired.

"Oh, that's Gilbert. Gilbert...Masey," Mrs. Wilkes said, while stuffing another square.

"Where does he live?"

"Oh, he has a place on the east side of Boston." Mrs. Wilkes waved her hand to the east.

"Have you ever been there?"

Mrs. Wilkes scowled. "Certainly not, he's my employee."

"Of course, silly of me."

"Does he ever stay here on the estate?"

"He has a room in the carriage house. He stays there from time to time."

"And Mrs. Burns stays on the first floor of the house. Does she have another place?"

"She lives with a sister when she isn't here. Why are you asking all these questions?" Mrs. Wilkes shoved a stuffed square at Sara.

"I'm just trying to get to know the people that I live with."

"Well don't concern yourself with the staff. You're here to serve me. Besides in a year's time you'll be gone, and someone will take your place."

Mrs. Wilkes abruptly ended the conversation, and Sara

didn't know any more than when she began the questioning, but she knew she had to visit the carriage house and the room once more.

— — — — — —

Clouds began to build on a summer Sunday afternoon. The air was sticky and hot when Sara went for a walk while Mrs. Wilkes was taking her nap. She returned drenched with perspiration, but the time she spent alone was worth it. After she mopped her face with a wash cloth, she searched for a book to read to pass the rest of the afternoon. She had only read a few chapters when she heard Mrs. Wilkes voice on the tube.

"Sara, Sara, are you there?"

"Yes, Mrs. Wilkes."

"Let's eat lunch. My granddaughter is coming by to spend the evening with me."

She snapped her book shut. "I can arrange that. I believe Mrs. Burns left us cold chicken and potato salad in the ice box. I'll be down to get you," she told her.

After Sara wheeled Mrs. Wilkes into the dining room, she went to the kitchen to collect their cold meal. "Is this all right?" Sara asked her, placing the plate before her.

"Yes, it's too hot to eat anyway. I'm anxious for you to meet my granddaughter Myra. I think you will get along nicely."

"How long is she planning to stay?" Sara asked, attempting to keep the weariness out of her voice.

"She usually stays here about a week and entertains me the entire time. We like to play the same kind of board games, and she wheels me to the park. I do get tired of being cooped up here in this house. After she arrives you can spend the rest of the day as you wish, and she can help me to bed."

"Thank you."

"You can go out if you wish."

"I really have nowhere to go for such a short time, but I do like to read."

"Very well. Whatever suits you."

Myra, a rather thin girl with ordinary features and unnaturally bright red hair, arrived soon after they finished eating lunch. Mrs. Wilkes showed a special joy at her arrival that Sara had not seen before. Strange that this lackluster girl would initiate such a response, but after all, Myra was her granddaughter.

Myra and Mrs. Wilkes spent the evening together in the parlor while Sara cleared the dishes and cleaned up the kitchen. When Sara heard Myra laughing with her grandmother, an odd sensation coursed through Sara. She had heard that voice before. But where? She hadn't recognized the thin girl and could not place her if indeed she was familiar.

Sara organized what she would prepare for supper and then retired to her room to read.

After a short nap Sara skipped down the stairs refreshed and delighted to find Mrs. Wilkes so animated. Myra and Mrs. Wilkes continued chatting about family affairs during the evening meal. Sara was pleased Mrs. Wilkes had someone to talk to.

"I'll leave you two alone for the evening," Sara said as she cleaned the dishes off the table.

Both were whispering together in the parlor when Sara brought in the tea and dessert for them. They seemed not to notice her. She excused herself and returned to the kitchen to wash the dishes. When she peeked in the parlor before she left for her room, Mrs. Wilkes and Myra were gone. Sara shrugged and assumed they had gone to their rooms.

Sara started upstairs just as a storm began to let loose its fury. She shuddered as she pulled the shade against the light-

154

ning piercing her window, but the thunder shook the house in defiance. A sudden thud, then a noise of flapping wood caused her to jump, but she ignored its significance until she heard it several more times. Knowing that there was no one to explore its source, she left the room and climbed the stairs toward its origin. The sound was definitely coming from the third level at the top of the stairs. She steeled herself as she continued to ascend the stairs.

The lightning lit up the sky and illuminated the upper room. Mustering every ounce of courage, she peered around the corner, listening for the banging sound. Her attention to the sound was diverted when she saw a quilt draped haphazardly across the rocker. Her heart beat wildly as she continued onward. Her knees were weak by the time she reached the chair and placed her hands on the seat. She detected a warm sensation.

Someone was just here. She collected her senses, hesitated for a few moments and walked quickly into the large room looking for some sign of occupation. No one was there.

The lightning cracked and thunder roared, deafening any other sounds in the house. She forgot about the banging sound, instead she backed herself up to the rocker and picked up the quilt as another flash of lightning broke the sky.

This can't be. Darkness enveloped her for what seemed like eternity before another flash of light illuminated the quilt.

It's the mission quilt. She would know that quilt anywhere. She had been there at the mission when they made most of the blocks.

Sara snatched the quilt and like a thief in the night, sneaked down the stairs to her room. Once inside, she shut the door. Quaking with the realization she had found the missing Jacob's Ladder quilt, she sat down by the lamp and searched for the quilter's initials added to the quilt. Sure enough, her Grandmother Red Bird's embroidered red bird was there on the quilt's edge. She ran her hands over Red Bird's handiwork, attempting to touch her grandmother's essence. The quilt had faded some, but otherwise was in good repair.

"What should I do with this quilt?" she asked herself out loud, trembling from head to toe. Someone must have taken it from the mission, but whom and how did it end up here?

— — — — — —

Sara did her best not to intrude on Myra and Mrs. Wilkes's time together. She was happy for the extra time to herself. Besides, Mrs. Wilkes seemed to enjoy her granddaughter's presence immensely. Meals were usually quiet affairs interspersed with desultory conversation. Sara liked it that way. Most of the time she was just too preoccupied with the missing quilt to chit chat.

After Sara had put Mrs. Wilkes to bed one evening, the roving spirit took a hold of her. She continued on up the stairs until she reached the top level where she could step out to breathe the evening's fresh, invigorating air. As she turned the corner, to where she liked to sit she stopped dead in her tracks. The lavender scent that had mystified her for the past few months lingered with two figured shadows occupying the space normally vacant. She remained rooted to the spot as she studied the two forms. The woman hunched over and sitting in the rocking chair barely showed any signs of life, and the woman leaning up against the chair was middle aged. It took a while for Sara to collect herself, and then she slowly backed away, retracing her former steps.

By the time she reached her room, she shook in tremors. Who were these people and why hadn't she seen them before? She wondered if these two strangers were a part of this house, but why the secrecy and what were they hiding? She admonished herself for not having the courage to approach them and demand who they were.

Weak in the knees by the time she crossed her room, she immediately sat in her bedside chair to sort out what she had just seen. *What is the matter with me?* She chided herself. *I'm overreacting.*

Perhaps Mrs. Wilkes or Mrs. Burns had forgotten to tell her about the two women guests. After all, she had been gone all day and she wouldn't have seen them arrive. She calmed herself by deciding to ask someone about what she saw. There was no sense arriving at wrong conclusions. It was just Lois's talk about ghosts and such that ran away with her imagination, she concluded.

Sara slept fitfully and awoke early to Mrs. Wilkes's demanding voice through the tube. "I'll be right there," Sara said.

After an hour, they entered the dining room for breakfast. No sign of any guests seemed apparent. Mrs. Burns served them their customary breakfast, a poached egg, tea, and toast for Mrs. Wilkes and toast and coffee for Sara. Mrs. Burns commented that Myra was sleeping in. A few desultory words concerning the weather were spoken among them but no mention of any guests was made.

Sara left without any answers to the two women she had seen last night. When Sara arrived at the hospital she searched for Lois, but couldn't find her. Realizing that they wouldn't be working together that morning, Sara did her best to concentrate on her assignment of preparing bandages and sterilizing equipment. The morning dragged until lunch when Sara could speak to Lois.

"My, you look disheveled today," Lois remarked as Sara sat beside her.

Sara rubbed her eyes. "I didn't sleep well last night."

"What did you do? See a ghost?" Lois laughed.

"I might have. How about two?"

Lois's eyes bulged. "Seriously?"

"Oh, I don't know. I went up to the observatory last night for a breath of air and I saw two women sitting where I usually sit. I don't think I'll sit in that chair again or maybe not even go up there anymore."

"Gosh, there really are ghosts in that house."

"They looked awfully real to me," Sara said.

"Did they fade before your eyes?"

"I left before they could. When I took Mrs. Wilkes to breakfast, everyone behaved the same as usual. I thought maybe the ladies were guests I didn't know about."

"Strange. Tell me more," Lois encouraged. "What did they look like? Could you see through them?"

"No, nothing like that," Sara said with an irritated edge. "They certainly appeared human to me. One was old and the other middle aged. I was going to ask Mrs. Burns about them at breakfast, but I'd appear foolish if I'm just imagining all this."

"Are you going to look for them tonight?"

"I don't know what to do."

Lois's eyes widened. "I'd get out of there, fast."

"They looked harmless enough. I just don't know who they are."

"Ask someone, then. In the meantime, lock your door."

"I intend to and I may just talk to Mrs. Burns about the two ladies I saw." Sara parted company, leaving Lois to look after her in a concerned state.

"My, you scared me," Mrs. Burns commented over her shoulder as Sara walked into the kitchen just before the evening meal.

Sara watched Mrs. Burns bustling around the kitchen preparing their supper. Sara realized she didn't know Mrs. Burns all that well and wondered what her response would be if she told them about the two women she saw last night. "Did you have any visitors yesterday or the day before here at the house?"

"No, why do you ask?"

"I want to ask you something."

Mrs. Burns bristled. "You don't like it here, do you? Mrs. Wilkes is getting to you like all the other girls."

"No, that's not it."

"Then what is it?" she asked impatiently.

"I went up to the observatory last night and I saw two women there, one elderly and one much younger. I retreated before they could see me. I've heard strange noises since I've come here."

"What kind of noises?" Mrs. Burns asked still tending to her tasks.

"A wailing sound."

"I haven't heard anything."

"Well, I have and I want to know who these women are?"

"Maybe...ghosts? It has been said this house is haunted."

"I...don't believe in ghosts." Sara stood her ground. "Have you seen any since you've been working here?"

"I haven't, but I hear that others have. Maybe that's why I jumped when you came in the kitchen and surprised me. Old houses conjure up stories of ghosts. I simply don't know what to tell you. Perhaps you've been working too hard."

"Have you ever heard anything out of the ordinary?"

"I have never heard anything of the sort." Mrs. Burns abruptly took the dishes from the cupboard and began to set the table, dismissing Sara's inquiries.

"Lois told me that some of the girls who took care of Mrs. Wilkes heard things, too." Sara insisted.

"It's all rubbish."

Sara scowled at the impasse and left the kitchen not believing what Mrs. Burns had just told her. She was certain there had to be an explanation. Determined to find the answer, she proceeded up to the third level of the house. She peeked around the corner and, seeing no one, entered the large room. She stood silent and listened. Unable to detect a sound, she moved about the room, inspecting the wood paneling for a secret passageway. She pushed and pulled on any section that appeared suspect, but to her dismay she could find nothing.

If only I could find a floor plan of the house, perhaps I could find a secret room, she thought. She had heard that some houses had secret passage ways.

"Ah, hah, but I do remember something," she whispered. She dashed down to the second level and entered the unused bedroom across from hers where she had seen a picture of the house hanging on the wall when she had first explored the second floor rooms.

Sara hadn't studied the picture at the time, but now she scrutinized it. The sketch was rather rough but something in it looked differently, but what was it? The sketch had been dated 1850 and had been signed.

"It's the turret," she blurted out loud.

In the sketch there were only two towers. The current Victorian had two towers and a turret. She tapped her chin in thought. She had been in the two tower rooms. Her room and Mrs. Wilkes bedroom were in one tower. The other tower room was over the parlor. A guest bedroom on the second floor was above that. That left the turret above a porch and the locked bedroom on the second floor. Did it connect to the third floor? She traced the spot on the sketch with her finger, assimilating it in her mind.

If there's an entrance to the third floor, it has to be right here, she decided.

Leaving the room, she revisited the third floor. She searched the wall where she contemplated where the turret room should be, but as she thought there didn't seem to be an entrance to the locked room from the third floor.

Just to be sure, she felt along the wall, searching for some sort of entry way to the locked room. Pushing and tapping against the wall yielded nothing. Disgusted, she flopped into the rocking chair to think while wiggling her toes back and forth.

How do the two women get to the third floor unless they used the stairs? She wanted to know.

She re-evaluated her discovery. The turret was above one of the porches so that would take care of the first floor, the second floor bedroom above the porch was locked or was it boarded off, too? Somehow she had to get into that room. She bolted from her chair to visit the porch and scampered down the stairs.

Peering up at the second level above the porch revealed nothing about the mysterious turret. She searched the base of the two towers. There was no outside entrance that she could locate, unless there was an underground entrance somewhere. She walked around the foundation of the house and couldn't locate anything. If there was an underground entrance it wasn't near the house, she surmised.

What am I doing? I'm behaving like a detective. She shook her head at her antics, but what would a detective do next? Footprints perhaps? She walked around the house looking for a worn path in the grass but couldn't find any evidence of that either. Scratching her head in defeat, she re-entered the house.

"Where have you been?" Mrs. Burns asked in an agitated tone. "Mrs. Wilkes is calling for you."

"Sorry, I had to run outside a minute." Sara fled from Mrs. Burns and entered Mrs. Wilkes's room out of breath.

"What are you up to now, Sara?" Mrs. Wilkes asked. "I'm beginning to wonder about you."

– – – – –

After seeing the women on the third floor, Sara contemplated the voices she thought she heard in Mrs. Wilkes's room the day Maud had come for a visit. Sara planted a thought in her own head that the Victorian possibly might contain secret walls and staircases.

There might even be a secret entrance to Mrs. Wilkes's room, she contemplated. But she never had the opportunity to search for it. Today presented that opportunity. Myra had taken her grandmother out for a Sunday walk in the park. Sara guessed they would be gone at least an hour or more.

When Sara was sure she was alone, glancing one more time toward the kitchen, she opened the door to Mrs. Wilkes room. She knew she was invading her privacy, but she just had to find out what was going on in the house. Quickly, she knocked against the walls searching for a hollow sound, but she found no walls that sounded suspicious. She rolled up the area carpets and searched under them for a trap door, but none were evident. There was nothing suspicious under the bed either. She moved the lighter furniture to see if something was hidden there, but again she found nothing.

About to give up her search, she thought of the closet. The door opened to an array of clothing, shoes, and hats. In its cluttered state, she expected to find nothing, but she gave it a once over anyway. Pushing clothes aside and kicking shoes out the closet door enabled her to reach the back of the closet. There was something different about the wall. She pushed against it, and it yielded to her touch. A small, narrow staircase appeared before her. Her heart thumped wildly.

"Oh my gosh," she whispered. "What does this mean?"

Sara cranked her neck through the small opening and listened. There wasn't a sound, but she felt a swoosh of air descending from up above and along with it the faint aroma of lavender. She had to find out where it led but did she have time? In a rush of excitement, she scooped the shoes back into the closet and closed the door. Amazed to find the interior of the staircase dimly lit by sunlight, she stealthy scaled the steep steps, stopping every few steps or so to listen. The steps curved ever so slightly until she reached a small slanted window. That explained the sunlight, she thought. She kept climbing, thinking she must be near the second floor. Since her bedroom was just above Mrs. Wilkes she wondered if she had access to the staircase, too.

With each step, she began searching for an entrance into her own room. She pushed and prodded on the wall, but nothing yielded. She kept going and tried again and this time a panel in the wall moved, and she fell into a closet. But this wasn't her closet! Reaching for the panel, she pulled it shut until she could get her wits together. She opened the closet door into the bedroom next to hers, and stood in wonderment at her recent discovery.

Did the residents of this house know about the hidden staircase? She wondered.

"Yes, they do," she said out loud. "That may explain some of the strange happenings, but who was entering and exiting without being detected? And who wore the lavender scent?"

Sara heard Mrs. Wilkes and Myra clatter into the house.

Oh, no, thought Sara.

In her haste she never straightened the shoes in Mrs. Wilkes's closet. Quickly, Sara darted to the closet, closed the door, and pushed against the panel. Out on the staircase, she nimbly descended the stairs to the first floor. Nearly missing the moving panel, she panicked and back tracked until she found it. Not only did the staircase connect with the first and second floor it appeared to descend to a lower level. With no time to check it out, she found the panel to the first floor, pushed on it, and dropped into Mrs. Wilkes closet. She heard voices and stopped dead in her tracks.

"You rest, grandmother. I'll go find Sara," Myra said.

"She may be resting, don't disturb her." Mrs. Wilkes

called after here.

Sara dared not to breathe. What was she going to do? She wondered in panic. There was no way she could straighten the shoes without making noise, and turning to ascend the staircase was risky, too. All she could do was wait and hope Mrs. Wilkes dropped off to a deep sleep.

Sara had no idea how long she remained immobile. She hadn't heard anything from Mrs. Wilkes and hoped she fell asleep. After she quietly straightened the shoes, she had to try and reach the second floor. As she opened the panel to the staircase it creaked louder than Sara had anticipated. She stopped and gritted her teeth.

"Susan is that you?" Mrs. Wilkes said in a state of grogginess.

Sara froze. Susan? Who was Susan? She stood still until she heard Mrs. Wilkes slightly snoring, and made another attempt to the stairs. Once on the stairs she pulled the panel behind her and climbed up the stairs to the opening in the bedroom next to hers. This time she counted the number of stairs.

Back in her room, she sighed with relief. There was definitely more to explore. She would do it another day. Thinking that Myra might be needing her, she straightened her hair and washed her face and willed her heart to quit thumping. Taking a deep breath and feeling rattled from her amazing discoveries, she went downstairs to find Myra in the kitchen.

"Oh there you are. I was looking for you, but when I found the door of your room closed I concluded you were napping," Myra said. "Grandmother said for me not to disturb you. My, you look flushed. Are you all right?"

"Why, yes. I was napping." Sara exhaled with relief that the door to her room had been closed.

"Grandmother must think highly of you."

"Why do you say that?"

"If it would have been anyone else she would have demanded I wake them up. And then she would have soundly scolded them that they dared take a nap." Myra peered over her shoulder at her. "You certainly have a hold on my Grandmother."

"We do get along rather well I think." After admitting their close relationship, Sara felt guilty that she was lying and sneaking around behind Mrs. Wilkes's back. In a sense betraying her trust.

– – – – – –

On Sunday, Myra had left after her week's stay, promising to return soon. Gilbert was gone for a day's respite. Sara had overheard Mrs. Wilkes and Mrs. Burns talking about his short vacation to the country. Mrs. Burns also would be out for the entire day to help her sister. Only Mrs. Wilkes and Sara would be in the house.

Sara was restless. A question kept stirring in her mind. Who was using the hidden stairs and how did they get in the house? She had little time to do much sleuthing, but she had to find the answers.

Today presented the opportunity, and Sara was going to take advantage of it. Once again she waited until Mrs. Wilkes fell asleep and then left for the carriage house. She didn't even stop to stroke Simon, instead she rushed to the door of Gilbert's room and found it unlocked.

Once again she peeked inside. Only a few shirts hung on hooks along with a couple of hats and a coat. She glanced at the photograph she had seen before. She was sure that the woman in it was Mrs. Burns when she was a younger woman.

But why would Gilbert have a photograph of Mrs. Burns? She wondered.

She didn't want to venture inside the room since it belonged to Gilbert at the moment. She was about to leave when she noticed a throw rug curled on one end, revealing a crack in the floor. Against her better judgment, she clenched her fist, entered the room, and kicked the rug aside. She gasped when she discovered what she was looking for, a trap door. She tugged at the small strap and pulled it open. Stale air whooshed through the room, assailing her senses. The hole was dark, and she had not brought a lantern with her. What was she going to do? Mrs. Wilkes could wake any moment, but an opportunity like this might not present itself again.

She left the room and hunted for a lantern in the carriage house. Finding a can of matches nearby, she lit a lantern and approached the trap door. The dim light revealed a stairway. Lifting her skirt and placing her foot on the second rung, she edged her way down to a tunnel that she discovered went in two different directions. One way went to the house, she guessed, but she had no idea where the other one led. Nor could she tell how long the tunnel could be, but she decided she had to make time to explore it.

She hesitated on embarking into the dark space and hoped she would not encounter any skeletons, animal or human. Where it would end, she did not know, but she climbed down. Testing the ceiling with her hands, she discovered the passageway seemed to be quite low. The walls molded around her, confining her to its dark abyss. Relieved that heavy wood beams supported the rough dirt walls, she took a deep breath and began to walk, slowly at first to get used to the ground underneath her feet. To her surprise, the path in the tunnel appeared well worn, like it had been used recently. She assumed by Gilbert, but whom else?

She proceeded warily until she became used to the dark space. The cold penetrated her bare arms and she began to shiver, not knowing if it was from the cool damp interior of the tunnel or the fear she was experiencing. She was about ready to turn back when she nearly slammed into another small stairway. Surprised that the tunnel wasn't any longer, she climbed the stairs and emerged in an abandoned shack. Where was she? She frantically looked out its small singular window for a landmark. All she could see was woods.

Carefully opening the door, she peeked out the door and seeing no one, she stepped outside to have a look. Nothing seemed familiar to her, but the warm sunshine felt good on her arms. If she had more time she would look outside the woods, but she knew she had to get back to the house. Besides, the kerosene in the lantern was running low, and she didn't want to be in the tunnel without light. Promising herself to search for the woods and the shack later, she rubbed her prickles from her arms and returned to the tunnel, and then hurried along the tunnel to the carriage house.

Once back at the carriage house, she closed the trap door, and placed the rug where she found it. Checking the clock on the bureau, she surmised she had been gone over an hour. Mrs. Wilkes would be waking soon.

— — — — — —

Sara waited anxiously for a week until Mrs. Burns left the house on her usual Sunday off. As usual, Mrs. Burns told her she would be gone the entire day and to take care of Mrs. Wilkes and prepare her meals.

She smiled to herself as she calculated a plan. Today was her opportunity to look for the shack in the woods. The thought made her giddy. Perhaps its discovery would help her solve this mystery that had been plaguing her for months. Something was going on in this house. She had seen two strange women in the house and to her knowledge, they were still there, somewhere. Also, someone had been to the mission and stolen a quilt. But who? What could be the motive? She was sure it wasn't sinister, but still she wanted to know.

Mrs. Wilkes insisted they work on the puff quilt after lunch. Since the day was warm, Sara did her best to dissuade her by suggesting a walk outdoors, hoping that she would tire quickly, but she insisted. Sara removed the nearly completed quilt from the cupboard. There wasn't much to do to finish it; however, Sara wasn't in the mood to sew the remaining squares together.

"Do you really want to spend the afternoon sewing?" she asked Mrs. Wilkes.

"I do. I want to give this quilt to someone, and I want to finish it before you leave."

"Before I leave?"

"I've detained you long enough as my nurse. I know you would rather be doing other things."

"Oh, I've enjoyed it here." She did enjoy the experience with Mrs. Wilkes, but when she discovered what was going on, she planned to ask Mrs. Wilkes some direct questions. It was her guess that the camaraderie that the two had briefly experienced would be jeopardized.

The minutes ticked by every so slowly while they sewed. Neither one was in the mood for conversation, so they sewed in silence. In about an hour, Mrs. Wilkes began to yawn. "Ready for a nap?" Sara asked attempting to keep her tone even.

"I think so. We have finished it, haven't we?"

"Yes, it is." Sara spread out the completed puff quilt. It's pretty don't you think?"

Mrs. Wilkes eyes sparkled. "Indeed it is. I'm happy you suggested working on a quilt. I forgot how much I had enjoyed it."

"It actually was Mrs. Burn's idea. I'm happy I took her suggestion." Sara folded the quilt and placed it in Mrs. Wilkes' lap and wheeled her to her room, tucking her in for the afternoon. She noticed that Mrs. Wilkes eye lids were exceptionally heavy.

Good, Sara thought. *Her lengthy nap would give her more time.*

When Sara grabbed a light wrap and stepped outside, the sunshine and a warm breeze was soothing. The day was lovely, a good day for a hike in the woods. She increased her step not to waste any of the precious time she was allotted for exploring. Instead of using the tunnel, she tramped due south of the building into the woods. All she had to do was find the shack. It couldn't be far.

Her steps felt springy on the damp spongy ground as she walked deeper into the woods. She kept an eye on the carriage house for she calculated that the tunnel had been built in a mostly straight line. The trees became thicker and blocked the bright sunlight as she hiked deeper into the woods. She began to shiver from either the dampness or the anticipation, she didn't know.

"It can't be much farther," she convinced herself.

She turned again to check to see if she was walking in a straight line from the carriage house only to realize that the trees were now too thick to see the landmark. Panic began to palpitate in her chest.

I could become lost if I don't find the shack soon.

How would she explain where she had been if she didn't arrive back to Mrs. Wilkes when she woke up from her nap? She had no idea how far she had walked, but she sensed that the tunnel wasn't this long.

It must have veered in another direction. Maybe if I swing a little to the left and walk back, I'll come across the shack. She struggled not to break out into a run and to keep herself calm. Time was fleeing, and she needed to get back to the house soon. Perhaps, she told herself, she should search for the shack later. This time she would use the tunnel to the shack so as not to get lost.

She turned to the left in an arc and walked, her eyes searching for a building. She almost gave up hope until she saw the dilapidated structure surrounded by tall bushes. Relieved, she approached it and when finding the latch askew, she opened the door. She cautiously lifted the trap door and peered into the tunnel. Voices! She heard voices and a slight scent of lavender filled the space. Her stomach leaped into her throat. She almost slammed the trap door, but caught herself in time and let the door down gently and scooted out of the shack. Her heart pounding wildly, she looked around for a place to hide. She had to see who came through the tunnel.

Wedging herself into the side bushes, she waited breathlessly. She had barely situated herself when two women burst through the door. One was dressed in a nurse's uniform and the other was an elderly woman. They appeared to be the same women that she had seen in the ballroom months ago. Tucked under the elderly woman's arm was the puffed quilt.

Well, I'll be, Sara thought, realizing that they had just seen Mrs. Wilkes. The elderly woman was "the someone" who Mrs. Wilkes had intended for the quilt.

"No, you can't take that with you." The big burly nurse argued with the elderly woman, who clutched the quilt and wouldn't let go. "We'll leave it here in the building and pick it up when we come back," the nurse said. Still the woman wouldn't let go, see-sawing the quilt back and forth between them. Finally, the elder woman released her hold, and the nurse gathered the quilt and placed it in the shack.

I have to follow them. Sara held her breath until the women were far enough ahead not to hear her. She crawled out of the bushes, straightened her skirt and walked quietly at a distance behind them. She glanced over her shoulder, trying to determine where she was, but all she could see was woods. In a short time, she found a well-worn path the women were following. She determined it was a path they had followed often.

She kept close to the trees in case she had to dart behind

one, but to her relief they never sensed someone was following them. The trees began to thin and soon the women approached a clearing on the edge of the city. Sara wasn't familiar enough with the city to know where she was. She looked back by the way she had come, determining she wasn't sure how to get back to the house and Mrs. Wilkes.

Torn by going back or pressing on, she kept following the women. She was too close to finding out where they were heading. About two blocks down a narrow street, the women came to a park. Both women sat down on a bench and remained there. Sara threw up her hands in disgust. A Park? They ended up in a park. She couldn't begin to comprehend why if they visited Mrs. Wilkes they would not use the front or back door. Why all this mystery?

Perplexed with the situation and unanswered questions, she turned back to the woods and chanced that she could find her way back to Mrs. Wilkes. It wasn't as difficult as she expected, although she ended up a block from the Victorian.

Once she entered the house, Sara heard Mrs. Wilkes's voice booming through the interior. Finding the door ajar, she rushed into her room to find her in an agitated state.

"Where were you? I was calling for at least a half hour."

Sara hadn't even thought of an explanation in case Mrs. Wilkes woke up early and called for her. She stammered for an explanation.

"Where on earth have you been? Your face is scratched and your skirt is torn?"

Sara was speechless. She hadn't thought to look in the mirror. She had no explanation other than to tell the truth. "I'm sorry I wasn't here. I...was out for a walk. Past the carriage house."

Mrs. Wilkes pursed her lips. "You know Gilbert disapproves of you gadding about the grounds."

"I know, but I'm looking for...answers."

"Answers to what?"

"Shall I wheel you out to the parlor where we can talk over a cup of tea?"

"Yes, I'm ready to get out of this bed. My bones ache so badly today."

Once Sara wheeled Mrs. Wilkes to the parlor, she rushed into the kitchen to brew the tea while thinking about her decision to tell the truth. The tea kettle whistled, and Sara filled the teapot, placed it on a tray with the cups and took it to the parlor.

"What questions do you have on your mind?" Mrs. Wilkes asked, taking the teacup from Sara.

"What I'm about to say is going to surprise you. I hope you don't think badly of me because of it."

Mrs. Wilkes glared. "Well go on. Out with it."

Sara swallowed hard, and then cleared her throat. "I saw the puffed quilt go out of this house."

Mrs. Wilkes narrowed her eyes. "You what?"

"I saw the quilt we made. An elderly woman was carrying it. She and another woman came out of a tunnel and headed into the woods, eventually arriving at a park."

Mrs. Wilkes sat silent, seemingly stunned. "I don't know what to say. What were you doing so far from the house?"

"Just looking around."

Mrs. Wilkes scowled. "What else have you seen while you've been here?"

"I apologize for being disrespectful and not minding my own business, but I found something."

"And what was that?"

Sara felt herself beginning to shake. "A quilt. A missing quilt from our mission."

"A quilt? Are you sure?"

"I'm sure. I found it on the third floor. It was draped over a rocking chair."

"Women make the same patterns all the time. You're probably imagining it's from the mission."

Sara shook her head. "I know it's ours. My Grandmother's signature, which is an embroidered red bird, appears on the edge. No one can duplicate that without intending to."

"I see."

"Please, tell me what it's doing here so far from the South Dakota mission."

Mrs. Wilkes sighed. "You are one inquisitive girl. I've never met anyone like you. The two women you saw were... friends of Mrs. Burns'."

"Why don't they use the door instead of coming and going through tunnels? Besides, I'm sure the large woman was a nurse and what were they doing with my quilt?"

Mrs. Wilkes paused. "The old lady is quite eccentric. I think the big lady pretends she's a nurse."

"I gathered the older lady was odd. She and the nurse were haggling over the puffed quilt. Finally, the nurse convinced the woman to leave it in the shack. Did you give the quilt to this old woman?"

"I...I put the quilt aside for Mrs. Burns to store," Mrs. Wilkes said. "She must have promised it to her friend instead. I'll have a talk with her."

Sara frowned. "What were they doing here when Mrs. Burns is out for the day?" Still not satisfied with the answers, she asked. "Did they simply pick up the quilt and leave with it, through a tunnel none the less?"

"They're strange characters. I can't really explain their actions. Now don't worry about it."

"You still haven't explained what they were doing with my quilt," Sara insisted.

"They may have picked it up at a store that sells used items," Mrs. Wilkes reasoned. "Someone else may have taken the quilt and brought it to Boston. It could have ended up as a cast-off. Mrs. Burns could have bought it in a thrift store without telling me."

Sara thought about Mrs. Wilkes explanation and determined it could be plausible. She did answer her questions. "You may be right. I've never seen such odd people before. I don't know why they don't just come in through the doors like everyone else."

Mrs. Wilkes shrugged. "I don't pay any attention to them. They're harmless."

"Well, alright," Sara consented. "Why are there tunnels?"

"It goes back to the days before the Civil War. Slaves were smuggled out through these tunnels to freedom."

"Have you ever been in them?"

"I should say not. Why would I want to use them?" Mrs. Wilkes voice grew stern. "I suggest you tame your wild imagination. You're getting ideas into her head. Ideas that aren't healthy. And cease your exploring. I want you here in this house when I call."

CHAPTER 13

Sara's last conversation with Mrs. Wilkes confused her. Mrs. Wilkes had told her the two women were probably friends of Mrs. Burns; however, when she saw them on the third floor the first time, Mrs. Burns attempted to convince Sara that the women were figments of her imagination.

Sara continued to feel uneasy about the situation at the Wilkes's Victorian, even more so, since she had seen the two strangers on the third floor. She ceased her exploring for the moment.

Once more she confided her suspicions to Lois while they were cleaning the hospital operating room. Lois was the only person she could trust.

"Sara, I don't believe any of what Mrs. Wilkes told you. What kind of people sneak around through tunnels? Friends of Mrs. Burns? I doubt it."

"She said they were eccentric people."

"They most certainly are eccentric," Lois shivered. "I don't know how you can live in that house. Aren't you afraid?"

"No, I'm not. Just curious."

Lois shook her head. "I think Mrs. Wilkes is trying to protect someone."

"You might be right, but how am I going to find out?"

"I don't think you should try to find out anything," Lois said firmly. "You need to get out of there and come live with me."

"Then I'd be like all the other girls. Leave before they finish with their assignment. I don't want to be like them."

"Sara, you're so stubborn. You are the bravest girl I've ever met, but I'm worried about you."

"I really don't feel like I'm in danger."

Lois ceased scrubbing and looked at her in disbelief. "How can you be sure?"

"It's just a feeling."

"I would have been out of there weeks ago."

Sara grinned. "Want to come and spend the night?"

"Quit teasing me. I'm serious."

"I know and thanks for worrying about me."

Lois rolled her eyes. "A lot of good it's doing."

Sara wiped down the last of the operating table. "Thanks for listening, anyway. I think we're finished here for the day."

"And it's earlier than usual," Lois removed her apron. "Any plans for the extra time off?"

"Not really. Maybe I can sneak upstairs and read a while before Mrs. Wilkes calls me."

"Good luck. See you tomorrow."

Sara seriously hoped she could sneak into her room without anyone noticing. *An extra hour to myself would be paradise,* she thought. *Although it will be hard to slip past Mrs. Burns and the kitchen. But if I used the tunnel and came into the adjoining bedroom on the second floor, I wouldn't be detected at all.*

She contemplated she could either enter the tunnel by

the carriage house or in the shack, a quarter-mile away. *Maybe not the carriage house,* she thought. Gilbert might be in his carriage house room, and she didn't want to risk an encounter. If she hurried she could be at the shack in a manner of minutes. She increased her pace until she arrived at the shack unnoticed. Once inside the building, she picked up a candle and match stored in a tin and lifted the trap door with the attached rug and descended into the tunnel.

She was about to strike the match to light the candle, but ceased when she saw a glimmer of light up ahead. She froze with the realization that someone else was in the tunnel ahead of her. Undecided whether to follow in the dark or wait until the light disappeared. She remained still for a few minutes, but while contemplating her strategy, a creaking noise and a slice of light slightly above her propelled her forward. Someone was coming in through the trap door above her! Her skin prickled and the hair stood up on the back of her neck. It was then she knew she had no choice but to stumble through the dark as quietly as possible.

Luckily, she had been through the tunnel before, but still she didn't know every hole or uneven piece of ground. Terrified of being discovered, she surged ahead of the light behind her toward the light in front of her. She had no idea if the person behind her had detected her presence. If she kept far enough ahead she had a chance to get to the hidden staircase and disappear.

The light preceding her vanished, indicating the person had reached the house. *If only I could be so lucky,* she thought.

She reminded herself to keep her head low as not to bump against the ceiling, but in spite of her caution, she whacked her head on a protruding rock. She heard a piece of ceiling clatter to the floor. Not daring to look behind her, she increased her pace against her better judgment. It seemed like she had been in the tunnel for an eternity before she reached the basement entrance and the staircase.

It was dark and she had no light to guide her. A quick look behind her, confirmed her suspicions that someone was gaining. She felt for the stairs at the house, found them and scampered up as quickly as she could. Without a light, she knew finding the panel for the second floor would be next to impossible. Whoever was behind her would surely catch her. Her hand flailed against the wall, indiscriminately searching for the secret panel, realizing she had no idea where it was. She looked backward one more time expecting to see someone looming above her, ready to snatch and expose her presence, but the light disappeared. No one was coming up the staircase.

Calming her uneven breaths, she dropped her arms and sat quietly regaining her composure. She searched again for the hidden panel to the second floor. She retraced her steps several times before she pushed against a section that opened into the closet of the adjoining room to her bedroom. Once inside the closet, she attempted to steady her shaking legs before she peeped through the partially open door into the large bedroom. Quietly, she moved toward the bedroom door and peered out into the hall. No one was within sight, and she scurried down the hall to her own room and closed the door. She leaned against the door for some time until she quit shaking.

Who was in the tunnel with her and where were they going? Her heart thudded rapidly in her chest. One person went to the basement she presumed, but the other? She had no idea. She spilled water into her wash bowl, wet a wash cloth, and mopped her face. Mrs. Wilkes would be calling for her soon, and she couldn't appear frightened or disoriented.

After changing her light blue skirt, which had accumulated dirt from the tunnel, she dusted her shoes and straightened her hair. By the time she finished, Mrs. Wilkes called for her. Reaching the bottom stair step, she caught a glimpse of Mrs. Burns in the kitchen. Mouth-watering aromas drifted through the house. Mrs. Wilkes was right. Mrs. Burns was a good cook.

In a sense of uneasiness and dread, Sara attended to her usual duties with Mrs. Wilkes and then brought her to the dining room. She apparently covered up her fright well for Mrs. Wilkes was none the wiser. Sara knew that both women had lied to her about the two strange women making appearances in and around the house, and realized she had no one she could trust while she remained there. Her stomach churned with confusion, wishing she could make an excuse to leave the dining room. She placed her napkin in her lap and while glancing down, she noticed Mrs. Burns' shoes. They were covered in dust just as hers had been. The edge of her navy blue dress was soiled with dirt. Sara's heart jerked with fear. Had Mrs. Burns been in the tunnel with Sara?

– – – – – –

The next morning the gardener lumbered into the solarium to speak with Mrs. Wilkes.

"What's the trouble, Gilbert?" Mrs. Wilkes abruptly woke up from a catnap and asked. "You look annoyed."

He loomed over her wheelchair, his face angry, and his shoulders slouching. "That girl that takes care of you is a snoop. I found her out by the stables several different times in the past few weeks. Did she ask your permission to go out to the paddock and see Simon?"

"No, she didn't. Usually the girls don't bother to go out in the back yard." She laughed. "I think you scare them."

"Well, I should. Nobody has any business out there. I even saw her go into the carriage house for a moment. I was ready to throw a scare into and warn her about snooping, but she came to the house about then."

Mrs. Wilkes straightened the blanket covering her. "She's a different one alright. Has more courage than any of the others."

Gilbert paced around the wheelchair. "You need to talk to her. Tell her to mind her own business."

"Won't that make her more suspicious? Besides, what is she going to find?"

"I don't like her in my way. She asks too many questions," he grumbled, and then turned to stare at Mrs. Burns walking into the solarium.

"Ready for your morning nap, Mrs. Wilkes?" she said.

"I've been nodding off already. The sun puts me to sleep. But before we go, I'd like to know if you think Sara is poking around our business too much?"

Mrs. Burns cast Gilbert a sideways glance. "She certainly asks a lot of questions. And I think she prowls around peeking into all the rooms."

"I think she's spying on us," Gilbert added.

"Nonsense," Mrs. Wilkes rebutted. "I hired her as my nurse, not a spy. Besides we aren't doing anything wrong."

"Personally, I think you should complain to the school and find someone else to take care of you," Mrs. Burns suggested.

"I like the girl," Mrs. Wilkes protested. "She's efficient and doesn't complain. I don't want anyone else."

Mrs. Burns bent down and stared her in the face. "If you want things to remain the same around here, you had better request someone else."

Mrs. Wilkes shrunk back from her threatening words. "I'll have to give it some thought, but first I'll try to talk to Sara."

"It's too late for that," Gilbert said.

Mrs. Wilkes gathered her courage. "I'm the employer here," she reminded them. "I'll talk to Sara as soon as she comes from the hospital."

Mrs. Burns wheeled Mrs. Wilkes to her bedroom without another word about Sara. She helped her in bed and then left her alone.

Mrs. Wilkes' hands shook more than usual. Mrs. Burns had never taken that tone with her before, and Gilbert had hardly ever said a word to her. *Why are they so concerned about me and the secret I am trying to hide? It doesn't affect them any,* she thought.

She remained awake until Sara came into the house. She knew Sara would be listening for her on the tube. Taking Mrs. Burns' advice to replacing her with another girl was out of the question. She liked Sara, and besides she didn't have the energy to break in another girl.

"Sara, I'm awake." Mrs. Wilkes said loudly into the tube. "You can come on down now."

Sara's voice rang with cheer. "Be right there."

Mr. Wilkes heard Sara running down the stairs and soon after that she opened the bedroom door. "Gosh, you don't look like you slept very much. What's wrong?" Sara asked alarmed.

"I had a confrontation with Mrs. Burns and Gilbert."

"A confrontation? Where?"

"In the solarium. I was nodding off when Gilbert came in and then Mrs. Burns joined him a little later to take me to my room."

Sara pulled up a chair next to the bed. "What did they want?"

"It has to do with you."

"Me? They're unhappy with me?"

"Yes. It seems they don't like you poking into someone else's business."

"How am I doing that?"

"According to Gilbert, you're a spy. Mrs. Burns says you've been prowling around the house, peeking into all the rooms."

Sara bowed her head in embarrassment. "It's true I have

been exploring some, but not spying."

"You go ahead and look around if you want. I have nothing to hide, but I suggest you do it when Gilbert and Mrs. Burns aren't around."

"I know. Gilbert got after me a few weeks ago when I was near the stables and carriage house. He nearly scared me to death. He is rather fearsome looking."

"He is, but he keeps my garden and my house in tip-top shape. I would hate to lose him as an employee and Mrs. Burns does her job well, too. If possible, I want all three of you to get along."

"I'll do my best," Sara vowed. "I'm sorry if I caused any trouble."

"I don't think you have, but be careful not to get in their way," Mrs. Wilkes warned.

"Do you want to try and get some sleep now?"

"Yes, I would. Now that you're here I feel safer."

Sara bent down and adjusted the covers. "Are you afraid of them?"

"I never was until now. Something isn't right, and I don't know what it is."

"Don't worry I'll keep an eye out."

"Just be careful." Mrs. Wilkes lay back on the pillows, her eyes uneasy.

— — — — — —

Sara simply had to know what was going on with the two strange women. She decided one evening to ask Mrs. Wilkes point blank while they were having their after supper tea and dessert.

"I know you didn't believe my explanation, but I wanted to spare you all the details," Mrs. Wilkes said. "You are too smart for your own good. I'll tell you the truth this time."

"I would appreciate it."

"This isn't anything like murder or underhandedness. It's a long story so you had better pour us more tea." Mrs. Wilkes downed a cup before she began. "It all starts with my mother, Henrietta—"

"Henrietta, the original owner of this house."

"How do you know?"

Mrs. Burns and Mrs. Wilkes weren't the only ones that weren't truthful, Sara reflected. She hadn't been honest either. "I did some research into the house's history."

Mrs. Wilkes lifted her brow. "Because of the house or because of me?"

Sara wasn't sure herself. "You have to admit there's some strange things going on around here," Sara said, remembering the frightened look on Mrs. Wilkes's face after she told her about the solarium incident.

Mrs. Wilkes nodded. "Yes, there are even things I can't explain. I guess I can't blame you for wanting to know." She paused before she continued. "You see...before I was born, my mother gave away a baby to an orphanage, many years ago. She was poor at the time and very young. She felt she had no other choice."

"But this house?"

"My mother didn't have this house then. Eventually she married into money. I was lucky enough to be born here, but her first daughter was not."

"How sad."

"Mother never forgave herself and spent years of her life searching for her daughter. She inquired at the orphanage but was told her daughter was adopted. Mother never gave up trying to find her. In fact, she was so obsessed with locating her that it affected her mentally."

"What does this have to do with the quilt?"

"Be patient. I'm getting to it." Mrs. Wilkes frowned. "Like I said this is a long story. Mother hired a detective later in life. He was successful in determining that the orphaned daughter left Boston to work at a mission out west. From the Missionary Society, he pinpointed the exact reservation."

Sara's face flushed. "What reservation?"

"The Cheyenne River reservation mission."

"Why that's...that's the same place I'm from. How could that be?"

"We thought so."

"We?"

"You see I sent my granddaughter Myra to look for my missing sister."

Sara could hardly ask the question. She thought she knew the answer already. "She found her?"

"She did. Her name's Cassandra. I believe you know her?"

"I do, but she was never adopted," Sara countered. "Cassandra said no one wanted her. She left the orphanage and came west when she was of age."

"Like I said, my mother inquired there, but they told her that her daughter had been adopted."

"The information they gave her wasn't true," Sara insisted.

"So that explains why mother could never find her. I wonder why the orphanage lied."

Sara's hand flew to her mouth. "Oh, my. I can't believe what you have just told me? Did Myra tell Cassandra that her mother and sister were in Boston?"

"She didn't at my request, but she took a quilt from the mission that Cassandra helped make. You see my mother wanted something from her orphaned daughter, not necessarily to see her. Mother is so ashamed of what she had done."

"Myra took the quilt?" In disbelief, Sara repeated what Mrs. Wilkes told her. "Now, I remember. A young woman came to work at the mission, but she didn't stay long. She was blonde and wore her hair differently. That's why I didn't recognize Myra. But the voice, I knew the voice, but couldn't place her."

"She didn't recognize you at first either. You have grown up she said."

"Explain why the people associated with this house come and go as if they're criminals?"

"What do you know about their comings and goings?" Mrs. Wilkes asked.

"I've discovered the hidden staircase. I know there's an entrance in your closet. In fact, I thought I heard quiet whispers in your room at one time?"

"I've underestimated you," Mrs. Wilkes said. "Mother and her nurse Susan stop in to visit from time to time. You see, Mother and I upset one another, so it's best to remain apart for most of the time." Mrs. Wilkes massaged her forehead. "Sometimes she thinks that I am the orphaned daughter. Her behavior distresses me."

Sara continued her barrage of questions. "What is so special about the third floor? That's where I found the quilt."

"Mother enjoys the view. She likes to look at the night sky. It calms her."

"Why is she hidden away? Couldn't she join us for meals and conversation?"

Mrs. Wilkes shook her head. "It can't be. You see my mother is deranged most of the time. Have you ever heard wailing and screeching?"

"I haven't, but Lois my friend who stayed here one night claims she heard something similar."

"No doubt that was my mother. There isn't much we can do for her. If we sent her away to a nursing home, she would be confined, maybe even tied to her bed. I don't want that for her, so we do our best here at the house."

"I'm curious, Mrs. Wilkes, how can you have girls living here if there were strange things happening in this house? Surely, others became suspicious like I did."

"You're different from the other girls we have had here.

Most of them were afraid. Anything unusual and they were ready to run. They wouldn't have confronted the strange goings on, but you…well, you are strong and fearless."

"I don't understand why you bothered with having student nurses here anyway."

Mrs. Wilkes sighed. "I need care, and I can't afford to pay for it."

"I had no idea. I just assumed you were wealthy."

"My fortune disappeared years ago."

"Where do your mother and her nurse live? I've searched everywhere."

"Mother and Susan live in the basement apartment."

"The basement?"

"Don't worry she's quite comfortable there. Susan even takes her out on walks, which you have witnessed. They visit the third floor occasionally, but it's risky. You saw them there."

"Have any of the other students seen her?"

"Oh, no. Most of the ones that have lived here didn't venture far from their room or mine. I'm sorry to have been so secretive, but I thought it was best for my mother."

"I haven't exactly been honest either, sneaking around like I did."

Mrs. Wilkes wore a weary expression. "I forgive you, if you forgive me," Mrs. Wilkes said. "I'm just glad that the entire mystery is out in the open."

— — — — — —

Sara performed her duties in a daze for the next week after learning the truth about Mrs. Wilkes, her mother Henrietta and Cassandra's connection to both. While waiting for Mrs. Wilkes to awake from her nap she spread dried rose potpourri about her and pondered the recent events.

What was she going to do with this knowledge? Mrs.

Wilkes never suggested that she contact Cassandra. In fact, she didn't bring up the subject again. Apparently she thought it best to leave things as they were. But could she leave what she learned alone and forget all about it?

In her heart, Sara knew that she couldn't dismiss the knowledge so readily. Should she write Cassandra and tell her she found her mother and sister, or should she let the revelation remain a secret? What a difference it would it make in Cassandra's life, but would it be for the better or for the worse? After much thought and sleepless nights, she opted to write Evangeline and ask her what she should do.

Dear Evangeline,

I have learned something extraordinary that I believe is my duty to share with you. I am in a dilemma of whether we should tell Cassandra about my latest discovery. What I am about to reveal is unbelievable.

Ever since I arrived at Mrs. Wilkes's home, strange things have been happening. You know my curious nature. I just simply have to have answers to everything. When Frederick hired Henry to check out the background of the house, it wasn't just for the house's history. I also wanted to know if there was something unusual about the house. I did my own investigating and discovered secret staircases, trap doors, and tunnels.

Now, don't be angry for me not telling you these things. Don't worry, I am perfectly safe. There is nothing sinister here. Mrs. Wilkes is trying to care for a deranged mother in this house without anyone knowing about it.

While sleuthing, I happened on our mission's missing quilt. You know the Jacob's Ladder quilt the mission women worked on when you came the first year. Red Bird helped with that quilt and embroidered a red bird on one corner. I know it's hard to believe, but that very quilt was left on a rocking chair on the third floor ballroom. Who would ever guess the quilt would be here in this very house? When I saw it, I snatched the quilt and returned to my room. I still have it and don't know if I should give it back.

One night, I saw two women on the third floor, one elderly woman attended by a middle aged lady. I didn't approach them and then I saw the same women months later come out of a tunnel about one-fourth mile from the house. It was then I approached Mrs. Wilkes about what I had been seeing. She was reluctant to tell me, but she knew I wouldn't forget what I had seen.

She told me her mother had given away her first daughter to an orphanage in Boston and always regretted her decision. Now brace yourself for this surprise. Mrs. Wilkes's mother's orphaned daughter is Cassandra. Mrs. Wilkes is Cassandra's sister. Can you believe it?

And there's more. Mrs. Wilkes's granddaughter Myra came to our mission looking for Cassandra several years ago. She found her but said nothing, which to me doesn't make sense. Why wouldn't she have told Cassandra who she was? Instead she took the Jacob's Ladder quilt Cassandra had helped sew to give to Mrs. Wilkes's and Cassandra's mother as a keepsake.

Now my question is— do we tell Cassandra? You should know Mrs. Wilkes's mother, Henrietta, is not mentally well. It would probably be an upsetting situation for Cassandra to face. Please tell me what to do.

Warmest regards,
Sara

Sara folded the letter and placed it in an envelope, and then she hid it in her dresser drawer until she could take it somewhere and mail it. She may have solved one mystery in this house, but she had this nagging feeling there were still unanswered questions.

Feeling weary, Sara sat down in the chair overlooking the gardens. She watched Gilbert weeding the flower garden. He was an odd sort of fellow, always watching her like she was the enemy. Why would it be so terrible if she found out Mrs. Wilkes was caring for her unstable mother? It had all been so secretive.

She leaned in closer to the window, watching Mrs. Burns picking her steps carefully through the garden until she came up to Gilbert and stopped short. She wished she could hear what they were saying. Both held their heads bent together deep in discussion about something.

What do these two have in common to carry on such a conversation? She wondered.

She pulled away from the window, her thoughts in a tangle of suspicion. An image of the photo she had seen in the room off the carriage house several months ago came back to her. I have to see that photograph again, she thought to herself. She was sure Mrs. Burns was in that photo, but who was the man?

And then there was still the locked room. She still didn't know what it contained, but she told herself it was none of her business anyway. Still, she ignored her reasoning and gave into her curiosity. Was there a secret entrance into that room, too? To her knowledge no one had ever entered the locked room; however, they could have when she was at the hospital in training. Suddenly, she became obsessed with the locked room and had to know what it contained.

She left her room to inspect the door to the mysterious room. Before she tried the door, she glanced at the floor to see if any foot prints were left in the dust. She saw none, so she wiggled the knob. As she suspected, it was locked.

With a sigh of frustration she left the second floor for the kitchen where she heard Mrs. Burns rattling pots and pans. Sara went in and watched her preparing a roast chicken for supper.

"What do you need, Sara?"

"I have a question."

"I thought all your questions have been answered and you'd be satisfied that your snooping paid off."

Sara reeled at the verbal slap. "I never meant to be a snoop."

"Well, you did. If I were Mrs. Wilkes I would be angry. You're lucky you never raised her ire." Mrs. Burns turned her back, ending the conversation.

Plainly, Mrs. Burns was not going to answer any more of Sara's questions, especially about the locked room. The only way to find out, if she could, would be to ask Mrs. Wilkes.

She didn't like Mrs. Burns or Gilbert's increasingly foul attitude, further raising her suspicions.

I might have to have a talk with Henry, she thought as she turned on her heels and left Mrs. Burns to her chicken.

CHAPTER 14

Sara left the hospital in the late afternoon during a rain storm. The situation with Mrs. Burns had been on her mind all day. Instead of immediately returning to the Victorian, she detoured to Henry's office, hoping to find him available.

She shook the rain off her umbrella before she entered the building, annoyed that her wet shoes squished with each step. The receptionist confirmed that Henry was in and led her down the hallway. After shaking Henry's hand and exchanging pleasantries she sat across from him while he shuffled papers on his desk in attempt to find a file.

"Ah, here it is. I have been meaning to get a hold of you. I did find some history on Mrs. Wilkes's Victorian, but I'm afraid it isn't much." He opened the folder. "It was built before the Civil War and looked differently from what it does now. The owner was an abolitionist and built tunnels and hidden staircases to aid slaves in escaping."

"I have found the stair cases and tunnels."

Henry opened his eyes wide with surprise. "Very good. I

guess you didn't need me."

"But I do. Mrs. Wilkes has two employees that in my judgment are suspicious. The cook and housekeeper, Mrs. Burns, and the gardener Gilbert do not like me because I have been snooping too much in their opinion. Gilbert has been quite vocal about it."

Henry lifted his brows. "Have you been snooping?"

"I have, but only in Mrs. Wilkes's interest. She's a very unhappy woman, and I've been trying to find some way to help her. She's very secretive about her life."

"What would you like me to do?"

"Investigate Mrs. Burns and Gilbert."

"And what's his last name."

"Reynolds. Gilbert Reynolds."

Henry jotted down their names on a scrap of paper. "I'll start with Mrs. Burns. Do you feel like you're in danger?"

"No, I don't, but I would appreciate your looking into the matter."

"I'll do my best. But if you feel that you're in danger, contact me immediately."

"I don't feel that way at all, really."

"You're a brave lady, but still be careful." His eyes softened in concern. "Stop back in about a week, and I may have something for you."

Sara rose to leave. She thanked Henry and walked back out into the rain in no hurry to get to the house. Sara dreaded the evening meal especially after the scene with Mrs. Burns in the kitchen. Her hostile accusations of being a snoop had upset her.

By the time she reached the Victorian, she was quite soaked. Since no one had noticed her entrance into the house, she scurried up to her room to change her dress and her spongy shoes, and then returned downstairs to find Mrs. Wilkes in the parlor.

"I thought I heard you come in. Your hair's all wet."

"It's a down pour out there. Are you ready for the dining room?"

Mrs. Wilkes nodded. Sara wheeled Mrs. Wilkes into the dining room in hopes that Mrs. Burns had mellowed.

"Ah," Mrs. Wilkes said, "I can smell the baked chicken. I think I detect sage, too. Mrs. Burns is a wonderful cook, don't you think, Sara?"

"Yes, yes, she is." Sara forced the compliment.

Mrs. Burns scurried around the dining room table efficiently serving Mrs. Wilkes and Sara. Beside roasted chicken, she served sage dressing, and carrots. "I have pumpkin pie for dessert, also," she said, clearing her throat. "I will not join you this evening. I have invited Gilbert to dine with me in the kitchen. Just ring if you need anything."

"Very well, whatever you wish." Mrs. Wilkes waved her away.

Mrs. Burns departed curtly, leaving the two women alone.

"Highly unusual for Mrs. Burns not to join us," Mrs. Wilkes croaked under her breath. "And to entertain Gilbert?"

Sara smiled. Apparently Mrs. Wilkes had her reservations about Gilbert, too. "It's my fault that Mrs. Burns has not joined us. She doesn't approve of my...inquisitive nature."

A slight smile turned up the corners of Mrs. Wilkes lips. "I see. I'm not sure I do either, but you have other qualities that make up for it."

"How long has Gilbert worked for you?" The question popped out of Sara's mouth before she even had time to think about it.

Mrs. Wilkes didn't seem to notice. Her focus was on her supper. "About four years. Mrs. Burns has been with me ever since Isabel died."

"Hmmm, I thought they might have been with you longer than five years."

193

Mrs. Wilkes waved her fork. "Help is hard to keep for any length of time."

Sara wanted to ask if Mrs. Wilkes knew anything about their background, but it was not the right moment. Mrs. Burns and Gilbert were in the next room within hearing distance.

Besides, she already asked Henry to look into the matter. Instead she turned the conversation to Cassandra. "Have you ever thought of asking your sister Cassandra here for a visit, to get acquainted?"

"I don't know if it's such a good idea to dredge up the past. Besides what would it accomplish? Mother is not responsive. She's stuck in the past. A past I cannot identify with."

"If you're interested in Cassandra, I can tell you a few things. In fact, when I first came here, you reminded me of her, though at the time I didn't realize it was Cassandra who you reminded me of."

"I lived without a sister for all these years. I can continue to do so."

Mrs. Wilkes disinterest in a sister disappointed Sara. Even if Cassandra would be interested, Mrs. Wilkes was definitely not. One thing for sure, both sisters possessed defeatist attitudes.

"I've been meaning to discuss the Jacob's Ladder quilt with you. The one you found. Mother misses the quilt dreadfully," Mrs. Wilkes said. "Would you consider returning it to her?"

"I don't know. I have attachments to the quilt also. It was the last quilt my Grandmother helped with."

"But you must have other mementoes of your Grandmother?"

"I do have some."

"My mother has nothing from Cassandra except this quilt."

Sara knew she should give up the quilt, but she just couldn't do it. "I could get another one from Cassandra. She wouldn't have to know what I want it for."

Mrs. Wilkes frowned and pushed her empty plate away. "It's too late. Mother is attached to this one."

"Alright, if you think it will make her happy. I can't deny her some comfort."

"I knew you would agree to the right thing to do." Mrs. Wilkes rang the bell for Mrs. Burns.

"You want dessert in the parlor?" she asked.

"Please."

Sara wheeled Mrs. Wilkes into the parlor for dessert as was customary after the evening meal. Mrs. Burns brusquely served the pie and tea and returned to the kitchen without a word to Sara.

"Don't mind her. She'll come around," Mrs. Wilkes said.

Sara poured the tea and handed Mrs. Wilkes a cup. "It's good that I'll be leaving soon. I believe I wore out my welcome."

"Maybe with Mrs. Burns but not with me. Before you leave, I'd like to make one more quilt. I found out I enjoyed creating something pretty. I doubt I'll find anyone else who will spend the time with me like you have."

Mrs. Wilkes suggestion surprised Sara, although she herself wasn't in the mood for quilt making sessions. "Do you have a pattern in mind?"

"Something we can stitch by hand. Perhaps an appliqué."

"I'm not really skilled at appliqué. We made mostly practical quilts at the mission."

"I have done many. I'll teach you."

"All right." Sara agreed. "Any particular appliqué?"

"There is. Victorian ladies."

"Is there time to finish such a quilt? It sounds quite involved."

"If I commit myself to working on it instead of always

napping," Mrs. Wilkes admonished herself.

"But you need your rest," Sara protested.

"We'll see. The best part is I have a pattern for it somewhere. It may be in one of the bedrooms upstairs."

"Which one?" Sara did her best to contain her interest, contemplating it was another opportunity to explore.

"I'm not sure. You may have to search in every room."

"Even the one that's locked?" Sara asked boldly.

"Oh, no it wouldn't be in there."

"Are you sure? I could look," Sara insisted.

"I'm sure."

Sara would have to be satisfied for now, but at least she could search through the rooms again. What she was looking for, she really didn't know, but she had a strong feeling there were still unanswered questions in this house.

The next morning, Sara informed Mrs. Burns at breakfast she would be searching the rooms on the second floor for the Victorian Ladies quilt pattern. Mrs. Wilkes explained her desire to use the pattern.

A gold rimmed plate Mrs. Burns held in her right hand slipped and clattered to the table. "That won't be necessary I'll search for the pattern. I'm sure you have better things to do, Sara." Mrs. Burns snatched the spinning plate and held it to her chest.

Surprised at her sudden change of attitude, Sara insisted she would look for the pattern, claiming it would be no trouble at all. She noticed a flush coloring Mrs. Burn's face, which made her more determined to stand her ground.

What was Mrs. Burns afraid of? She thought.

"Perhaps we could search together. It would save time," Mrs. Burns suggested rather hurriedly.

"I think that's a good idea," Mrs. Wilkes said, obviously

unaware of how her cook had reacted.

Sara shifted in uneasiness. "I need to find it today, so that we can get started. I don't have many months left to begin and finish a quilt."

Mrs. Burns produced a forced smile. "I can help you today. We'll begin right after breakfast if that's alright with Mrs. Wilkes."

"Certainly. Just wheel me into the solarium. I feel like sun this morning."

When the dishes were cleared away, and Mrs. Wilkes was made comfortable in the solarium, Sara and Mrs. Burns proceeded to the second floor. Sara stepped aside and let Mrs. Burns lead the way.

Mrs. Burns glanced from one bedroom door to the other. "Where should we start?"

"I have no idea. You know this house better than I." Sara said offhandedly.

"Well, I doubt the pattern would be any of these bedrooms used occasionally. More than likely the pattern would be in one of the rooms used mostly for storage. Let's do this one first." Mrs. Burns opened the door to the room with the armoires.

Sara waited for Mrs. Burns lead. "Do you come up here very often? To clean, I mean."

"Very seldom," she said curtly. "Go ahead and look."

Sara began with the armoire that stored the quilts. The pattern might be in that one, she reasoned. She didn't remember all that it contained, but when she opened the door she almost gasped. The quilts that occupied the shelf were gone. It took her a moment to regain her composure. Was she wrong? Maybe it was the second armoire. *No*, she told herself, *it was this one.* She rummaged through the armoire searching for a pattern and possibly misplaced quilts, but there was nothing but odds and ends of memorabilia.

She moved on to the second armoire while Mrs. Burns

explored boxes stacked against a wall. She remembered the second armoire contained women's clothes and accessories. She opened the door to find that everything looked the same as before. She searched the drawers and a few hat boxes but didn't find any pattern.

"There's nothing here that I can see," Mrs. Burns said. "Let's try the other room."

The women looked through the bureau drawers and the closet of the next room with the photographs on the wall but didn't produce any pattern. "There's one room left," Sara said. "The one at the end of the hall."

"That room's locked."

"Why is it locked," Sara asked innocently.

"I don't know, and it's none of your business. We might as well tell Mrs. Wilkes we can't find the pattern."

Sara followed Mrs. Burns into the solarium. "We were unable to find the pattern. We searched everywhere," the elder woman said.

"You know what?" Mrs. Wilkes touched her forehead. "I think I put that pattern in my sewing box in my closet. Sara, would you go have a look?"

Sara immediately left the women and found the sewing box in Mrs. Wilkes's closet on a high shelf just where she said it would be. She lifted out the top later of notions, and in the very bottom she found the pattern, which appeared to be hand drawn. She pulled it from its hiding place and entered the solarium with the pattern.

"Wonderful. Sorry I sent you ladies on a wild goose chase. We can start on the appliqué right after my morning nap."

"We have some scraps left from the puff quilt." Sara began thinking out loud. "We can begin with those. I could have Maud bring scraps by, too. Her seamstress uses fine fabrics, and I know Maud doesn't let her throw anything salvageable away."

Mrs. Burns cleared her throat. "I have work to do." And then she stomped off toward the kitchen.

"Have you had enough sun, Mrs. Wilkes?"

"I have and I'm ready for a little rest."

"While you're resting, I'll assemble everything we need."

"Take my sewing box. I have embroidery thread as well as an assortment of needles and other thread."

While Mrs. Wilkes napped, Sara collected the scraps of material she had saved and laid everything out on a work table in the parlor. She cut out several appliqué pieces while thinking about the missing quilts from the armoire.

What was it about missing quilts and this house? She wondered. But more importantly who took the quilts and where were they? Should she mention the missing quilts to Mrs. Wilkes? But if she did, Mrs. Wilkes would know Sara was sneaking around the house. Or even worse, Mrs. Wilkes might think Sara took the quilts. She cringed thinking of a lesson Evangeline had taught her when she was a young child. "A lie will grow like a rain cloud and eventually consume you in a storm," she told her once. That was exactly what was happening to her now. She had dug herself into a hole and had no idea how to get out.

- - - - - -

Sara's mind was still in a muddle over the missing quilts stored in the armoire when Mrs. Wilkes and Sara met to begin their next quilt project. Sara had prepared the first appliqué block for her. Mrs. Wilkes began stitching the Victorian lady's flared skirt onto a white fabric square. Sara admired her delicate stitches, but she couldn't imagine why Mrs. Wilkes chose a Victorian appliqué, so she asked her.

"My mother drew this Victorian Lady pattern. You see my mother liked to be creative with her quilts. She designed most herself."

"Fascinating. Where are her quilts now?"

"I…sold most of them. I stored a few others."

Sara couldn't imagine selling heirlooms like her mother's quilts, but she thought she asked too many questions as it was. She didn't know whether she should tell her the stored quilts were missing from the armoire, besides she didn't know for sure if the quilts were stolen. Perhaps Myra took the quilts from the room.

As they sat in the parlor, Mrs. Wilkes demonstrated how to fold the edges under and sew the pieces to the square in careful neat stitches. As Sara struggled to perfect the stitches, she realized the Victorian lady quilt wouldn't be easy and would be wearisome to sew. She panicked knowing she only had a few more months to stay in this house to finish this quilt and solve the mystery of the missing quilts.

As she glanced at Mrs. Wilkes's skillful stitching, she thought of Cassandra who was also an expert at sewing.

"I know you'd rather not discuss your orphaned sister, but it has just struck me how alike you two are."

Mrs. Wilkes peered over her spectacles. "In what way?"

"You both are very good with a needle and thread. Cassandra said she learned to sew at an orphanage."

"My mother taught me, and her mother taught her. Both were excellent quilt makers and seamstresses. As I told you before, my daughter Isabel, was better than I. Unfortunately, Myra isn't the least bit interested in sewing."

"Does that bother you? I mean that you can't pass on your talent."

"Not any more. My days are numbered anyway. I'm no longer interested in passing on my skills to my family. Not that I have much to give anymore."

"You shouldn't say you have nothing to give," Sara admonished her. "I think we can give until the day we die."

"You mean if we try. I haven't been able to do anything but complain."

"I don't mean to judge you. I'm not in your situation."

Mrs. Wilkes glanced up from her sewing. "Does Cassandra have a daughter?"

"Just a son, but Cassandra taught me everything I know about sewing. I look forward to learning more someday."

"Do I resemble Cassandra? Not that it matters. Just curious."

"You're similar. You both are...rather stern, not given to excess smiling."

"We come by that naturally. Mother was quite strict. Anything else?"

"You both are slim." Sara hesitated. "Cassandra is tall."

"I would be tall, too, if I wasn't an invalid."

Sara was relieved when Mrs. Burns came in with their afternoon tea. Today wasn't the best time to talk to Mrs. Wilkes about her sister.

Mrs. Wilkes put down her sewing and waited for Mrs. Burns to pour her tea. "I would like you to get my candelabra from the locked room upstairs," she told Mrs. Burns.

Mrs. Burns appeared startled, nearly spilling the tea. "The candelabra. Why do you need the candelabra?"

"My banker is coming over tomorrow. I would like him to look at it."

"But you already sold it."

"I didn't sell it."

"Please excuse me for being impertinent, but I know you sold it."

Mrs. Wilkes' eyes burned with ire. "I may be infirm, but I still have my mind. Please go at once and find it." She reached into her sweater pocket, pulled out a key and slapped it in the housekeeper's hand.

Mrs. Burns set down the tea service and immediately left. Sara wanted to follow her and see where she went, but knew she had to remain in the parlor with Mrs. Wilkes. Maud's comment of several months ago resurfaced in Sara's mind.

201

Maud had brought to Sara's attention that Mrs. Wilkes had few decorative objects in her home. *Had she sold some of them?* Sara wondered. Just now, Mrs. Burns suggested that she had sold the candelabra. Sara had never thought that Mrs. Wilkes was in need of money until she had told her so. She had just surmised with three staff members, including herself, she was financially secure.

Mrs. Burns returned to the parlor with no candelabra in hand. "It's not there."

"If I could I'd go look myself. It has to be somewhere," Mrs. Wilkes insisted.

Mrs. Burns stood silent offering no more comments.

"Tomorrow, you and Sara will take inventory of the room. I want to know what's left."

So there were valuables in the locked room, Sara thought to herself.

––––––

The next morning, Sara awoke to a quiet house. She heard no sounds from the kitchen nor did the aroma of brewing coffee drift up the stairs. She slipped on her robe and hurried downstairs to the kitchen. Alarmed that Mrs. Burns was not there preparing breakfast, she tried the door of her bedroom off the kitchen. The door yielded and Sara carefully pushed it open to a room in disarray. Drawers were left open, the bed was unmade, and trash littered the floor. A further search confirmed Sara's suspicions. Mrs. Burns had left with her belongings.

Amid the turmoil in her head, Sara heard Mrs. Wilkes calling for her. She dashed to her bedroom and opened the door. "Mrs. Burns has left," Sara blurted.

"Left?"

"Her clothes are gone and her bedroom is a mess."

"No breakfast then?"

"No. I'll make us something as soon as we get you ready for the day."

"At least I have you," Mrs. Wilkes grumbled.

After Sara helped Mrs. Wilkes into the wheelchair she pushed her into the dining room while she prepared breakfast. Mrs. Wilkes was looking out the window, when Sara brought in coffee and toast. "Why did Mrs. Burns leave? She never said anything to me."

"I bet Gilbert's gone, too. There's nothing going on outside."

"I suppose so," Sara agreed. "I know I shouldn't have been snooping in the carriage house, but I saw a picture in his room on the bureau. I believe it was of him and Mrs. Burns. It looked like a wedding picture."

Mrs. Wilkes's face crinkled. "So you think they were husband and wife?"

"I suspect so, but why didn't they admit it?"

"I have a feeling those two were up to no good."

"Why do you say that?"

"The candelabra. I know I didn't sell it. It should have been in the locked room."

"The locked room?"

"I stored all my valuables in the locked room and those of Isabel, too. You see, after she died her husband and Myra moved to a different house. They had to get away from the memories. He gave me all of Isabel's silver, her china, and her jewelry. I had so many different girls come through here. I wasn't able to keep an eye on things, so I put everything together in one room and locked the door. Recently I have been selling off a few pieces to pay the bills. I let Myra get the pieces for me when I needed them.

"You think she stole the candelabra?"

"Yes and probably other things." Mrs. Wilkes handed Sara the key. "I want you to take inventory like I suggested yesterday. Mrs. Burns and her...husband skipped out because there are more missing pieces."

"They were robbing from you. That's incredible."

"It doesn't surprise me, although I'm going to miss her cooking."

"What are you going to do now with no help? I have to get to the hospital this morning. By the way is the banker coming by or did you make that up?"

"I made it up. I suspected something and thought it would draw them out."

"It worked, but now you're without help."

"I'll see if Myra can help out a while."

"Does Myra like quilts?"

"Why do you ask?"

Sara hung her head. "I have another confession. I found some quilts in an armoire some time ago, but when Mrs. Burns and I went looking for the Victorian Lady pattern the quilts were gone. I thought maybe Myra had them."

Mrs. Wilkes shook her head. "Myra would have told me if she took them. I doubt if she would have been interested in the quilts themselves, just the fact that her mother made them."

"Are quilts valuable?"

"The ones I had would certainly be. They were very intricate. But the worst part is that Isabel made them."

"I'm so sorry. Such dreadful and uncaring people."

"Run along upstairs and see if there's anything left."

"But, how will I know what's missing?"

"Good point. I'll jot down the most valuable pieces while you wash the dishes."

Sara hurriedly washed the dishes and took the list from Mrs. Wilkes when she finished.

"I want you to bring down the jewelry boxes. I hope there's something left."

Sara unlocked the door of the room that held so much mystery for her since she had first arrived. From the doorway she could see that the storage boxes had been jostled around. Contents spilled over the sides. Some of the dishes were out of boxes, silverware boxes were emptied, and art work was strewn across the floor. She located the jewelry boxes which appeared to be stripped clean and gathered them together and set them near the door. Taking the list Mrs. Wilkes had made, she checked off very few items on the list that were still in the room. The exotic vases and silver pieces were all gone. Only one painting was left and that was of Mrs. Wilkes as a young lady.

How did the thieves get into the room? Sara wondered. *If Mrs. Wilkes had the key, how did they steal from the locked room?*

She searched the closet looking for a trap door that might lead to another secret staircase. She was about to give up when she found the secret panel that opened and led to an unexplored staircase. She decided not to investigate the staircase as her first responsibility was to Mrs. Wilkes's list.

After an hour of careful searching the room, she locked the door and went downstairs to report to Mrs. Wilkes.

Mrs. Wilkes turned toward Sara as she entered the parlor. "Just looking at your face tells me the story."

Sara handed her the list and the jewelry boxes.

Mrs. Wilkes frowned as she scanned the list and then she opened the boxes. "They took everything of value. The diamonds, the emeralds, the rubies." She held her face in her hands. "How did they get into the room? I had the key."

"I found an entrance in the closet that leads to a secret staircase. It was easy for them."

"I had no idea there was one there. Did you explore it?"

"No. I didn't take the time. But I will," Sara promised.

"You had better report this to the police. They might be able to catch them and recover some of the stolen items."

"Yes, I now know what they have stolen, but how am I going to continue to keep living here? I have no money."

CHAPTER 15

A heady fragrance of lilacs, roses, and peonies perfumed the late spring air when Maud and Sara went shopping in downtown Boston for dresses. Sara insisted she didn't need anything, but Maud played on her sympathy. "But I don't have anyone to go shopping with," she pleaded. "Besides, Evangeline will think I neglected you if I don't send you home with something new and stylish."

Sara doubted that Evangeline would feel the way Maud described, but to humor her she agreed to go shopping.

"Sara, I'm worried about you. You look so weary," Maud said after Sara tried on her first yellow dress trimmed in white piping. "Evangeline will be angry with me for letting you get so run down."

Sara hadn't confided in Maud about the turmoil going on at the Victorian. "It's just that so much has been happening with Mrs. Wilkes. And of course training has been no easy matter."

Maud straightened the collar on Sara's yellow dress,

frowning. "I hope it's been worth it all. I'll be happy when you fulfill your commitment to Mrs. Wilkes. I don't think caring for her has been a pleasant experience for you. I should have stepped in and rescued you."

"Don't blame yourself. If I wouldn't have been there, no one would have known that her help was stealing from her."

"Stealing? " Maud lowered her voice. "You lived in that house among thieves? Now I know I should have done something."

"It's over now. The police are searching for Mrs. Burns and Gilbert. They took off when they felt Mrs. Wilkes was on to something."

Maud shook her head toward the dress Sara was modeling and handed her another one. "What were they stealing?"

"Art work, vases, silver, jewelry—"

"I knew it." Maud's eyes shone with assurance. "The house looked like it had been stripped clean."

"I would have never noticed if you hadn't said something. I'm not used to living in a house with all those fine things." Sara said from the dressing room while wiggling into another dress of Maud's choosing.

"I should have had Henry investigate," Maud said chastising herself.

"Mrs. Wilkes wasn't the one doing bad things. She had her valuables locked up in a room and was selling them to pay her bills." Sara lifted her brows at the white and black dress she was wearing with too many bows and ruffles. "It was her help taking advantage of Mrs. Wilkes. They used a secret stairway and entered the room through a secret panel and cleaned her out."

Maud pulled another dress off the rack. "And you discovered all this on your own?"

"Mostly. I... visited with Henry and he helped me out a bit."

"You did? Did he find out anything for you?"

"He helped me connect Mrs. Wilkes to her parents, the previous owners of the house. Henry determined her father built the stairways and tunnels during the slave days. We even detected Mrs. Wilkes's mother could be still living."

"Well, I'll be. I never knew any of this was going on."

Sara waved off another dress Maud had selected. "Luckily, Mrs. Wilkes became wise to her employees. I knew something was wrong but didn't know exactly what it was."

"Now what is she going to do?"

"Her granddaughter is with her now, but she has no money to keep going. She also sees to it that her mother is cared for. Henrietta lives in seclusion at her house with a nurse who looks after her."

"Goodness sake. No wonder you look worn out."

Sara plopped down in a chair with another new dress across her lap. "I'm tired and I want to go home for a while before I continue my nurse's training, but I don't know how the school will like that idea. And besides, Mrs. Wilkes depends on me. I can't leave her just now."

"But you have to think of yourself. There are institutions for people who need help."

"I know, but Mrs. Wilkes wants to stay in her home and provide the proper care for her mother. Her mother is deranged. She doesn't want her mistreated." Sara thought it best not to tell her about their connection to Cassandra. Maud was already beside herself, knowing that she had been living in a house with thieves.

"You should have stayed with us in the first place. Just think what horrible things could have befallen you."

"Nothing happened to me and the Victorian's mystery is solved. I just wish Mrs. Wilkes wasn't in need of money."

Maud shook her head. "A most unfortunate situation."

"I appreciate you taking me shopping, but I don't think I'm in the mood." Sara left the chair and handed Maud the dress she was holding. "If you don't mind I think I'll go back to the Victorian and check on Mrs. Wilkes."

"I see you're not having any fun." Maud sulked. "John can drive you back to the Victorian. I just thought you would want a break from Mrs. Wilkes and that house."

"Oh I appreciate your concern, but I've noticed that after Mrs. Wilkes discovered she had been robbed of her assets and her special mementos, she has become gloomy. It seems her quilting project and Myra are her only interests. When we sit during the evening hours and sew, she does little visiting. Even Myra can't rally her grandmother."

"Very well, then, be off with you. Tell John to drive you home."

It was nearly lunch when Sara arrived at the Victorian. Myra was already in the kitchen preparing something to eat.

"Back so early?" Myra commented.

"I just wasn't in the mood. Dresses and such don't mean that much to me, although it was nice of Maud to invite me for an outing."

"Want to get the vegetables for a salad?"

"Sure." Sara brought the vegetables from the bin to the sink and began to wash them. "Have you seen your great grandmother since she came to live here?" Sara asked Myra.

"I have, years ago, but not in the past few years. Grandmother would rather I remember the way she was before she became too confused and tormented. Why do you ask?"

Sara removed a peeler from the drawer and began to peel the carrots. "The thought of her being isolated in this house bothers me. She should see a doctor. There might be something he could do for her."

"Grandmother fears that the doctors will give her shock treatments. That's why she hid her away. She wanted no one interfering with how she takes care of her mother. I believe Grandmother is a bit paranoid about her care."

"I understand that. Your grandmother has sacrificed a lot to make sure your great-grandmother is well cared for."

"I know. She may seem hard and uncaring on the outside, but she has a tender heart, but she doesn't let too many people see it."

"I was becoming to see that side of her."

Myra filled a pan with water and placed it on the stove, and then turned toward Sara. "I'm sorry I stole the quilt from the mission. I just wanted to bring something back to my grandmas."

"You're forgiven." Sara paused. "But I don't remember you being at the mission."

"I was younger then. My hair was blonde. I put a henna rinse in it when we heard you were coming. Just in case you had met me before."

"What did you think of Cassandra?"

"She reminded me a lot of Grandmother. Don't you think?"

"Yes. They are very much alike. I probably shouldn't ask, but why didn't you tell her who you were?"

"Grandmother told me not to. She just wanted me to see how see was doing. If she was happy."

"Did you think she was happy?"

"It was hard to tell, but then again it's difficult to determine if my grandma is or was ever happy."

Sara agreed. "Neither is given to demonstrate joy, but for some reason I'm drawn to both of them."

- - - - - -

Myra was the one that broke the news to Sara that Mrs. Wilkes mother passed away during the night. As soon as Sara heard the news, she went to Mrs. Wilkes' room where she found her in her wheelchair staring out the window at the neglected gardens. "I'm sorry to hear about your mother."

Mrs. Wilkes continued to stare at the grounds while she answered. "It's for the best. She has suffered far too long. Now I must face the fact that the house has to be sold, and I must enter a place where they can care for me."

"Is that what you really want?"

"No. I'd rather remain in my own home. I have lived here most of my life. Not all the memories have been good, but it is my home."

The mention of the word home pierced Sara's heart. She too, wanted to go home. Weary wasn't nearly a strong enough description of how she felt. When she had first come to nurses training she was so sure of what she wanted. Now she was confused.

One dilemma had been solved, however. There was no need to tell Cassandra about her mother or even her sister. Henrietta was dead, and Mrs. Wilkes seemed to have no desire to see her sister. Dredging up the past would serve no purpose.

"I can help you with whatever you wish," Sara offered.

"Thank you for your loyalty." Mrs. Wilkes finally turned from the window. "Myra will make the funeral arrangements, and then she can find a nursing home for me. We'll sell the house with the furniture. What few personal items that remain can be divided between Myra and you."

"I see you have given this a lot of thought. I plan on returning home for an extended visit within a few months."

"I want to finish the quilt before I leave this house."

"Will you take the quilt with you?"

"I'll give it away."

Sara realized how important the quilt was to her and assumed she would give it to her granddaughter Myra as a parting gift.

"Will you be able to stay with Maud and Frederick when you leave here?"

"Oh, yes, they're anxious for me to move back in with them."

"Good," Mrs. Wilkes said. "I would worry if you didn't have proper accommodations."

Sara detected the scent of lavender, the same scent that been alluding her for months. She whirled around to see where it was coming from. It arrived with Henrietta's nurse Susan.

"Susan, come on in and meet Sara, my nurse." Finally, after all these elusive moments Sara was meeting the mysterious woman who had puzzled her for all these months.

She nodded to Susan, a large boned woman with the countenance of granite. The nurse handed the Jacob's Ladder quilt to Sara. "Mrs. Wilkes said for me to return this to you."

Sara took the quilt and stroked it smooth. "Thank you."

Without any change of expression Susan spoke to Mrs. Wilkes. "My duties have ended. Sorry for your loss."

"Thank you for your loyal service. I would keep you on if I could afford it, but I can't."

"I understand."

"I will mail you a check. Have you taken your things?"

"I have."

"Very well."

Susan turned and left without a backward glance. The lavender scent followed her out the door. Sara regretted the scent would no longer wander the secret staircases and the hidden tunnel anymore. Mystery had been the essence of this house since the slaves used it to escape to freedom. Strange to say, but she would miss it.

Within minutes, she heard voices from the open doorway and scurried to see who the visitors were. Henry and two policemen in uniform tipped their hats to her, just as Myra came from the kitchen. Each officer was carrying a pile of quilts.

"We're here to see Mrs. Wilkes," the younger of the policemen said.

"I'll bring her into the parlor," Sara said. "Have a seat we'll be right in." She hurried to Mrs. Wilkes bedroom and told her two policemen were waiting in the parlor with quilts.

"The stolen ones, I presume."

The policemen stood as Sara pushed Mrs. Wilkes into the parlor.

"We've brought something of yours." A policeman laid several quilts across her lap.

Mrs. Wilkes examined them. "They're mine. Where did you find them?"

"Your two employees were married and living in a flat a few blocks from here. We searched their apartment and found several of the stolen items. We have more with us, but unfortunately they have sold the greatest share."

"I didn't expect to see anything returned. I'm grateful for what you recovered."

"We'll bring in the rest."

"Any jewelry?" she asked

"I'm afraid not."

Henry, who had been quiet until now, approached Sara. "I apologize that I'm too late with my information."

"What did you find out?" Sara asked.

"Do we need to meet in private?"

"No, Mrs. Wilkes and Myra need to know, too."

"Very well." Henry selected a chair in the parlor and sat. "I shared my findings with the police. I was worried about your safety. As the police told you the man and woman who worked for you were married and were using fictitious names. Their real names were hard to determine. Both have been fleecing the elderly for a period of years, using different names for each employer."

Mrs. Wilkes frowned. "Why were they never caught before?"

"I guess they were too clever for most. And they didn't have anyone living in the house as vigilant as Sara."

Sara blushed. "It's my curious nature."

Henry winked. "Young lady you can work for me any-time."

"Thanks but no thanks. I have more than I can handle now."

"Very well." Henry bowed to the ladies. "It was a pleasure meeting you all. I shall be off."

After the police and Henry left, Mrs. Wilkes opened up the quilts. Sara gasped at the fine workmanship. "These quilts are masterpieces."

"I could never use them. They're just too beautiful. Like works of art." Mrs. Wilkes refolded the quilts and handed them to Myra. "Here's your mother's legacy. Take care of them."

"I never knew how much they meant to me until they were gone," Myra admitted. She took the quilts from her grandmother and carried them up to her room, while Sara wheeled Mrs. Wilkes to the solarium. "You can leave me alone for a while. This is my favorite room. I shall miss it."

Sara left her and returned to the second floor. She noticed that Myra's door to her room was shut and that the door to the locked room was open. There was still one thing she had to clear up in her mind. Where did the staircase from the locked room lead? She picked up a candle from her room and walked down the hallway to the infamous locked room. She stepped inside and shut the door before she entered the closet and moved a wall panel to reveal the staircase.

Lighting her candle, she poked her head through to see that the stairs went up. The stairway was remarkably wide compared to the other set of secret stairs. She climbed through the opening and followed it until the stairs ended. She pushed and prodded the wall in front of her. Eventually it yielded and opened into the ballroom on the third floor. She was puzzled why they didn't join the other staircase that eventually led to the tunnel joining the carriage house tunnel. *Possibly*, she thought, *Mrs. Burns or Gilbert took the booty out of the locked room, entered the hidden staircase, and entered the ballroom with the stolen goods. Then she or he simply used the main stairs to remove the booty from the house.*

If Mrs. Wilkes was sleeping she would never know what her employees were up to. The thieves could have joined up with the tunnel on the lower level, and then moved the treasures through the remainder of the tunnel to the shack in the woods and then to their flat.

Remarkable, she thought.

Still there was one question unanswered. How did Susan get Henrietta to the third floor ballroom? None of the secret staircases she discovered led to the third floor. Besides, even if there was one Sara hadn't found, Henrietta was too old to navigate such narrow stairs.

The ballroom must have been used when the house was first constructed, she reasoned. Gatherings usually furnished food for the guests. She asked herself a question while drumming her finger on her cheek. Would the kitchen staff climb the stairs to the third levels with platters of food or would they use the popular dumb waiter? Maud and Frederick had one in their house, Sara recalled. She hadn't spent too much time in this kitchen, but she never noticed a dumbwaiter.

With that thought, Sara scampered down the stairs to the kitchen. She searched for a panel in the wall that could be raised up to reveal an elevator contraption to deliver food, but she found nothing in the kitchen. Maybe it was taken out, she reasoned.

The door to Mrs. Burns' room was still open and caught Sara's attention. She hadn't had the time to explore earlier, but now she had. Sara stepped over the mess Mrs. Burns had left behind and scrutinized the closet where she searched but found no hidden panels or trap doors. Shaking her head in bafflement, she then ran her hand over the dark paneled walls of the room.

A recent remodeling project in the house, she guessed. The dark walls didn't match any of the house's other wood.

On the next to the final wall, she noticed a large painting of a pastoral scene, rather badly done. It covered a large portion of the wall. Lifting the painting at the corner, she peered underneath to see an outline of some sort of door. It took all her strength to dislodge the painting from the wall. After tugging and pulling, she stumbled backwards and fell onto the bed with the painting pressing against her. Shoving the painting off to the side, she saw the door to an elevator. She scrambled to her feet, and pushed a button to open the elevator door. She wasn't sure if it worked or where it went, but she had a good guess.

Casting caution aside, she stepped into the rectangular cube and pushed the button. A motor ground and some sort of cables lifted the elevator a distance and then stopped. The door opened and she stepped out into a narrow room with no windows and one make-shift door. Disoriented to where the elevator had stopped, she anxiously opened the door. She found herself standing near the back wall of the ballroom. So this is how they got here? She whispered to herself. She turned around to see where the door was concealed in the wall. Right in the middle of the fountain mural. How could she not notice it?

Sara stepped back in the elevator and pressed the button to descend back to the kitchen, but when the door opened she discovered she was in the basement. It had never interested her where Henrietta and Susan spend the last few years, but here she was. She hesitated before she left the elevator and set foot in Henrietta's small world. The two rooms where she and her nurse lived were furnished with sofas, upholstered chairs, beds and bureaus. No wonder, she thought to herself, why they took excursions either to the ballroom or to the park.

She searched for the entrance to the tunnel. In a coat closet, she found the hidden staircase, which could be taken to either the first or second floor, or to the tunnel. It was here where Mrs. Burns took Henrietta out to the park.

Having seen enough, she stepped into the elevator and pushed another button, hoping it would stop in Mrs. Burn's old room. It did, and she skipped off, satisfied that most of her questions had been answered.

Why hadn't Mrs. Wilkes said anything about the elevator? She rushed downstairs to the solarium to ask her, but Mrs. Wilkes had nodded off in the warm sun.

Oh well, what difference does it make? She thought.

———————

Sara confided her concerns for Mrs. Wilkes to Myra one morning when they cleaning up the kitchen after breakfast. "I'm worried about your grandmother. She forces herself to work on the quilt, but other than that, she seems to have no interest in anything these days."

"I could usually cheer her up, but I can't seem to do that anymore," Myra confessed.

Sara dunked the washed dishes in the rinse water. "She won't last a month in a nursing home with the defeated attitude she has now."

"I feel the same way, but what are we going to do?" Myra asked, taking the dishes out of the rinse water and draining them.

"She simply has to stay here where she's lived all her life. Otherwise, she will be very unhappy."

"How is she going to do that if she has no money?"

"I've been giving it some thought," Sara said. "If she could rent out the empty rooms to nursing students, then perhaps she could afford to hire a cook and a gardener. Now that all the secrets are exposed, there should no longer be any fear of staying here."

"It might take some convincing. I'm afraid my grand-mother and this house have a reputation."

"I'll see if I can talk to the nursing students myself. Convince them there's nothing to fear."

"That's a great idea, and Grandmother could still have student nurses care for her. Couldn't she? That way she could save money."

"I don't see why not." Sara pursed her lips in thought. "Now let's see. How many rooms could we fix up to rent?"

"There are three on the south side of the second floor and three on the north. Some don't have beds, but we could probably find some. A little painting and wall papering and they could be ready. Let's talk to Grandmother." Myra threw the dish towel on the counter. "See what she says."

Mrs. Wilkes was working steadily on the quilt when the girls came into the parlor. "What are you two up to? Looks like you're bursting at the seams with something."

"Grandmother, I think Sara and I have come up with a way for you to stay in your home and not go to the nursing home."

Mrs. Wilkes ceased her sewing. "Really? Well, what is it?"

"Sara, tell her."

"We thought if we fixed up the rooms on the second floor you could rent them out to nursing students. The school is always short on places for them to stay. With that money, you would be able to afford a staff once again," Sara said.

"Are you talking about all the upstairs rooms?"

"Yes, we thought so." Sara sat across from Mrs. Wilkes, her eyes bright with the new idea.

"What am I going to do with all those girls running around?" Mrs. Wilkes jammed the needle into the quilt. "I can't supervise that many. I didn't even know Mrs. Burns and Gilbert were robbing me blind. Just think what trouble young girls can get themselves into."

"I have thought about the possibility," Sara said. "One of your staff members will have to be a house mother and watch over them, set curfews and such. She could do other duties, like cook or clean. And I'm thinking the young ladies will be too tired after working at the hospital all day to get into trouble."

Mrs. Wilkes shook her head. "I don't know. You know I have a reputation, as well as my spooky house."

"I can help rid the myth concerning the house. Maybe, you could become–"

"Friendlier?" Mrs. Wilkes added.

Sara grimaced. "It would help fill up the rooms faster."

"Don't you want to stay in your home, Grandmother?" Myra frowned in concern.

"I do, but I'm not sure about this arrangement. I can't afford to have someone get the rooms ready. I haven't been in them for years. Certainly they need a good cleaning."

"We would do the cleaning for you," Sara said. "We could even paint or wallpaper if need be."

Myra patted her grandmother on the shoulder. "Give it a try, Grandmother."

"I don't have the energy to interview applicants for the staff."

Sara glanced at Myra. "We'll do that, too."

Myra nodded her approval.

"You'd do all this for me?"

"Sure, why not?"Sara said.

Mrs. Wilkes sighed. "You two have certainly given this idea of yours a lot of thought. Since I trust your judgment, I'll give it a try."

Myra bent down and hugged her grandmother. "I'm

so pleased. I know you'll be happier here than in a nursing home."

"We'll see. Will you have time to do all this before you leave, Sara?"

"I won't leave until I do."

Mrs. Wilkes shook her head. "I don't think I should detain you."

Sara waved it off. "It's no trouble. I want to do this for you."

"Let's get started with our plan, but where do we begin?" Myra asked.

Sara stood and then bent down to check Mrs. Wilkes progress on the quilt. "For today, we can begin the cleaning. Tomorrow, we'll go to the school and tell them our plan. See if we can get some renters."

"What about staff?" Myra asked.

"There's no money to pay them right now. You and I will have to be the staff for a while. Can you stay here a little longer?"

"I think so," Myra consented.

"Good. Fill some buckets with hot water and soap and let's get started."

Myra filled the buckets with hot soapy water while Sara searched for brooms, mops, and cleaning rags.

A bewildered look stretched across Myra's face as she picked up the buckets, one in each hand. "Which room do we start with first?"

"How about the ones that have beds in them and could be rented out soon? Let's start with the one across the hall from me. It's a pretty room."

Sara and Myra lugged their cleaning supplies up the stairs and opened the door to the room with the rose bedspread and the photographs of Isabel and Mrs. Wilkes. They dragged the rugs out into the hall, so they could sweep and mop the room.

"What should we do with these photographs on the wall?" Myra asked, dusting them off with her hand. "I don't suppose the renters will appreciate them."

"I suppose we should take them down. We'll ask your grandmother where we should hang them. Or maybe you should take them. Do you have pictures of your mother?"

Myra removed the pictures from the wall and cradled them in her arms. "I have copies of these."

"This one of the Victorian should hang in the parlor, I think." Sara held up the picture for Myra to see. "I'll ask Mrs. Wilkes...Mattie. She said I could call her Mattie when no one else was around. You know, this painting of the house gave me a clue that something was added to the house after it was first built. Do you know what's missing from this painting?"

Myra studied it for a moment. "It's the turret."

"Henry guessed that Mr. Cummings, your Grandmother's father, had it added to distract attention from his real building project."

"And what was that?"

"Tunnels and secret passageways to move slaves to freedom."

"I have heard something about it. I was thinking maybe the tunnels and stairways should be closed up or filled in."

"It's your family home, but I think it's something that should be kept as it is. Although a few locks placed here and there might be a good idea."

"Perhaps you're right. I'll have to speak to Grandmother about it."

In a few hours Sara and Myra had finished the first room, and then they moved across the hall to the masculine looking bedroom where they agreed the décor would do for now. Sara's bedroom and Myra's bedroom were in good shape. A light cleaning before they left was all that was needed. Only two rooms remained without beds and they were the formerly locked room and the one with the armoires.

"Starting tomorrow, we have two rooms that can be rented out," Sara said as she sat down on the bed exhausted. "I'll visit the school tomorrow."

Cliff Point Nursing School was delighted to hear additional boarding rooms would be accessible. Already, Cliff Point assigned two students to rent the two available rooms at the Victorian. One of the students would become Sara's replacement. Since the rent money would be paid up front, Sara calculated that two beds could be purchased and placed in the two rooms that had been previously used for storage.

Sara couldn't wait to tell Mattie the good news. Sara stopped on her way home to the Victorian to buy two pails of yellow and blue paint for the room that had been locked and the room with the two armoires. Mattie was sleeping by the time she arrived at the house, so she told the good news to Myra who was upstairs cleaning out the armoires. Myra sat on the floor, a forlorn expression on her face, her mother's dresses and hats piled in her lap.

"Oh, Myra, this must be so difficult for you." Sara hadn't even thought of the feelings that Myra's mother's possessions would stir in her heart. "Any plans for your mother's things?"

Sara tossed a few of the hats to the side. "I'll keep a hat or two and donate the dresses and other things to charity. I know Grandmother couldn't part with them, but I believe I can. I have her quilts."

"Here, let me help you with her things, and then we can get started." Sara folded the dresses and placed them in a box. Myra sorted out two hats and added the rest to the carton.

"I never liked to come in this room because of the memories," Myra said. "I'm glad we're cleaning out these things and moving in a different direction with this house. It'll seem nice to see normal living taking place. People coming and going through regular doors, not tunnels and secret passageways. Perhaps I'll visit more often."

"Oh, dear, we haven't kept a room for you."

"Not to worry. A bed on the third floor will do me. Grandmother needs the money."

The young ladies moved to the room next door that had been locked for so long. They set to painting the neglected walls, which Myra had previously washed down. It wasn't long before the room took on a bright new glow. "And to think this is where Mrs. Burns and Gilbert stole Grandmother's and my mother's possessions," Myra said. "It almost makes me shudder to think of robbers pawing through their things. I never suspected Mrs. Burns. She was nice to me. Gilbert? Well, Gilbert scared me a little."

"I kind of wondered about Gilbert, too. But I didn't suspect Mrs. Burns at first. Mrs.—I mean Mattie told me once Mrs. Burns had threatened her in the solarium. From then on I didn't trust her."

"Well, it's over," Myra said. "Thank goodness."

"All these weird goings on bothered you, didn't they?"

"They did. Of course, I didn't fear my great grandmother exactly, but she was strange and the thought of her wandering around with her nurse unsettled me." Myra shuddered. "And then there was Gilbert. His appearance and the way he slunk around bothered me. I slept with my door locked, but I never knew for sure if there wasn't a secret passageway into my room."

Sara dipped her paint brush in the pail of yellow paint. "Once we get a bed and an armoire from the room next door, this room will look different."

"I suppose so. What we going to do about the panel in the closet to the secret stairway?"

"Nail it shut," Sara said.

"But it should be disguised somehow."

"It should, but I'm not sure how. Have you ever been on the secret stairways?"

"No, I never have. Mama was always going to take me, but we never got around to it."

"I'll take you if you want," Sara offered.

Myra's tone betrayed panic. "Right now?"

"Let's go. We have one wall finished."

Myra hesitated. "I don't know if I want to."

"I think it best to face your fear. The tunnel and the secret passageways are unusual but not frightening. Nothing sinister has happened in this house that I know of, except robbery."

Myra's face paled. "Oh, all right. I'll go. I trust your judgment."

Sara and Myra wiped the paint off their hands, borrowed a lantern from the kitchen, and opened the panel in the closet. "Go first," Myra said.

"This passageway is short," Sara said from inside. "I don't even know why it's here."

"Where does it end up?" Myra asked as she stepped on to the stairway."

"You'll see shortly."

"In just a few minutes Sara and then Myra stepped out on the third floor.

"The ballroom?" Myra exclaimed.

"When Mrs. Burns and Gilbert helped themselves to the treasures stored in the locked room, they would bring the pieces out to the ballroom and take them out through the house."

"I'd say that was bold."

"I thought it was strange at first, but then I got to thinking. When Mattie was napping, all they had to do was come down the stairs with the stolen goods. She would never know they were robbing her."

"There are more secret stairways, aren't there?" Myra asked.

"There are." Sara wagged her finger. "Follow me and we'll enter through the closet in the room between our bedrooms."

Once inside the closet, Sara wiggled through the small space that opened to the secret stairway and held the lantern for Myra to see.

"My this is cramped," Myra said. "How did Gilbert and Mrs. Burns get through here?"

"I don't know if they even used these stairs much. The stairs are narrow so be careful," Sara said, leading the way. "We should be about where Mattie's bedroom is. If we feel along this wall, we may find the panel that goes into the closet," Sara explained as she searched for the entry. She lifted her lantern near the wall. "Here, there's a mark. I never noticed it before. Someone marked the panel."

"Are we going into her closet?" Myra asked horrified.

Sara stumbled. "We won't go into her closet now. If we follow the stairs we'll eventually end up in the tunnel."

Sara heard a commotion behind her.

"My foot, it's stuck on something. Can you help?" Myra cried out.

Sara retreated back up the stairs to find Myra tugging on a large cloth object wound around her foot. Sara held the lantern high to see what it was. "This is what I stumbled on. It looks like a quilt." Sara unwound the quilt holding her foot and bunched the quilt up and set it to the side. "That's odd," Sara said. "I've never seen it before. We'll get it later."

They continued on down until they came to the ground floor where the stairway continued to descend a short distance to the tunnel entrance. "See there." Sara pointed. "We could enter the tunnel from here or from the carriage house. Still want to go through the tunnel?"

"Not really, but I suppose I should. Lead the way. I can't believe you explored this alone," Myra said as they crept inside the cool dark tunnel. "It's kind of creepy."

"Don't worry I haven't found anything to make me scream. Look above," she said after several moments of walking. "See that trap door. If we opened it we would be in the carriage house room where Gilbert stayed from time to time."

"That's creepy. What if Gilbert comes back with intentions to harm us?"

"Your concern has crossed my mind, too. I doubt it will happen. He should be locked up by now. Still, I think we have to prevent others from getting into the house without our knowing it."

"Good, let's get it done soon." Myra shivered. "How much farther? I'm getting cold."

"Not too far and we should be coming to the shack in the woods. Don't worry we won't miss it. The tunnel ends there."

Sara heard Myra stumbling behind her. "Are you all right?"

"Yes, it's just this uneven ground."

"I think I see the end up ahead. This time we'll leave the tunnel, and I'll show you where the shack is located." A few more feet and Sara reached up and pushed the trap door. "Help me, it feels stuck. Myra reached up and both of them heaved the trap door upward. "We got it, now let's get out."

"I can't believe the tunnel ends here." Myra scrambled upward as fast as she could. "I've seen this shack when I used to go riding but I never thought much about it."

Sara brushed the dirt off her hands. "Now you know all about the tunnel. It's up to your family what you want to do with it. We'd better get back before Mattie awakens. She doesn't like to be kept waiting for her tea."

"Do we have to go back through the tunnel?" Myra's voice whined.

"No, we'll just walk it from the outside."

Once inside the house, Sara and Myra trouped back to the bedroom next to Sara's. Myra waited while Sara opened the closet and crawled through the secret panel to the stairway. She climbed in to retrieve the quilt they had stumbled on. Sara pulled it out and laid it flat on the floor.

Myra wrinkled her nose, picking at it with her fingers. "It looks old. It's been used a lot."

"I agree. I don't know much about quilt patterns. Maybe Mattie can help us." Sara folded the quilt and carried it downstairs to the parlor. "You heat the water for tea and I'll check on Mattie. Sara scrambled to her room and listened through the tube. She detected Mattie stirring.

"She's awake," Sara told Myra as she bypassed the kitchen. "We'll meet you in the parlor."

Sara wheeled Mattie into the parlor where Myra had the tea and cake set out on the side tables.

"What have you girls been up to? You have paint on your faces, and I think I can smell the fresh scent of paint drifting down the stairs."

Sara touched her face and laughed. "Oh we forgot. We were painting one of the bedrooms, and then we got distracted."

"Sara took me through the secret stairs and into the tunnel. Have you ever been through it?"

"When I was a girl I went through the tunnel with my father. I didn't care for the eerie thing and never went into it again."

"It's creepy alright, but kind of interesting, too," Myra said. "Imagine slaves using it to escape. The stories it could tell."

Mattie pointed toward the floor. "What's that bundle doing here? Looks like it should be thrown away."

Myra picked up the folded quilt and brought it closer. She unfolded it in front of her grandmother. "We found it in the stairway. I caught my foot in it."

"It must have worked its way out of its hiding place," Sara said.

Mattie bent forward for a better look. "It certainly is old. I think it may date back to the Civil War era." She pointed to the quilt's pattern. "See the three strips, framed on the corners with triangles? It was called Hard Crackers."

"Why did it have that funny name?" Her granddaughter asked.

Mattie shrugged. "The Civil War soldiers were fed a lot of crackers."

Myra's eyes grew wide. "Really, do you think your mother could have made it?"

"Possibly. She was a quilter, too. I wonder what it was doing in the secret stairway. Do you suppose someone stole it?" Mattie asked.

"Or maybe it was given to someone as a gift," Sara said on a more positive note.

Myra wrinkled her nose. "What do we do with it? It's in bad shape."

"Perhaps a museum would give us a little money for it," Mattie suggested. "If not we will donate it. Fold it up and store it somewhere for now."

Sara reflected it would be a shame to give a piece of history away, especially if an ancestor had sewed it. She folded the quilt, thinking where to put it.

"I'm ready to warm up these stiff bones. One of you wheel me to the solarium?"

Myra stepped forward. "I will Grandmother."

Sara remained in the parlor staring at the folded quilt. The more she thought about it, Sara was certain she couldn't give the Hard Crackers quilt away. She spread the quilt out on the parlor floor and carefully studied it. The tattered edges defied repair. Perhaps the quilt was a lost cause as Mattie thought.

Sara doubted her ability to tackle the task of restoring the quilt. She wished she could ask Cassandra what to do. Mattie wasn't the least bit interested. She would be of no help. Mattie was only focused on her current project of the Victorian Lady.

Sara had to admit that at the moment the quilt wasn't pretty to look at. It had been soiled by either use or having been wadded up under the stairway for forty years. But the pattern itself was in good condition. She thought if it was carefully washed the colors might appear brighter. Or it was possible the quilt would fall apart when washed.

Myra appeared in the doorway, crunching on an apple. "What you doing, Sara?"

"Looking at this old quilt. Just wondering if I could fix it."

"Really? I think it's done for. Why you so interested in keeping it around?"

"It's a part of the house's history. It's a shame to throw it out."

Myra shrugged. "I wouldn't think twice about tossing it."

"The worst part, I don't have time to do anything with it. I'll be leaving after we get the rooms ready."

"Take it with you."

"Take it to the mission with me?"

"Why not? Grandmother doesn't want it around anyway."

Sara's eyes remained focused on the Hard Cracker. "I'm already taking the Jacob's Ladder quilt with me. I don't even know if I have room for that one."

"I bet we could find another trunk in the carriage house. Let's have a look."

The girls checked on Mattie before they scampered outside to the carriage house. She was snoozing peacefully.

"This time I don't have to worry about Gilbert sneaking up on me," Sara said as they entered the building.

Myra laughed. "It's a relief not to have him around here anymore."

The girls poked around the relics stored in the space. Myra sneezed. "This dust is getting to me. I don't think these things have been moved in years."

Sara rattled a few objects. "I may have found something. Come over here."

Myra joined here near a corner of the carriage house. "Wow, a couple of trunks."

"Help me pull them out."

Sara and Myra tugged until two dusty trunks emerged from their hiding place.

"I wonder which relative of mine used these." Myra sneezed again.

"Let's carry them outside, so we can see them better." Sara snatched a rag from a pile of junk and wiped the dust off the trunks as best she could. "Do you suppose there's a treasure in here?"

"I doubt it. If it was valuable Mrs. Burns and Gilbert already sold it," Myra said wryly.

Nonetheless Sara felt a prickle of expectation as she worked the rusty latches and lifted the domed lid with Myra's help. The trunk was nearly empty except for a small box tied with string. Sara nodded to Myra to lift it out.

"What could be in here?" Myra asked. "I'm almost afraid to look."

"Open it."

Myra slowly drew the string off the box and removed the lid. Inside were photographs. Old photographs of Negro people. Myra handed them to Sara. Sara sorted through about a half dozen photographs and then reshuffled them again. "Look, Myra," Sara blurted out in excitement. It's the Hard Cracker quilt."

Myra scrutinized the photograph. "I believe the white woman in the picture holding the quilt is my great grandmother Henrietta. But who's the colored woman next to her?"

"I would guess someone very special to her. Sometimes the wealthy white people became attached to their servants." Sara took the photograph from Myra and looked at it intently. "Can you believe we found a photograph of the quilt? Amazing."

"Let's take these to Grandmother. I bet she can identify some of these people," Myra suggested.

The young ladies dusted off their skirts and rushed to the solarium where they found Mattie nodding off. Myra awakened her grandmother and told her about their discovery. Her grandmother frowned about being bothered, but became more interested when her granddaughter thrust the pictures in her face. She determined that most of the pictures were taken when she herself was quite young. She admitted that she vaguely remembered a few house servants. One of the colored women, she identified as possibly being her colored nanny. She doubted if she ever saw the slaves being smuggled into or out of the house. "My parents were very protective of me," Mattie said with pride.

"Oh, Grandmother, these pictures are such a treasure. I'm so glad we found them," Myra said in a state of bliss.

"I guess. But it's just old history to me."

"Would you mind if I took the one with the quilt in it to show to Cassandra," Sara asked. "I promise to bring it back with me. It's a good picture of her mother." Henrietta appeared quite young in the photograph. Sara would have described her as genteel, dressed in the style of a Victorian lady. Her kind face showed through the wealthy trappings of their society.

Uncanny, she thought, *Cassandra nor Mattie resembled her.*

"Sure. If it's alright with Myra?"

Myra nodded. "I trust you to bring it back."

Sara held the photograph near her heart. She just couldn't believe her good fortune.

———————

In the next two weeks, Sara and Myra had painted the last two rooms, washed windows, and curtains, and made the beds Sara had purchased just days before. The girls had complimented each other on the rooms' transformation from drab and eerie to beautiful and fresh.

The first two renters came just days after the rooms were ready. Sara, Mattie, and Myra agreed not to say anything about the tunnels and secret passageways, which had recently been secured against intruders. Best of all, Mattie agreed to be on her best behavior.

Sara brought her replacement, Edith, to meet Mattie. "Just call me Mattie," she instructed her new nurse. Sara smiled at the changes which had taken place, including Mrs. Wilkes's new attitude. She left them alone to become acquainted and escorted the other nursing student to her room.

"We have six rooms on this second floor," Sara said to the new student, Amelia. "Two are still occupied by myself and Mattie's granddaughter, but we will be leaving soon. Feel free to select from the other four bedrooms.

Sara could tell Amelia was impressed with the bedrooms. Her eyes lit up with each one she inspected. "What a hard decision," she said. "But I'll take the one with the rose bed spread and rugs."

"I'll let you get settled, and then I'll show you and Edith around the house tomorrow." Sara left her alone to unpack, remembering the first time she saw the house and met Mattie. So much had happened since then. She peeked in on Mattie and Edith. It appeared Mattie was being charming for the moment at least.

The cook Sara had interviewed would come tomorrow and assume her duties as cook and house mother. Sara expected the gardener who would also assume the duties of maintenance man tomorrow, also. The gardener she had hired would come to work only a few days a week, especially during the colder months. But the summer months would probably occupy him every day.

Myra had agreed to stay on an extra week after Sara left to see if the arrangements were running smoothly.

While Edith and Amelia were preoccupied, Sara retreated to her room to pack before she began the evening meal. She tucked a few more items in the trunk she had brought with her from the mission. Sara and Myra had cleaned, aired, and sprinkled the trunk found in the carriage house with lavender and rose petals. She bent down to sniff its interior.

It is beginning to smell better, she thought.

She folded the Jacob's Ladder quilt and wrapped it in tissue paper and placed it near the trunk. She planned to slip it in the day she left for home, along with Hard Crackers which she had laundered a few days ago. She hoped Cassandra would have ideas for repairing it. She scanned the room, which was beginning to look bare. The closet had been emptied as well as the bureau drawers. Satisfied she had made progress, she left for the kitchen.

Sara prepared an evening meal for a table full of people. The chatter of the young girls seemed to brighten Mattie's spirits.

Maybe this is what she needs, Sara thought to herself.

Edith and Amelia helped clear the table and after excusing themselves, they climbed the stairs to their rooms. Sara heated the tea water and cut slices of cake to take to the parlor.

Myra had already rolled Mattie's wheelchair into the parlor for the evening routine and then left Sara and Mattie alone. "We won't have many more evenings together," Mattie commented wistfully.

Sara noticed Mattie holding the Victorian Lady quilt in her lap. They had finished it two days ago. "No, but I'm coming back. There will be visits. Perhaps not every evening like we used to, but it's not forever."

"I have something for you to take back to the mission." Mattie held out the quilt.

"For us?"

"I hope you all enjoy it, but it's for Cassandra."

"Cassandra?" Sara did her best not to sound too surprised.

"I have a notion you thought I didn't care about my sister. I do care, but I still think it best not to dredge up the past. Do you realize how she would feel? I have been raised in luxury. She grew up in an orphanage alone, without knowing her family. I don't think I can face her knowing that."

"Did you intend all along to give her this quilt?"

"I did. My mother—her mother designed the pattern when she was a real Victorian lady. She dressed and lived the part. Hard to believe she was destitute at one time and was reduced to such poverty that she had to give her little girl away."

Sara sat stunned, never knowing the depth of Mattie's emotions until now.

"She may not even want my gesture. If not, the quilt is yours."

Sara nodded in agreement. "She will be certain to appreciate your handiwork."

"I will miss our quilting sessions. It has been good for me to keep my fingers busy."

"Perhaps, one of your renters will be a quilter."

"Possibly. But for now I think I'll take a break. I can't believe we've completed two quilts in one winter. Now, if you will put me to bed."

After Sara settled Mattie in for the night, she scooped up the quilt from the parlor and skipped up the stairs to her bedroom. Another quilt for the trunk. She smiled as she put it beside the other two, waiting for their trip to the mission.

CHAPTER 16

Talk of the South Dakota cattle empires crumbling from losses and encroaching homesteader had made Tex nervous. He didn't want to be left high and dry. He knew Texas had plenty of land. After all Texas was the largest state in the United States. There had to be a ranch for him somewhere among the millions of acres of grazing land and he was going to look for it.

It didn't take him long to book passage on the train going south. He was on his way home to Texas to buy a ranch. Reluctantly, Ed had let him go for a few weeks on the condition that he would be back before the fall roundup.

Tex had assured his son Curt he would be back as soon as he could. Curt gave his word he would keep his eyes on their interests at the Bar Double B. In turn Tex promised him he would find a ranch big enough for both of them.

Tex had plenty of time to think about the recent changes in his life as the train clung to the track, devouring the miles. As hard as he tried to push Louisa out of his mind these past few weeks, her image flashed before him when he least expected it. She had written to him several times while she was in Texas; the letters padded his pocket. However, none of her correspondence gave him any hope that she would be home soon. In fact, it seemed to him she was in no hurry to get back to her South Dakota Ranch. He could look for her ranch in Texas and visit while he was there, but what would a visit accomplish.

For now, he had to put her out of his mind. Netty, Curt, and the family's future were at stake. Tex had wired Netty to meet him in San Antonio. According to the train conductor, the train would arrive in another few hours. He leaned his head back on the seat and closed his eyes. No use worrying until his feet hit the Texas soil. He had enough connections to help him find what he was looking for.

The blaring whistle awakened him and informed the citizens of San Antonio the train had arrived. Tex sat upright, rubbed his weary eyes and stared out the window at the adobe buildings, topped with tiled roofs, and detailed with arched windows and doors. He spotted Netty on the platform. Tex smiled in contentment. She was a good girl and pretty, too.

Not what you would call striking, he thought, *but wholesome looking.* His sister-in-law Martha had done wonders with her.

He barely cleared the last step of the coach when Netty rushed into his arms. "I've missed you father."

"And I you," he answered in a husky voice. He tipped his hat to his sister-in-law and walked into the Spanish style depot with them.

"What brings you to Texas this time of year?" Martha asked. "I thought you had work to do."

"I'm looking for a ranch."

"You're coming back to stay?" she asked. "What brought this on?"

"Yeah, I might. Have to find a ranch first."

After Tex retrieved his luggage, Martha's driver took them to her modest adobe home in the city.

Martha removed her hat once she was inside the house. "I've prepared a light lunch for us. Are you hungry Tex?"

Tex detected the odor of hard boiled eggs. "Oh, I can always eat." He noticed how much his sister-in-law reminded him of his wife, a practical woman, not flashy.

"Do you know where you're going to begin your search for a ranch?" Martha asked.

"I have a couple of men who know about land. I'll look them up tomorrow. Today, I plan to spend with Netty. Catch up on her life."

Netty smiled at her father while she set the table. Martha made sandwiches and produced a salad from the icebox. "I think we're ready," Martha said.

After Tex heaped potato salad and cold roast beef on his plate, he turned to his daughter. "Now then Netty what would you like to do today."

"Oh, we don't have to do anything. Martha has the nicest courtyard. Why we can sit out there all afternoon and sip lemonade if we want."

"Isn't it a little warm to sit outside today?"

"There are the nicest shade trees and a place where we can feel a breeze."

"You'd rather stay here?"

"I do. I want to spend every minute visiting rather than sightseeing."

"Alright then, if that's what you want."

After thanking Martha for lunch, Netty and Tex retired to the outdoors to Netty's favorite magnolia tree. "You must sit here often," Tex commented as he arranged two wrought iron chairs in the shade."

"It's so peaceful here. You should have seen the magnolias blooming this spring. The entire town smelled like heavenly perfume." Netty pulled up a wrought iron table for their lemonade.

"You do appreciate nature. You're like your mother in that way. When you were a little girl you would run through the bluebonnets and Indian paint brush in the spring looking for the best blooms for a bouquet."

"I still visit the hill country in the spring. Nothing is more beautiful." She poured more lemonade. "Tell me everything about South Dakota."

"You go first. I want to know what you're doing."

"Later. I want to know why you're here looking for a ranch."

"Oh, that." Tex twirled the corners of his mustache. "Well, some of the cattlemen think the open range is about over. Maybe a few more years and then we'll be out of luck. I thought I'd get a jump on things and find us a ranch."

"Curt wants to come back, too?"

"Not so much a question of wanting to, but having to."

"You like South Dakota?"

"I do, but time to face the facts. There may not be a future there anymore. Texas is a big place. There's got to be a ranch for us somewhere." Tex stroked his chin. "Or would you rather live with Martha?"

"I like Martha, but you know I want to be with you and Curt." Netty sipped her lemon aid. "Curt didn't find himself a lady?"

"No. He tried but she wasn't interested."

Netty shrugged. "There are plenty girls in Texas."

"I'm not worried, either. He's still young. And how about you?"

"Nothing serious."

"No proposals?"

"None. Don't worry. I'm still young," Netty insisted.

Tex and Netty visited all afternoon until the katydids began singing in the treetops. "It can't be fall already," Tex said.

"I just got here."

Netty laughed and dismissed herself. She had enough of the afternoon heat and went to lie down before the evening repast. Tex left her to rest while he strolled about the neighborhood. He pulled the last letter from Louisa out of his pocket. The letter contained information and directions to Louisa's father's ranch. He tapped the letter in the palm of his hand, thinking. Her ranch, Rancho del Alvarez, was located west of San Antonio on the Rio Grande River. Should he try to find her before he began his search for a place of his own? He had to know if she wanted to be a part of his future, but yet there were Curt and Netty, his grown children, to consider.

– – – – – –

Tex left Netty and San Antonio without explaining any details to his daughter. All she knew was that he would be looking for a ranch. He didn't intend to tell Netty about Louisa. He wasn't sure if there was anything to tell, yet.

She seemed troubled to see him leave again, but he promised to be back within the week. He bought a train ticket traveling west as close to the Alvarez ranch as he could get. After miles and miles of sagebrush the train finally arrived at the end of the line in El Paso. There he boarded a stage coach to a small settlement near the Rancho del Alvarez.

"I know the place," a talkative male passenger shriveled from age and sun informed him.

"Good, then I know it exists," Tex said.

"My name is Pablo Martinez." He extended his hand.

Tex shook it. "Pleased to meet you. I'm Tex MacMurray originally from Texas. Farther east of here." He wiped his face with his kerchief. "So tell me more of the Alvarez family."

"Ah, yes, Miguel Alvarez and his forefathers have been here for many years. His ranch has been a landmark for over a century. You know Miguel?"

"No. I met his daughter Louisa in South Dakota. I've been ranching there for several years."

"I haven't seen her for a long time. She is well?"

"As far as I know. She came back to Texas to be with her father. I understand he is ill."

"Too bad. You'll never meet a finer man."

"And how do you know the Alvarez family?" Tex asked him.

"I'm a merchant in the nearby town. My family has been there for years, too."

"I'd like to clean up before I go out to the ranch. Do you have a hotel in town?"

"Sí, Senior. I will take you to it personally."

"I also need to know the best way to get to the rancho." Tex pulled the map Louisa had drawn for him from his pocket. Pablo studied it and nodded his head in approval.

"This is right. I'll point out this road when we get to town."

After hours of agonizing ruts and bumps the stage stopped in front of an adobe building. The stage driver jumped down from his perch and threw down the luggage onto the dusty street. Tex picked up his bag and followed Pablo to another adobe structure with only a few rooms for rent. On the way, Pablo showed him what road to take out of town to the rancho.

Tex thanked Pablo, stepped inside the cool adobe, and signed the registry. He inquired as to a bath. The clerk pointed to a public bath house down the street. After inspecting his room furnished with heavy dark furniture and brightly woven rugs, he folded his clean clothes, tucked them under his arm and proceeded to the bath house.

On the way, he noticed the cantinas that served food and

tequila. He thought he'd stop in one before he retired for the night. After a meal that ignited his taste buds, he entered his room and flopped on the hard bed, softened with his exhaustion. He slept and woke feeling rested.

Louisa's map indicated that he would be able to arrive at their ranch in a day's ride. After dressing and filling his canteen with water and purchasing some tortillas, he stopped at the livery where he rented a horse for a few days, and then took the trail Pablo had pointed out.

The sun blared down on him for miles on end before he came to the Rio Grande. He had never seen this river before. He thought it an impressive sight as it coursed through the desert straight as an arrow. It was wide and long, just like he had heard from others who had seen it.

He stopped and dismounted to study its current, contemplating a swim. Instead, he dipped his hat in and poured the river water over his perspiring head. After shaking off the excess and relishing the sensation of a cool spring rain, he pulled out the tortillas from his saddle bag, rolled them, and ate them while watching the water flow steadily to the Gulf of Mexico.

The tortillas satisfied his rumbling stomach. The river had cooled him. Leaning back against a rock, he pulled the map from his pocket and determined he had only a few hours left before he saw Louisa. By now, he realized his bath and his clean clothes, sticking to him like cactus juice, had been a waste of time and money.

Stiff from riding, he swung his leg gingerly over the saddle and set off for the ranch. He rode beside the river, using it as a guide. It was over an hour when he spotted buildings in the distance. Referring to his map once again, he was sure he was in sight of the Rancho del Alvarez. Before he angled away from the river, he dismounted and taking his blue kerchief from his neck he stooped toward the water, wet his kerchief, and wrapped it around his forehead.

As he neared the ranch headquarters, grazing long horn cattle began to appear along with a few vaqueros. The land seemed rough and bleak, but the cattle were thriving.

Soon he came to a well-watered valley where a low adobe hacienda sprawled across the bottom land. He removed his kerchief and wiped his face before depositing the kerchief in his saddle bag. As he slowly rode up to the front door, he saw a hitching rail, with two horses tied. He dismounted and tied up his horse, entered a well-kept court yard, and knocked on the door. His heart fluttered in wait. Soon he heard footsteps. A woman came to the door and inquired as to who he was. When he identified himself she lifted her brow in curiosity, but let him in anyway.

She left him standing in a cool dim room filled with dark ornate carved furnishings. Earthenware vases and tapestries lent a colorful contrast to the otherwise dim room. He turned when he heard her voice.

"Tex, you've come." Louisa moved toward him and took his hands in hers. "I didn't know if you would." She was dressed in a turquoise skirt and blouse. A turquoise barrette held her hair piled high off her exquisite face; her dark skin released a spicy fragrance.

Tex leaned into her. "I'm sorry but I just couldn't keep away. Even though it would have been for the best."

"For the best?" She drew back seeming offended.

"You have to admit, our situation is complicated."

"Come in and sit. I'll have Rosita bring us some refreshments." She grasped his hand and led him into the great room. She pulled a bell rope. Soon Rosita came and listened to Louisa's instructions.

"How's your father?" Tex asked, unwilling to let go of her hand.

"He hasn't changed much since I have arrived. I'm pleased that he does know me."

"You're not planning on coming back to South Dakota soon?"

She shook her head. "I cannot leave while he is ill. I fear he will not improve."

"I thought as much. That's why I'm here."

"I hoped you would come and visit, but what you say is true. How can we be together?"

"I don't know. I thought I would look for a ranch in Texas. Ed is worried that the open range days are coming to an end." He studied her face seeking a response.

She averted her eyes, left her chair and paced the room. "Ed is a smart man. He sees things that others would rather not face."

Tex cleared his throat. "I have to ask you something."

She came and sat beside him and stroked his hand. "What is it?"

"Ed and I've been talking. We both think that you're the anonymous stockholder for the Bar Double B."

She dropped her eyes from his gaze. "You both are perceptive. How did I give myself away?"

"You really didn't. We just figured it out, but why did you keep it a secret?"

"I didn't want anyone to know it was a woman. Nor did I want anyone to know about this ranch in Texas. As you can see, the Rancho del Alvarez is worth much money. I can afford to be a stockholder and keep my husband's dream alive."

"Ed thought that was the reason." Tex's shoulders slumped. "You must have loved your husband very much."

"I did. But he is gone. I only have his memory left."

Tex didn't know what to say. Could he compete with the memories of her dead husband? He broke the sudden silence between them. "And what is your prediction for the open range?"

"I'd rather not predict. I may be wrong."

"I'd like to know." His voice was uncertain.

"I don't want to be the one to give the death blow to a way of life you love."

Hard lines appeared at the corners of his lips. "Ed has prepared me."

"I think next year, I will remove my support." She expelled her breath. "No matter how hard I want to fight the changes taking place, I can't."

"I know. I'm not sure what to do."

"Nor I. When my father passes, my brother Carlos will inherit this ranch. Father gave me a dowry when I married. That's my share."

"When your father...dies you will have to leave this ranch?"

"Yes."

Tex played the scenario in his mind. If he bought a ranch in Texas and married Louisa, both of them would not be obligated to anyone. Her sons could keep the ranch in South Dakota and Carlos would own the family ranch. But would Louisa marry him?

— — — — — —

Before the evening meal, Louisa walked Tex to his room where he could freshen up. "Would you like to see my father?" she asked abruptly.

"Is he able to have visitors?"

"He's not able to visit, but he can at least meet you. I'd like him to see the connection between us. He's always worried that I'm still unattached."

Louisa's words touched his heart. She had referred to them as a couple. "I'll see him, then."

Louisa smiled and left Tex at his bedroom door. "I'll come back for you in an hour."

The room where she had left him was immaculate, furnished with the typical dark wood furnishings, a bright woven bedspread covered his bed and a magnificent view of the ranch appeared out the window. He gazed on the far reaches of the Alvarez ranch, and then rummaged through his bag for something suitable to wear for dinner. To his consternation, he decided he hadn't brought anything along that could equal the lifestyle of the Alvarez family.

When Louisa returned, Tex noticed she had changed into a shimmering heavily embroidered red dress. He apologized for his apparel. "You're handsome to me," she simply said, sliding her arm through his.

He thought she was stunning as he strode beside her down the hall to her father's bedroom. Tex adjusted his eyes to the dimly lit room when they entered. A man with a full head of gray hair, framing Latino features, lay propped up on pillows.

"Father," Louisa called, attempting to nudge him out of his sleep. Her father's eyes opened into tiny slits. "I want you to meet Tex, a dear friend of mine." She motioned for Tex to come closer. "He's a manager of one of the ranches we've been funding in South Dakota." Tex noticed her father moved his hand toward hers. She lifted it next to her face and kissed it.

Louisa cooed soft murmurings of conversation to her father, then fluffed the pillows and kissed him on the cheek before she left his bedside. She motioned to Tex they should go. Outside in the hall, she said, "Father understood. I know, even if he couldn't say it."

Tex hadn't seen her so vulnerable and so tender as before now. He bent down and kissed her. He felt her respond, and then she gently pushed him away. "We must go. The cook doesn't like to be kept waiting."

Juan and Carlos were already seated at the table sipping wine. Grins spread across their faces when Tex and Louisa entered the room furnished with a massive table and an open cupboard filled with earthenware dishes. A bright red rug covered the dark stained floor.

"Tex, this is Carlos my brother. And you already know

Juan," Louisa said, completing the introduction.

Tex shook hands and sat across the table from them with Louisa at his side.

"Louisa has told me a lot about you, Tex," Carlos remarked.

Tex shifted uncomfortably in his chair. He wondered how much Louisa told him. Did she mention that the two of them were quite fond of each other? But if he hadn't known, he would know now. It was quite evident. Tex had traveled many miles to see her. "She has mentioned you, too. I'm sorry about your father."

"Old age may descend on all of us." Carlos passed a platter of enchiladas the cook's assistant had brought to the table. "It's a fact of life."

"You have quite a spread here." Tex scooped up an enchilada and placed it on his earthen tone glazed plate.

"Thanks to my grandfather and my father. It's been in the family for years," Carlos explained, handing Tex a spicy looking sauce.

"I'm looking for a Texas ranch. Any ideas of available land?"

Juan dropped his fork. "You leaving the Bar Double B?"

"I don't want to, but Ed has been telling me that the open range days may be numbered."

Juan shook his head. "And I was looking for a job there."

"The operation isn't going to end tomorrow. I just want to be prepared when it does."

"You looking for land, you say?" Carlos asked, downing a glass of water, his face flushed.

"I'm originally from Texas. I had a small place after my days on the trail. When my wife died, I sold it and came to South Dakota. But now I want to come back."

Carlos waved his hand. "There's land all around us. Some more suited to cattle. If you want I could take you around tomorrow and show you some of it." He lifted his brows and glanced toward his sister. "You want land near this ranch?"

Tex began to sweat. He hadn't even talked to Louisa about the location. "Maybe, I like this area," he said lamely.

After the meal, Carlos invited Texas to go riding, but Louisa interrupted. "He's only here for a few days. He's staying with me."

Secretly Tex was glad Louisa spoke up. He did have only a few days, and he had something important to ask her. Something he would have to build up to.

After Juan and Carlos left, Tex and Louisa strolled hand in hand around the ranch headquarters. Ordinarily he would have taken in every detail but at the moment he only had eyes for her.

"Are you looking for a ranch close to us?" She lifted her eyes to meet his.

"It depends on you. Would you like me to be close by?" He touched her lips with his finger.

She smiled. "Of course I would."

"I do have to help with the fall roundup at the Bar Double B. Maybe Juan could take my place when I come back to Texas. That is, if you can get along without him here."

"I can tell Juan is itching to leave. Carlos and Juan don't always see eye to eye."

Louisa led him to a bench in the shade where they sat side by side. Her fragrance and their nearness were too much for Tex. He took her in his arms and kissed her ardently. This time she didn't pull away. "Louisa, would you consider marrying me?" He blurted out the question without intending to.

"Do you think we could make it work? I mean with our families."

"I believe we could. We'd have our own place, other than Curt and Netty might be with us for a while. It won't be as grand as the Rancho del Alvarez, but we could be happy."

"I don't need all of this. Remember how I worked on the

South Dakota Ranch? I enjoy the comforts of the Alvarez, but it isn't necessary."

"So what do you say?" He held her at arm's length.

"I have never felt this way since my husband died. I say yes. Yes, I will marry you."

"I don't have a ring," Tex apologized. "I wasn't sure how you felt."

"I wasn't certain about you either, but I still can't leave my father."

"When can we get married? I'll have to return to the Bar Double B soon."

"Either before you leave or after your return?"

He grabbed her shoulders. "I don't want to wait."

"I don't either. Let's have the priest come to the house and marry us."

"Can we do that? I'd like to have Netty here at least." His eagerness turned to concern.

"Wire her and see if she can come. It won't take long to arrange something. Perhaps some of our friends and neighbors will attend, and we'll have a grand fiesta afterwards. And the best part, Father will see us married."

Tex realized he didn't have the proper clothes in which to wed. He wired Netty again with his measurements, entrusting her to bring what he needed. Within several days Netty arrived with Aunt Martha, who didn't seem too friendly toward Tex.

"Shame on you, Father," Netty berated him when she saw him. "You never told me of a woman in your life."

"I'm sorry, but I didn't know if she'd have me. I'm not of her class, but luckily she doesn't seem to notice." He laughed and helped Netty with her luggage and packages.

"I do hope everything fits," Netty fretted. "Martha helped with the selections."

"He bowed slightly to his dead wife's sister. "Thanks for your help Martha."

"Anything for my Netty," she said.

Louisa appeared on the stairs, dressed in royal purple. Her hair held a Spanish comb.

Tex extended his hand toward her. "Come Louisa and meet my family."

She descended the stairs gracefully and held her hand out to Netty. "You must be Tex's daughter. I see the resemblance."

"And this is my sister-in-law Martha," Tex said. "Netty has lived with her from time-to-time." Martha stiffened, but extended her hand to Louisa.

"I'll have the maid show you to your rooms. Christina, please take them upstairs and see that they are settled comfortably. As soon as you wish you may come downstairs for refreshments."

Tex picked up the luggage and followed the young Latino maid. "I'll take these up for them," he told Louisa.

Netty dropped back to walk beside Tex. "Louisa's beautiful. I see why you pursued her."

"You're not mad at me for finding someone else. I know how much you loved your mother."

Netty patted his arm. "I know you did, too. She's been gone for quite a while. It's time for you to find happiness."

"What's wrong with Martha?" Tex whispered.

"I think she does have a problem with you remarrying. She rather you be the miserable widower."

Tex bent his head toward his daughter. "I think she doesn't want to lose you. She's been like a mother to you."

"I never thought of that."

Tex took the luggage into their rooms and then went downstairs to be with Louisa. "You look especially pretty," he told her, and then kissed her. "How are the wedding plans coming?"

"Quite well. I sent for a dress when I first arrived here in Texas. Since I haven't worn it yet, I'll save it for our wedding. The invitations have been sent out and the food will be prepared on time. We'll tidy up the courtyard and be married there. Any suggestions?"

"None. Just that the priest shows up."

Louisa laughed. "He will."

Netty and Martha joined them in the dining room, where a light repast had been prepared for their arrival.

"How lovely," Netty said. "You didn't have to go to all this trouble."

Louisa bustled around seating her guests. "I know how dreadful the food can be when you travel."

Once the food was passed and the blessing said, Netty asked her father about the ranch he was searching for.

"Carlos and me went riding one blasted hot day. He showed me a place not far from here with a decent adobe house and sheds. The grazing looks good, too. He didn't bother to tell me it was his uncle's place until afterward."

"It's for sale then?" she asked.

"It is. If we can reach a deal, Louisa and I will have a home, and so will you Netty."

"Is it far from here?"

"Not far. I could take you over after lunch. You too, Martha, if you want?"

"I doubt if I'll ever come to visit. It's just too far away." She yawned. "A nap is what I want."

"Louisa, want to come with us?" Tex asked

"I would, but I have too many things to do around here. You two go on." She shooed them with her hands. "Take whatever you need from the stable."

After lunch Netty changed into riding clothes while Martha retired to her room. Tex asked Louisa once more to go along, but she declined. He kissed her on the cheek and departed with Netty to the stable. "Want to ride or shall we take the buggy?"

"I'm a little rusty when it comes to riding. I just don't have the opportunity anymore."

"The buggy then?"

"I would prefer it."

There were more buggies than Tex needed. He searched through them choosing the one most comfortable for Netty, hitched it to two shining sleek black horses, and headed toward Carlo's uncle's place.

"You are certainly full of surprises," Netty said, staring intently at her father. "I can't believe you're getting married, and I had no idea you wanted to come back to Texas."

"I didn't either girl. Things can change in the blink of an eye."

Netty nudged him. "One of them being Louisa?"

"Yeah, her and the news that the open range is heading for doom changed my future plans."

"What's happening with the open range?"

"The blizzards for one thing and the other is the homesteaders wanting the public domain. Remember how worried I was about that?"

"I do, but I just didn't think it would happen so fast."

"It'll take a few years to take place. But I'll want to come back from the reservation as soon as I can."

"When will that be?"

"I told Ed I'd help with the fall roundup and then I'm coming back to Texas. When can you join us?"

"I've been thinking...you and Louisa need to be alone. I think I'll continue living with Aunt Martha. You've seen her. She'd be lost without me."

Tex abruptly turned toward her. "But I counted on you living with us at the ranch?" His voice contained regret.

"I know you did, but I changed my mind. I'll come for visits."

"Martha said it was too far."

Netty smiled. "For her maybe, but not for me."

"I told Curt I'd get a ranch big enough for the two of us. I think I did." Tex pointed toward the adobe situated near a group of scraggly trees."

"Looks a little neglected."

"Maybe some, but Louisa and me will get it in shape in no time."

— — — — — —

While Tex dressed for his wedding, he brooded about Netty not coming to live with him and Louisa. He regretted that Martha had assumed the mother figure that Netty had needed since her mother died. He was hoping Louisa could be her mother now. But he had to admit the area he had chosen to live with Louisa was desolate and far from the conveniences that Netty now enjoyed. Perhaps she had seen this with her own eyes and had made the decision that very day he showed her his new ranch. She had a point though. Louisa and he needed to be alone for a while. True, Netty could come for a visit, and in turn, he and Louisa could visit her.

Right at the moment, his musings were interrupted by his fumbling fingers. He needed someone to help with his tie. He opened his bedroom door and yelled down the hall for Netty, and then ducked back in his room. He stood in front of the bureau mirror, struggling with the narrow piece of material slick as a wet bar of soap in his large hands. He heard footsteps and expecting to see Netty in the mirror beside him, he gasped when Curt appeared dressed fancier than he had ever seen him before.

Tex turned around. "Why, why, Curt what you doing here? Going to a wedding or something?" His face broke into a silly grin.

"Surprised?"

"I'll be jiggered. Didn't expect to see you."

"Louisa wired me. Told me you didn't have a best man."

"Well, Carlos was going to be."

"But you wanted me. Right?"

Tex pumped his son's hand. "Sure I do."

"Let me help you. They're waitin' for us."

Curt tied Tex's tie and looked him over from top to bottom. "You're looking good for an old man."

Tex slapped him on the back. "At least I'm getting myself a wife."

"You beat me there," Curt said, as they scooted together to the court yard.

The priest and the guests had been seated, and were waiting somewhat patiently for the wedding party. The male guests tugged at their shirt collars when they thought no one was watching and the women frantically fanned themselves with ornate fans. Tex chuckled to himself and assumed his position with Curt beside him near the fragrant rose bed and the priest.

Tex's eyes swept the wedding guests. His eyes landed on Carlos and Juan who grinned at him. Martha sat staunchly in the first row. Other than them, he knew no one else in attendance. The organist played the wedding music from the next room and Louisa's bridesmaid, a friend of the family, stepped through the doorway in a royal blue gown. Louisa followed in a crème colored gown, carrying a bouquet of red roses. She was wearing a matching traditional mantilla lace veil held high with the Spanish comb. A dizzy sensation overtook Tex, and he reached for Curt's arm to steady himself.

After the wedding vows and the presentation of husband and wife, Louisa led Tex upstairs to her father's bedroom. They both knelt at his bed, seeking his blessing. The old man opened his eyes and barely lifted his hand, indicating his blessing on the newly married couple. "We've made his day,"

Louisa said, kissing Tex for her father to see. A faint smile played across her father's lips before his eyes closed again.

"I wish Father could join us in the festivities. He loved to entertain his friends," she said as she lifted her skirts to walk down the stairs.

"He did see you marry again. Guess you'll have to settle for that."

Downstairs, the servants had moved the furniture from the living room for dancing space. The Mexican folk band struck up lively music in which almost everyone participated, dancing to the guitars, trumpets and violins.

Louisa and Tex danced the first dance, followed by the bridesmaid and the best man. Soon other couples joined them. Even the unattached Carlos had gotten the reserved Martha to dance to the infectious music.

"I don't believe it." Texas discreetly motioned toward the couple.

Louisa smiled. "Carlos is a lady's man. No one has caught him yet."

"He's not thinking about heirs."

"I guess not. Do you suppose Martha can change his mind?"

Tex laughed at the idea.

"You know how to throw a party." Tex drew her close.

"I do at that. Our guests seem to be enjoying themselves. That's the true test, but I, for one, need to sit this next dance out."

Arms linked, Tex and Louisa stopped at the refreshment table to visit with Netty. Louisa laughed. "And to think this is where we first met, at a refreshment table."

"You did?" Netty beamed.

"Tex came to a Christmas dance and latched on to the refreshment table for security," Louisa teased.

"She's right," Tex admitted

"Why Father, I thought you weren't afraid of anything?"

Tex shook his head. "Not of ornery cattle or bad men, but dancing and women is something else."

"Anyway," Louisa continued with a smile, "We've been seeing each other since."

"I wish you a long happy married life," said Netty as she hugged Louisa.

"Tex says you're not going to be living with us?"

"I think it best for now I remain with Martha. She has no one."

"If you change your mind, remember you are always welcome."

"I'm just guessing here, but by the looks of things, Martha may not be alone for long." He pointed to Carlos and Martha dancing. This time she had snuggled in a little closer.

CHAPTER 17

Maud and Frederick had made the arrangements for Sara to return home to the mission with the condition that she promised to live with them when she returned to finish nurses training.

While on the train Sara mostly slept, dreaming of hidden staircases and tunnels that led to nowhere. When awake, she wrestled with her conscience. She had so much to explain about her time in Boston. What was she going to tell Cassandra and the rest of them about the quilts she was bringing back?

Within a few miles of the steamboat landing, her heart began to race in anticipation. She had only been gone half a year, but it had seemed like forever. The world she had once known had been so distant. There were times she felt that it wasn't real, and she desperately wanted to reach out and touch it once again.

The railroad hadn't crossed the Missouri River yet, still requiring the steamboat ride from Pierre to the landing near the mission. She didn't mind. It gave her a chance to find a sense of peace in the rolling currents and to breathe deep of the river water, the aroma a mixture of mud and fish. She laughed at herself for missing something so ordinary.

As she neared the landing, the steamboat sounded its bugling horn. Sara shaded her eyes and searched the shoreline for a glimpse of her family. She wasn't sure who would be there to pick her up and take her on to the mission. She spotted a toddler in a blue dress darting back and forth.

Could that be Willow? She wondered.

Willow would be old enough to be walking, and yes, she saw Evangeline was more beautiful than ever, her blonde hair tied in a bow, wisps of her hair blew in the wind, and there was Elijah, too. She jumped up and down on her tip-toes when she saw them.

Barely able to wait for the boat to dock, she gripped her satchels. It took all of her patience to let the elderly depart first, but she crowded in close behind them, her heart pounding. As soon as Evangeline saw her, Sara smiled and waved, edging closer and closer to her awaiting arms.

"Mama told me you needed rest," Evangeline said, hugging her. "I can see she was right. Welcome home, daughter."

"I had no idea I would miss home so much." Sara laughed.

Elijah snatched the luggage from her. "You were under a great deal of stress. The mission is peaceful now that the students have left for the summer. Rest is on your agenda."

"I have two trunks this time," Sara told Elijah.

"I'll go get them."

Secretly, Sara was glad school was not in session for the summer. She looked forward to undivided attention. For certain, Evangeline would spoil her. She hadn't experienced any of that while working at the hospital or for Mrs. Wilkes.

"I won't argue with that for a while." Sara smiled and coaxed Willow into her arms and planted a kiss on her cheek before they jaunted to the wagon.

"I hope you don't mind but we have planned a welcome home party for you this evening," Evangeline said. "Cassandra, Minnie, and Bea are cooking up a feast. Everybody who knows you will be there."

Sara pressed her hand to her chest. "For me?"

"Yes, for you. You are loved very much," Evangeline reminded her.

"I do look forward to visiting with everyone," Sara said, boosting Willow up first and then boarding the wagon. She so preferred the wagon to Frederick or Henry's motor car. While the wagon creaked and jolted along the trail, Sara breathed in deeply of the verdant prairie. It held a special fragrance that she hadn't found in Boston. Her eyes darted to all the familiar landmarks, Swift Bear's old camp, the river where she played as a child, and the horse pasture. She thrilled at each swell and hill. All held pleasant memories for her. With eagerness, Sara watched for a glimpse of the mission. The smoke rising from the chimney brought the joy of familiarity to her.

We're nearly there, she thought. *Home at last. No place on earth could ever replace it*, she vowed.

"What do you want to do first?" Evangeline asked as Elijah pulled the team into the mission.

"Where will I be staying?"

"You have two choices," Evangeline said. "Either with us or the dormitory. You can have your pick of rooms there."

"I choose the dormitory. Then I won't be under your feet."

"You won't be under our feet, but you will enjoy more space and solitude if you wish."

"Let's make our first stop the dormitory, then."

"Consider it done," Elijah promised. After he pulled the team to a stop, he helped the women and Willow from the wagon. The wind whipped Sara's skirts and threatened to dislodge her hat. "Now I know I'm home for sure." She laughed. "Can't say I missed the wind all that much."

Evangeline held the door against the wind as Sara and Willow wedged through it. Cassandra was waiting on the other side. "Welcome home child." Sara startled at the sound of her voice. It sounded so much like Mrs. Wilkes. "Let me help you with your things. You will be staying here at the dorm?"

"I will."

"You have your pick of rooms. But first Minnie and Bea want to see you." Cassandra led her into the kitchen. A sweet aroma drew her to its source. Minnie wiped her hands on her apron and embraced her. "Sara, Sara, it's so good to see you." Bea joined in with heartfelt greetings. "Evangeline probably told you we're planning a party in your honor."

"It isn't necessary, but I will enjoy seeing everyone."

Minnie pulled out a chair from the table. "Now sit down and sample a few cookies while we catch up."

"There isn't much to tell." Sara broke off a piece of cookie and popped it in her mouth.

"I find that hard to believe," Cassandra chided.

If she only knew, Sara thought. More had happened to her than most people would experience in a six month period. How or what she should tell all of them was still unclear in her mind.

"Training mostly involves helping at the hospital. Unfortunately we do many of the clean up jobs. What I really enjoy are the academic classes, but there aren't enough of them."

Minnie's eyes softened in sympathy. "We hoped it would be pleasant for you."

"Oh, I didn't mean to give the wrong impression. I think I'm just tired."

"Rest is what you need." Evangeline patted her shoulder.

"Will you be working with Doc while you're here?" Cassandra asked.

"I finished my internship with Mrs. Wilkes when I left, but I need to do more. Cliff Point has made arrangements to intern with Doc. That way I can stay here for a few months."

Evangeline smiled. "Wonderful."

Minnie poured coffee and filled the cookie plate. "How was the time you spent with Mrs. Wilkes?"

Sara dashed a glance at Cassandra, and then averted her eyes. "It was interesting. She was a rather demanding lady, but we learned to get along."

Evangeline shifted uneasily in her chair. "I think Sara should choose a room and rest a while before the party. What do you say to that, young lady?"

"I agree." Sara pushed back the chair and stood. "The cookies are delicious, ladies. I look forward to all the other surprises you have in store for us."

Evangeline, Willow, and Sara stopped near the entrance picked up her luggage and walked down the hall of the dormitory.

"Perhaps a room some distance from the kitchen," Evangeline suggested.

"Good idea. How about this one? It faces north so it won't be so hot."

"You have the quilt?" Evangeline asked once Sara selected her room.

"Yes, you'd like to see it?"

"I would."

Evangeline nodded as Sara opened the trunk and lifted out the Jacob's Ladder quilt she packed at the very top. She shook out the folds.

"It's in surprisingly good condition," Evangeline said as she bent to examine it.

"It was a favorite of Cassandra's mother."

Evangeline pointed to the open trunk. "You brought others?"

"It's a long story. I'll tell you and Elijah about it in a day or two." She sighed deeply. "What am I going to do about Cassandra? Do I tell her what I discovered?"

"I just don't know. Elijah and I have talked this over many times."

"That's all I think about any more."

"We have to reach a decision soon so you can get some peace of mind. But for now, put your thoughts aside and rest." Evangeline picked up Willow and moved toward the door.

"Thanks, Evangeline. It's good to be home." Sara softly shut the door after them, and then retreated into peaceful slumber.

A few hours before the party began, Sara slipped out of the dorm unnoticed and followed the well-worn path to the cemetery on the hill. She felt rested and found a spring in her step that had been missing for the last few months. The mourning doves called her onward, awakening both sadness and joy in her soul, sad because she would be leaving the mission after a while.

Sara was grateful Evangeline thought so much of the mission that she had spent one summer beautifying the mission cemetery. The wind whistled through the cedar trees Evangeline had planted. They had put on some growth, and the iris showed evidence of past spring blooms. Sara ran her hands over the gleaming headstones Evangeline had placed at the graves of Red Bird and Swift Bear.

Sara eased down beside their graves in meditative thought. She closed her eyes, as the wind stirred the prairie grasses into whispers of long ago. She listened to the voices of what used to be; living in Swift Bear's old camp, sharing the tepee with Red Bird, and living at the mission. She had existed in two different worlds, one Lakota and one white.

At times she had grown confused at the pull each had on her, but she was beginning to reconcile the differences. She would study the white man's medicine and return to the mission to heal her people.

The sounds of whinnying horses and rumbling wagons drew Sara's attention. She looked down from the hill top to the buggies and wagons jostling down the mission road to welcome her back. She stood, leaving Red Bird and Swift Bear, ready to answer the many questions she was sure to be bombarded with.

Sara slipped in behind the church and joined the throng of people. She was most anxious to talk to Doc to see how he was doing with his patients. Most of her Lakota people distrusted him and his methods from the very beginning of his practice. She had accompanied him to see many of his patients before she had left for Boston with the hopes she could win some of her people over to the white medicine. It had worked for only some of his patients. Many still practiced the Old Ways.

But it wasn't Doc that approached her first, it was Curt. "My, you're a sight for sore eyes." Curt swaggered toward her, his spurs jingling.

Sara furrowed her brow. "And what do you mean by that?"

"Oh, it's a compliment. I haven't seen anyone that can hold a candle to you."

"Then, you haven't been anywhere," she retorted.

"Just as spunky as ever. I like that." His eyes gleamed with mischief.

"And what are you up to nowadays?"

"Working at the Bar Double B. We merged our cattle ranch with theirs. Thought we'd have a better chance at the leases."

She twirled a lock of her raven black hair. "You spend a lot of time at the mission?"

"A far amount. Attend church on Sundays."

"And Tex, how is he?"

"He's here somewhere. Found himself a Texas born lady. Her name's Louisa. She's in Texas right now with her sick father."

"Don't think I know her."

"Probably not. Lived a piece from here." Curt kicked at a spot on the floor. "Tex married her in Texas on her father's ranch. Bought a ranch of his own next door. He'll be going back soon."

"Then you'll likely be returning to Texas before too long?"

"I'm not sure. Depends."

She flashed her eyes. "Depends on what?"

"On things."

Doc walked up behind her and tapped her on the shoulder. "Welcome back."

She spun around. "Oh, Doc, I was looking for you."

Curt frowned. "See you around." He jammed his hands in his pocket, and sauntered away, his neck tucked deep into his shirt collar.

"Sorry, didn't mean to interrupt anything," Doc apologized.

"You didn't. Thanks for taking me on to intern."

Doc nodded. "No problem. I need your help."

"I'm anxious to visit our patients."

"They will sure be glad to see you."

"Are your visitations going any better?"

"Many have come around, but there are others who insist that you visit." Doc removed his spectacles and cleaned them with his handkerchief. "Some practice the old medicine. Sometimes it works and other times it doesn't. In most of those cases I could have done better."

Sara touched his shoulder. "Don't blame yourself. You do the best you can."

He held his spectacles at arm's length and peered through them. "I have better luck in the dormitory. We've had several cases of contagious diseases. Everyone rallied and we got through it okay."

"Of course you did. We're thankful you're here for us."

"Thank you." He bowed slightly. "When will you be ready for a trip to the country?"

"Anytime. Just let me know."

"Good. It may be as soon as tomorrow." He removed his glasses and cleaned them again. "I promised to play the fiddle so best be going. So good to talk to you."

Poor Doc, Sara thought to herself. If only she could make him feel more confident. Sara moved into the group of people who had gathered on her behalf. She chatted amiably, answering some questions and avoiding others.

Cassandra saw her and pulled her aside. "I get the feeling you have been avoiding me."

"Why would I be avoiding you?"

"I don't know, but that's the feeling I get."

"It's just I haven't had time to really sit down and visit. Evangeline insisted I rest before the party, otherwise I would have been over to see you." Sara hoped her explanation was satisfactory. Perhaps, she was avoiding Cassandra, but only because of the secret she hadn't shared.

"I'm sorry. I don't know what come over me. Since I found out you were coming home, I have lined up a few projects for us. We need a few more quilts for the boarding school students. Some students love their quilts so much that they take them home. That runs us short on quilts."

"I'll certainly help you when I have a few free moments. I do have to spend time making the rounds with Doc. The school insisted it was the only way I could come home for a few months. But I will have time to help you."

"Good," Cassandra mumbled. "I miss our time together."

Doc found her just before the party concluded. "Come

by my office tomorrow. I have some new equipment. You might be interested."

"I'm sure I will be. Will we have time to go on a few visits?"

"I'll arrange it if you wish."

She smiled. "See you in the morning."

As the party began to break up, many of the visitors came by to wish her well. The last one to speak to her was Curt. "I'd like to spend some time with you before you leave," he said, staring at the floor.

"I have an internship to finish, and I promised to help Cassandra with quilt projects. I just don't know if I will have time." She hoped he would be satisfied with the explanation. She didn't want to be rude.

"You have no interest in me, do you?" he asked bluntly, twirling his hat in his hand.

"It's not that, Curt. I have other plans for the next few years. I can't complicate it with a relationship. Spending time with you will give you the wrong impression."

"I promise I won't pressure you. Just a ride in a buggy, a walk by the river."

"Oh, Curt, give up on me. I'm not the girl for you. Believe me, this is the best way."

Curt slapped his hat against his leg, bowed his head and stomped away.

— — — — — —

The next day, Sara made a tour of the mission before she stopped at Doc's office. She noticed several changes at the mission since she had left. One was a new livery stable. The pounding of iron drew her to the new building. She peered in at the forge, a bright orange ball of fire and a muscular man bending over the anvil striking a heated piece of iron. The reddish-orange glow drew her attention. She strolled over to see it was Sam.

"Samuel, I thought that was you." Sara remembered Samuel had left Swift Bear's camp to help at the mission when Elijah went to Santee to study.

He looked up from his work. "Your aren't Sara, are you?"

"I am. Didn't know you liked blacksmithing."

"Tried to farm my allotment, but found out it wasn't for me. I like horses and wagons. Elijah mentioned the mission needed a livery stable."

"I never dreamed the mission would be growing like it has. Who knows what it will look like when I come back again."

Sam nodded and returned to his project.

Sara heard more pounding down the road. She walked a little farther to see workmen constructing a building. As she came closer she noticed Kat standing, hands on hips, looking up at the workers and shouting commands. Sara stopped to visit.

"What's going on here," she shouted to Kat.

"Sara, how good to see you again. Back for a vacation?"

"For several months, I hope." Sara placed her hand above her eyes and looked up at the frame building. "Is this yours?"

"It will be a hotel one day. I sold my business in Deadwood."

"I hope it will be a success."

"Me, too. I have a notion the mission is growing into a town. Just hope the railroad comes through here someday. We'll all prosper if it does."

"So do all the other small towns, I imagine," Sara mumbled.

"Annabelle and Miranda are living in Deadwood, now. Several of the ladies bought a small building together, which they are turning into a sewing shop. I have always been grateful to you for becoming such a good friend of Miranda's while she was at the mission with me."

"I did have a good time with her," Sara said. "She sure liked the little kittens."

"Heard about your coming home party," Kat said. "Sorry we didn't make it."

"It was a nice time. I have really missed everyone. Are you staying at the mission?"

"I will for most of the summer. I'll use one of the rooms for myself."

"Maybe it will be finished before I return to Boston."

"I sure hope so." Kat wiped her brow with the back of her hand.

"Better let you get back to work," Sara said, and then continued on to Doc's office.

"I'm ready," Sara announced when she entered the office smelling of iodine.

"Come on in. I'm not quite ready yet. Had a patient early this morning."

She smiled, watching Doc scurrying to collect his thoughts as well as his medical supplies. "Who are we visiting today?"

"A family with sick children. Some sort of flu. Another woman is having a difficult pregnancy, and another family needs food. They're practically malnourished."

"What can I do to help you out?"

"By the door are few bags packed with food. Want to carry one?" He handed her the lightest one. "What do you think of my office? Don't you notice anything different?"

Sara glanced around. "I sure do. You have some fine looking furniture and up to-date-medical equipment. Are your patients paying their bills?"

"Not really. Evangeline has helped me out."

"Medical care is so important. We're lucky to have you here."

Doc blushed. "Now then, if you want to stay here, I'll get my horse and buggy at the livery and then we'll be on our way."

"I walked by the new livery. A good addition to the mission."

"Did you notice the blacksmith?" he asked.

"I did. It's Samuel. I had no idea he was interested in blacksmithing."

While Doc left for the livery, Sara explored his office. She congratulated herself in being able to identify most of the medical tools and equipment. She had cleaned and sterilized most of the same during her training. She sighed at the thought of the daily drudgery.

Upon hearing the rhythmic clip-clopping of the buggy horse, she left the office and climbed into the buggy beside Doc and handed him his black doctor bag.

"Oh, I almost forgot," he said slightly embarrassed.

She smiled to herself, wondering how far he would have gotten until he remembered he had left his bag on the table. After a few miles out on the open prairie, Sara closed her eyes, drew in a deep breath and released it. "It's great to be out here in the open air. I've missed it." She hadn't felt this relaxed for a very long time.

Doc focused his eyes straight ahead. "How has training been going for you?"

"It's hard work for women. We're given the menial jobs of cleaning up the messes, to put it bluntly. I was hoping to actually study medicine."

"The academics are mostly reserved for doctors."

"I found that out. Are there many women doctors?"

"A few, not many."

"I've been giving nursing a lot of thought lately. Do you think I could become a doctor?"

His eyes met hers, momentarily and then darted back to the road. "I've never doubted what you can do. The program is rigorous. Are you willing to devote every waking moment to years of study?"

"I believe so."

"Believing isn't good enough," he said sternly. "You have to know you can."

"All right then. I know I can," she said adamantly, surprised at his seriousness.

He adjusted his spectacles, and then cleared his throat. "This is none of my business, but if you are planning on marriage and a family, I would put it aside until you get your degree."

"I have no one I'm interested in and for me marriage and family aren't a priority."

"I thought so."

"What about you?"

"Me?"

"Have you thought about marriage?" she asked.

"No," he said rather forcefully. "There aren't too many women who would want to come out here and establish a home. Most of them would rather remain closer to civilization."

"But it must be lonely for you." She boldly stated.

His face flushed. "Sometimes."

"Have you ever thought about returning east?"

He laughed nervously. "Many times. I know it's a while yet, but do you plan on coming back to practice medicine?"

"I would like to."

"There will be a place for you here. I guarantee it," he said without turning his attention from the road.

— — — — — —

Evangeline removed the letter from the dresser drawer that Sara had sent her several months ago. Sara had written Cassandra was Mrs. Wilkes's sister. Evangeline re-read it several times to make sure she understood. She and Elijah would have to make a definite decision on what to do. Soon Sara would be asking their opinion.

She was expecting Elijah home for supper and would wait then to discuss its contents. She sat in her chair watching Willow play while her thoughts drifted to Cassandra and their history together. She remembered when she first met Cassandra she was an embittered woman. In fact, Evangeline didn't even like her. Cassandra seemed to resent Evangeline and her idealistic ways. At the time she didn't understand why Cassandra behaved so surly. She had always thought it had something to do with her husband Ben leaving her and Elijah. For sure, that had to be one of the reasons.

But the real reason for her unhappiness wasn't only being left by her husband. When Evangeline learned that Cassandra was raised in an orphanage, she began to understand how this affected Cassandra's negative attitude. Since then, she tried harder to understand her. Eventually they patched up their difficulties and became friends.

In fact, it was Cassandra who told Evangeline that Elijah had feelings for her. Marrying Elijah had changed her and Cassandra's relationship. Then when Willow was born, Cassandra became even happier. Willow was her life.

Evangeline rose from the chair, picked up Willow, and peered out the window, searching for Elijah. She definitely didn't want to see Cassandra hurt. Would it be necessary to upset her life with this news? Just when she was finding happiness. What purpose would it serve now?

To Evangeline's relief, she saw Elijah coming home for supper right on schedule. She plunked Willow in her high chair and stirred the pot of soup bubbling on the stove.

"Ah, it smells like chicken and noodles. I'm hungry." Elijah kissed the top of Willow's downy head and snatched his wife up in his arms.

Evangeline laughed. "Good day. I assume."

"Every day is a good day when you're near." He grinned.

She let Elijah enjoy his meal as they chatted about the day's events. But right after supper, Evangeline placed the letter on the table. "Sara will want our opinion. What are we going to tell her?"

Elijah picked up the letter and seeing it was the letter sent by Sara some time ago, he said, "I've preached many sermons about how God works in our lives, but this...this is incredible. It has to be more than mere coincidence. How does one explain it?" He thumped the letter with his finger. "What are your thoughts?"

"I don't think we should complicate Cassandra's life any further. Perhaps it should be left a secret."

"You don't want to give her any more pain. I can understand that, but I tend to think the other way. This didn't happen by chance. These events happened for a reason. Cassandra has to know. We just have to trust what has happened is for the best."

"I trust your judgment. You're her son".

His eyes shone dark and serious. "The events have unfolded in such an ordered fashion as not to have some significance. My mother must know."

Sara knocked on Elijah and Evangeline's door early the next morning. She peeked in through the window to see if anyone was awake. Elijah opened the door yawning and rubbing his eyes.

"I didn't get you out of bed did I?"

"No, just made a pot of coffee. Sit down and have some. What got you out of bed so early?"

"Is Evangeline up?"

He smoothed his coal black hair with his fingers. "She will be when she hears your voice."

"Sorry to come so early, but I wanted to catch you both before you began your day."

"You did that." Elijah yawned. "Now what is this about?"

Evangeline appeared in the bedroom doorway, her blue robe drawn about her. "I hear you have something important to discuss."

"What shall I tell Cassandra? She's accused me of avoiding her, and she's partially right. I can't look her in the eye while I'm withholding the truth from her."

Elijah poured the coffee and then sat down across from her and took hold of her hands. "Evangeline and I have discussed this, and we have come to the conclusion that you tell her the truth. The events are just too incredible to ignore."

"It won't be easy."

"We'll be there with you," he promised.

"Good. I don't want to do this alone."

"Right after we get dressed, we'll stop by the sewing room. You can tell her what you've learned."

"What if she takes the news badly?"

"It's a chance we have to take. I believe it's destiny," Elijah reassured her. "No matter what the outcome is."

While Elijah and Evangeline dressed, Sara replayed the conversation with them in her mind. She hoped they were right. In no way did she want to hurt Cassandra.

Evangeline came from the bedroom bouncing Willow on her hip. "Luckily Willow woke too. I'll drop her off with Minnie before we see Cassandra."

Within a half hour, the three of them walked into the sewing room to Cassandra's surprise. "What's happened?" She whirled around to meet them.

"Nothing has happened. Sara has important news for you."

Cassandra pushed her sewing aside and stood. "And you two had to come along?" She furrowed her brow. "Please tell me it isn't about Ben."

"It's not about Ben," Elijah answered with a disgusted edge to his tone. "Sara wanted us here. Let's sit down. Sara has a lot to tell us."

Sara had rehearsed in her mind what she was going to say, but now that the moment arrived her mind failed her. She gathered her thoughts and began. "While I was caring for Mrs. Wilkes in Boston I learned something quite extraordinary. You are going to find this hard to believe, Cassandra, but it's the truth."

Cassandra's eyes grew wide and fearful.

"When I took the job with Mrs. Wilkes I thought there was something familiar about her, but I couldn't figure out what it was until later. She had a reputation for being mean and demanding of her nursing students who came to care for her as part of the training. I never totally feared her— actually we got along quite well. Although, I admit there were some strange things going on in that Victorian house of hers. One night when I went up to the third floor to look out on the city, I saw a quilt draped across the rocking chair. I thought it looked familiar so I went to see. I couldn't believe my eyes; it was the missing Jacob's Ladder quilt from the mission."

Cassandra gasped. "Our Jacob's Ladder quilt? In Boston?"

"Yes. I warned you what I had to tell you was extraordinary. But I haven't even come to the best part." Sara stirred in her chair and took a deep breath. "I had to find out how the quilt got there. I asked Mrs. Wilkes and she told me a fib at first, but later I found out her granddaughter Myra came to the mission, right here, worked for a while and took the quilt with her."

"Myra, I don't remember that name. There was a blonde girl who was here briefly." Cassandra said.

"She's probably the one. What was her name?"

"Mona, I believe."

"She changed her name then. I hardly remember her," Sara said. "She has red hair now."

"What did she want with the Jacob's Ladder quilt?"

Sara glanced over at Evangeline and Elijah for permission to continue. They both nodded. "It took me a while to find this out, but Mrs. Wilkes's mother was continually looking for the babe she had taken to the Boston orphanage. She finally tracked her down to our mission." Sara ceased speaking, waiting for Cassandra to draw a conclusion.

"To this mission? A babe at an orphanage?" Cassandra's face turned white. "Are you talking about me?"

Sara nodded.

"My mother was looking for me?"

"Yes, she sent her great granddaughter to find you."

"But Mona, I mean Myra, never said anything to me?"

"Mrs. Wilkes told her not to. Myra took the quilt as a remembrance."

Cassandra shook her head in disbelief. "I don't understand."

"I know it's hard to grasp. Your mother Henrietta was so distraught over giving you away and so obsessed with finding you that she eventually had a break-down. She hung onto that quilt as if it was her last hope."

"You saw her?"

Sara slowly shook her head. "It was some time before I knew that Mrs. Wilkes was secretively keeping Henrietta in the house with her nurse. You see Henrietta was deranged. Often times she would shriek and scream. She scared the student nurses half to death. Mrs. Wilkes didn't want her in an institution, so she kept her hidden in the house. I never saw Henrietta up close, only at a distance. Unfortunately, she passed away right before I left."

"You mean she was living until just recently?"

"She was. Lived into her nineties."

Cassandra frowned as in disbelief. "Where was she hidden?"

"Mrs. Wilkes's Victorian was designed with secret rooms, staircases, and tunnels. Her mother lived in the basement with her nurse. Mrs. Wilkes had to keep Henrietta out of sight in order to keep the nurses coming to take care of her. You see, Mrs. Wilkes is an invalid and needs care also."

"They kept her in a basement?"

"Not all the time. Her nurse Susan took her to the third floor where she could look out on the city. And they went for walks, using the secret tunnel."

"This is all too much. And you were living in the midst of it all." Cassandra's face assumed its stoic expression. "And who is Mrs. Wilkes?"

"She's...your younger sister. Henrietta's other daughter."

"I...have a sister?"

"Yes. That's why I thought Mrs. Wilkes looked familiar."

"And her first name?"

"Mattie."

"I have a sister Mattie. My mother's name was Henrietta."

"There's more to tell—"

Evangeline held up her hand. "Another time, perhaps."

Sara nodded in agreement. "Another time."

Several weeks passed before Sara attempted to approach Cassandra about her mother and sister. Always when Sara came over to visit and help with the quilts in the sewing room, both women carefully avoided any mention of the conversation they had of Boston and Mrs. Wilkes's Victorian.

Sara and Cassandra silently worked on a quilt for a new boarding school student who would enroll in September when Cassandra initiated the conversation while threading her needle. "My mother was looking for me. I always thought she didn't care."

Caught unaware of Cassandra's reflective mood, Sara ceased her sewing and blurted out something that had been bothering her. "I should have told you sooner. Wrote you a letter. Maybe you could have come to Boston to see Henrietta."

"No." Cassandra waved her off. "It's better this way. I wouldn't have wanted to see her so distraught and behaving like a madwoman." Cassandra inserted her needle into the quilt's border. "It means a lot to me to know that she regretted putting me in an orphanage. But then again, I was the source of her pain for all those years."

"You can't blame yourself. Life just happens sometime. We just do the best we can."

Cassandra continued basting the quilt's border. "You're wise for a young woman your age."

"We weren't sure if we should even tell you, but Elijah thought you should know even if it would be difficult to hear."

"He was right. It's best to know the truth even if it hurts."

"I'm not sure I agree. I think sometimes it's best not to know."

"Wait until you grow older, you may change your mind."

Cassandra hadn't asked about her sister, but Sara thought she'd bring her name up anyway. "Your sister Mattie was in financial trouble for some time. That's why she needed the student nurses to come in to care for her. She was selling off her heirlooms one by one, even her dead daughter's possessions that she had stored in a locked room. It turned out that her cook and groundskeeper were stealing from her. They found a secret entrance into the locked room and stole the things that Mrs. Wilkes was going to sell."

Cassandra held her needle in midair. "Mattie's daughter died? From what?"

"She and her daughter were thrown from spooked horses. Her daughter was killed, and Mattie was severely injured."

"Is she still able to live in her home?"

"Yes, her granddaughter Myra and I came up with an idea, so she could stay. We cleaned and fixed up the upstairs rooms to rent out to nursing students. There never seemed to be enough places for them to stay. The money she collects from the boarders can be used to maintain her home."

"How sad. It appears my family has had their share of grief."

"It does. What I found interesting is that you and Mattie are alike in some ways."

"How's that?"

"You look somewhat alike." She thought secretly that they both were somewhat somber, but she didn't mention that similarity. "You both like to sew. I made two quilts while I was with Mattie."

"You said the student nurses thought she was mean?"

"They did. She's was…brusque. I didn't find her mean, though. For some reason I was drawn to her, probably because she reminded me of you."

Cassandra frowned. "I hope you don't think I'm mean."

"No, I don't mean it like that." She laughed at her play on words. "You both have the same mannerisms."

Cassandra smoothed her basting with her hand. "I suppose sisters resemble one another in some way."

"Would you be interested in seeing her?"

"I think it best to leave the past alone," Cassandra said without apparently giving the idea much thought.

Hmm, Sara reflected, *sisters think alike, too.* Disappointed that neither sister seemed interested in one another, Sara dropped the subject.

"I would like to see the Jacob's Ladder quilt," Cassandra said. "You have it with you?"

"I do. It's in my dorm room. I wasn't sure how I should present it or whom to present it to."

"It does belong to everyone, doesn't it?" Cassandra said.

"I guess so. Everyone contributed to it. If I give it back to the mission, I will have to explain where I got it."

"That's true. I'm not sure I want anyone else to know about my estranged family."

"I could say I found it in a Boston thrift store, but that would be lying."

Cassandra nodded. "It would."

"Or I could just give it to you and not say anything about it."

"You could keep it, too. Your Grandmother helped make it."

Sara threw up her hands. "So what do we do?"

"Let's think on it a while. I have to get used to all this shocking information."

"When you come over for supper, I'll take you to my room and show you the quilt."

"Has it been abused?"

"There's a little wear. It was Henrietta's favorite," Sara reminded her.

"I'm glad it's not in tatters."

Sara glanced at the clock wishing the hands would turn a little faster. What could she and Cassandra talk about for another hour? There was more she could say about Cassandra's sister, but she didn't seem interested. Furthermore, Sara had a surprise for Cassandra in her dorm room, but she didn't know if she should give it to her. Sara wished she could read Cassandra's mind. She had done her best to read her expression when they discussed Mrs. Wilkes and Henrietta, but Cassandra hadn't revealed any emotions.

No longer able to sit and quilt as if there were nothing to discuss, Sara blurted out a suggestion. "Let's look at the quilt before supper."

Cassandra raised her brow. "Why the hurry?"

"I'm anxious for you to see it."

Cassandra put the quilt aside. "I suppose a break wouldn't hurt. Lead the way."

All the way to her dorm room, Sara debated about the surprise. She couldn't make a decision what to do. Once in her room, Sara took the folded quilt from the closet and laid it out on the bed. She watched as Cassandra stroked the material flat. "This quilt has lived an amazing story," Cassandra admitted.

"The most amazing part is your mother and how she loved this quilt because it was connected to you."

Cassandra sat on the edge of the bed, stroking the quilt.

"Why does life have to be so difficult at times?" Sara murmured.

"You should know Sara, your life hasn't been easy either."

"I don't think about it much. It doesn't do any good to grieve or feel sorry for myself." Sara returned to the closet and pulled out another quilt and handed it to Cassandra.

"What's this?"

"Your sister and I made this quilt together. I had no idea what she would do with it once she completed it. I thought she would give it to her granddaughter Myra." Sara unfolded the quilt.

A sound of approval escaped from Cassandra's lips. "It's a beautiful appliqué. I've never attempted one."

"It's Victorian Lady."

Cassandra sighed deeply. "My sister and my mother were Victorian ladies, I imagine. I never was and never will be a Victorian lady."

"Before I left Boston and said goodbye to Mrs. Wilkes, she gave me this quilt to give to you?"

"For me? But why?"

"Your mother designed the Victorian Lady pattern. I believe Mattie wanted to give something to you that would, in a sense, be from your mother. Mattie had to sell all her valuables to pay for her servants, including your mother's nurse. There were no jewels or anything left."

"So you're saying she had nothing from my mother to give me?"

"Exactly. I didn't know we were working on this quilt for you. Of course she knew all along. Some days I could tell she was in pain, but she never gave up our quilting session."

"Did she ever say she wanted... to see me?"

"She's just like you. She saw no reason to dredge up the past."

Cassandra fingered the quilt. "This is much too pretty for me. You keep it."

Sara winced. "It's for you. I would think you would want a remembrance of her. In fact, I don't understand the two of you. If I had just found out I had a sister, I would go to her." Sara immediately regretted speaking out in such an authoritative tone, but she couldn't keep still any longer.

"I know it's hard for you to understand, but it's easier this way. I'll accept her gesture and leave it at that."

"You mean you won't even write her a thank you note?"

Cassandra shrugged. "I could."

Sara felt her face warming. "I don't mean to be disrespectful. I like you both too much to keep quiet. You know that you and I get along just fine with our quilting and have grown to like each other. I admit it took some time to develop feelings for Mrs. Wilkes, I mean Mattie. She's a little crusty to begin with."

Cassandra smiled. "Kind of like me?"

Sara nodded. "I'm returning to Boston and the end of the summer to continue my school. Why don't you consider going back with me to visit your sister. As always you may stay with the DuMonts and me."

"I don't know. I'll have to think about it."

Sara didn't understand what Cassandra had to think about, but she would have to accept her decision for now. She had one more surprise quilt to spring on Cassandra.

When should she do it? She contemplated.

Sara waited a few more weeks to give Cassandra time to adjust to the shocking news of her family, and then she approached her about the Hard Cracker quilt. Cassandra was bent over the sewing machine sewing the backing on a boarding school student's quilt when Sara entered the sewing room.

Cassandra snipped the thread and met Sara's eyes with her own. "I have a feeling you're not done with me."

Sara lowered her head. "I have another favor to ask you."

Cassandra's head bobbed toward the bundle Sara was carrying. "What do you have there? Appears to be another quilt."

Sara unfolded the quilt before her.

"Looks to be in bad shape. Where did you get this?"

"From Mattie's Victorian. Myra and I found it in the hidden staircase."

"Oh, the Victorian again." Cassandra frowned. "What do you want with me?"

"I was hoping you could help me repair it."

"I hate to ask, but what's so special about it?"

"It's a Civil War quilt. It must have had a lot of history. Besides, there is a good chance your mother made it."

Cassandra turned her back to Sara and resumed her sewing. "Why do you keep reminding me of my mother?"

Sara pleaded. "I...I'd like to repair this quilt and take it back to Mattie. It belongs to the Victorian. I thought you could help me."

Cassandra sighed deeply. "Let me see it again." She reached for the quilt for a better look. "It'll take some doing, but I suppose we can fix it up a bit. Don't expect perfection. It's badly damaged in some parts."

"Thanks, Cassandra. I knew you'd help."

Cassandra laughed. "You have a way of talking me in doing things I wouldn't ordinarily do."

Sara reached in her pocket and pulled out the photograph carefully wrapped in paper. "I have something to show you."

Cassandra took the photograph from her hand and studied it. "Is this the same quilt?"

"It is. You'll never believe where I found it."

"At the Victorian," Cassandra said wryly.

"In an old trunk stored in the carriage house."

"Will wonders never cease?" Cassandra rolled her eyes.

"The person holding the quilt is Henrietta, your mother." Sara thought she could discern a slight tremble as Cassandra brought the photograph closer for another look.

"This is my mother. I can't believe it. After all these years. Why she doesn't look like what I had envisioned?"

"And how was that?"

"Unkempt and poor. She looks so regal."

"She was poor at one time. That's why she had to give you away, but she never stopped looking."

"Life can be so cruel." Cassandra's expression stiffened.

"I know it's a shock." Sara gathered up a portion of the quilt and held it out to her. "Your mother made this quilt, and you can help restore it back to its former self." Sara studied the expression on her face, hoping she hadn't pushed Cassandra too far. "Will you help me?"

Cassandra met Sara's inquiring gaze. "I don't know about all this. You're asking too much of me."

"I'm sorry, but restoring this quilt means so much to me. I want to give this to Mattie."

A pained look swept across Cassandra's face. "Why is it so important to you?"

"I don't know. It's just that I feel so sorry for her. I want to give her something, something that's whole, repaired, a part of her heritage."

"You think that much of her, do you?"

"I do."

"Very well then, I'll help." Cassandra sighed deeply and returned to her sewing. "I have one side of the quilt binding to sew and we can start. In the meantime look through the scrap box and see if you can match up materials."

When Cassandra finished the quilt, she studied the scraps Sara had selected. "It would be best to use materials from the same time period, but I just don't have them. We'll just do the best we can. You said you found this quilt in a stairway?"

"Yes, it was a hidden stairway. I haven't told you the Victorian had secret stairways and tunnels used to help slaves escape."

"It did?"

"I learned your mother and her husband built the house and then later added the stairways and tunnels for slaves to escape."

Cassandra laid a replacement piece over a worn one and began stitching. "You've been through them?"

Sara watched how Cassandra sewed on the piece and attempted a repair on her own. "I have. Like I said there were strange things happening in that house. I just had to figure out what was going on."

"What things?" Cassandra's curiosity piqued.

"Remember I told you Mattie was hiding your mother away with her nurse Susan in the basement. I haven't told you the details. Mattie used student nurses for her own care, but they didn't like to stay there."

"So the student nurses never caught on what was going on?"

"They heard things. Many of the student nurses couldn't wait to get out of there. I suppose they thought the house was haunted and Mattie was often grumpy and demanding."

"Did the staff use the tunnels and staircases?"

"The tunnels mostly. Mrs. Burns the cook and Gilbert Reynolds the gardener used both."

"The two thieves?"

Sara nodded. "They were stealing Mattie blind. Only she had the key, but Mrs. Burns and Gilbert found a secret entrance to the room from the third floor. When Mattie was sleeping, they entered the room and stole valuable pieces and took them out of the house. It was a long time before we discovered what was going on."

Cassandra ceased sewing, looking at Sara intently. "You lived among thieves?"

Sara shrugged. "I did but I never felt like I was ever in danger. They were a husband and wife team who had done this before. I even hired a detective to look into their background, but they left when they knew Mattie and I had figured out what they were up to."

"So then, my...sister was left destitute, but you said she is still living in the house?"

"Myra and I came up with the idea of fixing up the bedrooms on the second floor and renting them out to nursing students. When I left, two of the rooms had been rented out, and Mattie actually seemed happy with the arrangement. One of the girls will be taking care of Mattie."

"You are indeed a brave girl. I'm proud of how you handled the situation."

"Thanks, but I'm glad it's all over with. I did promise Mattie I would return for visits."

"You must think highly of her."

"I came to appreciate her and her situation. A person would have to have great strength to endure what she has had to do."

CHAPTER 18

The katydids sang in the treetops informing Sara that autumn was fast approaching. She had enjoyed the summer with Doc, helping him in his clinic and traveling the countryside with him visiting patients. She admired his skills and his genuine concern for those sick and ailing. She thought he had won some of his patients over to trust him and the strange new methods he used to heal. The past few months with him confirmed her desire to become a doctor. She wanted to return to Boston and study even if it took her away from the home she loved. Doc had hinted for her to return and help him.

"Maybe someday we can build a hospital," he had told her. The idea appealed to her.

The mission bustled with planned activity, a party to welcome Kat back to the mission and to say goodbye to Sara and Tex. Sara had discovered she had been moping. She would leave the next day for Boston, knowing she could not achieve her dreams otherwise.

Sara took one last walk around the mission before she dressed for the party, doing her best to remember every nuance of this place she loved. Kat's hotel was about completed and ready for paint and flooring. She stopped by and shouted encouragement to Kat. A blue scarf tied up Kat's red hair and paint smudges covered her, but her grinning face confirmed she was enjoying every minute of her project. Jet stood there with her, scratching his head over her instructions. Sara laughed and waved, thankful they were happy.

Sara heard the whirl of Cassandra's sewing machine as she passed near the sewing room. What would Cassandra do if she couldn't sew anymore? She pondered. Sara hadn't bothered her anymore about returning to Boston with her. She left the decision entirely to her. Sara had told Cassandra everything she knew about her family and the adventures she experienced at the Victorian. Had all she told her fallen on deaf ears? She didn't know, but at least she tried. She smiled remembering the many moments spent together completing quilts for the boarding school students and repairing the Hard Cracker's quilt. It was finished and neatly folded for its return trip to Boston.

She waved to Samuel in his livery stable. She didn't expect him to attend the party. He was too shy for large gatherings, but she stopped by to invite him anyway. He seemed to be comfortable with his new business. She agreed he wasn't a farmer.

Tex and Curt rode up to the mission's dormitory. They waved to her and then dismounted and sauntered into the dormitory. *Apparently Tex and Curt have finished up the fall roundup*, she thought.

Tex would be returning to Texas after the party, anxious to see his new bride and ranch. Curt had told her he decided to stay on with the Bar Double B. She felt sorry for rejecting him, but there was no place in her life for a man right now, but at least he had a place at the Bar Double B for now.

As usual she saw Elijah at the church, preparing a message for the party. She saw him through the doorway with Willow. He called her over. "One last look before you take off tomorrow?" he asked her.

She nodded. "Not that I would ever forget." Her gaze dropped to the ground. "I guess I'm saying goodbye."

He placed his hands around her shoulders. "It's not forever. You'll be back for visits. And someday you'll be back for good."

"I know, but it's not the same."

"We'll be right here waiting for you."

Her voice grew thick. "I know, and I appreciate everything you have done." She bent down to kiss Willow and continued on to Tater's store where she stopped in to say hello and to personally invite Tater to the party.

"You want me there? He asked.

"It's not only for me, but for Tex and Kat," she explained.

"Yeah, I'll be there. Got to give Tex a hard time. He thinks I'm mad at him."

"Haven't you gotten over him using you and others to get land?"

"Don't tell him, but yeah I guess I have. He's seen what he did wrong."

"Bet you'll miss him."

"I will at that. But I still have Curt to keep an eye on."

"See you there," she said, realizing Tex and Curt had been his family. She wondered if they realized it.

Before her last stop at the dormitory, she detoured to Elijah and Evangeline's little house. She saw Evangeline outside cutting flowers from her flower garden. *For the party,* she thought to herself. She had been Sara's support since she was a little girl. She wouldn't be embarking on a medical career if it wasn't for her.

"Ah, Sara, out for a walk I see." She stood with a bouquet of flowers in her hand.

"I'm out visiting."

"Come into the kitchen with me while I put these in water."

Sara sat at the table and watched Evangeline fill a glass jar with water and arrange the orange and red flowers. "Evangeline, how did you manage to leave your home in Boston and come here to stay?"

"Are you fearful you won't be able to stay away as long as it will take to finish your degree?"

Sara dropped her head.

"You forget I left the mission and married James. I didn't come back for seven years."

"But you did leave Boston again."

"You're young. When you mature a little more, it will be easier for you to leave. Just focus on the future." Evangeline smiled. "I have an idea you will be so busy that the years will pass faster than you realize."

"I hope you're right, but you do know I'm thinking of becoming a doctor."

"I suspected as much. We do know you want to immerse yourself in medicine. We have no doubt you will be able to accomplish what you set out to do."

"It will take years of study."

"I know. We'll come for visits and you will have to visit at least one during the year. Now run along and make yourself beautiful for the party. I have some cooking to do yet." Evangeline kissed her cheek and scooted her out of the house.

When Sara stepped outside she detected the aroma of delicious food drifting from the dormitory's kitchen. She walked over and pushed open the kitchen door and offered her help. "No," Minnie said. "You are the guest of honor. You just sit and watch."

"I can't do that. Please just give me some sort of job."

"Well if you insist. Slice the bread and make sandwiches."

Sara took the bread out of the cupboard, placed it on

the breadboard, and began slicing. Jeremiah slinked in the doorway, winked at Sara in conspiracy and sampled the goodies while Minnie's back was turned.

Minnie turned and in exasperation shooed him out of the kitchen. Sara chuckled, admiring the elderly couple who made themselves useful even in their old age.

Such friends they all had been to her over the years. They had all nurtured her without her even realizing it. She sat in the kitchen for the remainder of the day listening to the voices of contentment and goodness. She only hoped that one day she could contribute as selflessly to the mission as they all had.

———————

The next morning, Sara awoke to her last sunrise at the mission for a while. An aroma of breakfast drifted under her doorway, urging her to leave the comfort of her bed. She slipped from the covers and padded to her window. The prairie she loved so much lay undisturbed in a sunburned slumber. She dressed in her brown traveling suit and combed her dark hair into a bun, pulling out a few wisps to frame her face like Evangeline had taught her. She left her room and walked down the hallway to the kitchen.

"Ah, there you are," Minnie said. "What can I get you? I have pancakes, eggs, and bacon."

"Pancakes and coffee, please."

"That's it?"

"I'm not terribly hungry this morning. My stomach always gets jittery when I have to travel."

"It can be grueling. Someday the railroad will come closer to us. Perhaps when you're about to graduate." Minnie laughed. "Then we can all come for the big day."

Evangeline, Elijah, and Willow entered the dining room to join Sara for breakfast before they took her to the steamboat landing. Sara thought their smiles and merry faces appeared contrived.

"You look nice, Sara. So professional looking," Evangeline complemented her. "Mama and Father can't wait to see you. They're so glad you'll be staying with them."

"I look forward to seeing them, too. I think I even miss Maud and her shopping sprees." Sara laughed.

"No more secret stairways and tunnels to discover," Elijah teased.

"Indeed not, but I do intend to visit Mattie as soon as I get to Boston."

Minnie brought breakfast over to Evangeline and Elijah. "Eat hardy," Elijah encouraged them. "Might be a spell before lunch."

"Am I late?" Cassandra shouted out, clamoring into the dining area, carrying a rather large satchel.

"Cassandra, are you coming with me?" Sara jumped up.

"I am. I'm certainly not going on a trip by myself. After listening to all your stories about the Victorian, I've decided I have to go and see it myself. Maybe you made the stories up."

Sara stared at her. "I can't believe you changed your mind."

"I've been known to be quite stubborn." She winked at Elijah. "But I am coming back. The mission is my home, and my family is here."

"We will always be here for you," Evangeline assured her, a grin spread across her face.

Cassandra pointed toward Evangeline. "Exactly why I need to visit my sister. I realized I have been blessed. Look what I have here." She tweaked Willow's nose. "I may have been an orphan, or thought I was an orphan, but I have lived a good life. Mattie, well Mattie has no one but her granddaughter who lives elsewhere. She must be lonely with only sad memories of her mother and daughter."

"I'm proud of you Mother," Elijah said, smiling. "Come back when you're ready."

Cassandra gasped. Her hands went to her face. "I forgot. I didn't ask you who would fill in for me—"

"Oh, I can do it," Minnie piped up.

"But you already have too much to do," Cassandra said.

"That's okay. Bea can pick up the slack here in the kitchen."

"There it's settled," Elijah said. "Stay as long as you want."

Cassandra waved away breakfast and settled for a cup of coffee, of which she hardly drank. Sara suspected it took every ounce of courage for Cassandra to face her past. Sara rested her hands on her chin, realizing that she and Cassandra were similar in many ways. Both had been orphans, but luckily they were rescued by loving hearts. True, the early years hadn't been easy for either one of them and left scars of struggle they had learned to overcome. The struggles made them stronger, more appreciative of the good in their lives, she reflected.

Sara was doing her best not to notice Evangeline's forced smiles. Evangeline, too, had encountered her share of anxiety since she had left Boston as a young woman, she realized. Sara had no doubt Elijah, Evangeline, and Willow would be right here waiting for her.

Sara sighed, contemplating life's ups and downs. Here they were, leaving the comforting arms of the mission to venture out on a journey of discovery, Cassandra to discover and embrace her heritage, and Sara to venture forth in the world of medicine. Like Cassandra she was certain she would return. Her family and all she loved were here—at the mission.

Jacob's Ladder

More Books from AQS

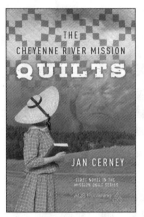

#1544 $14.95

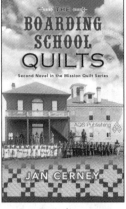

#1645 $14.95

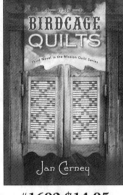

#1692 $14.95

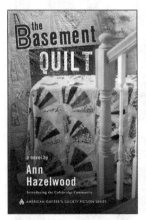

#8853 $14.00

#1256 $14.95

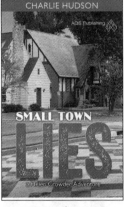

#1258 $14.95

Look for these books nationally.

1-800-626-5420

Call or Visit our website at

www.AmericanQuilter.com